THE MONSTER KEEPS ME SAFE

KITTY THOMAS

The Monster Keeps Me Safe

Kitty Thomas

Burlesque Press

The Monster Keeps Me Safe

Previously Published as:

Tabula Rasa

Printed in the United States of America

ISBN-13: 978-1-938639-83-8

Wholesale orders can be placed through the author.

Published by Burlesque Press

Contact the author at kittythomas.com Please use the "licensing" link in the top menu bar.

PROLOGUE

SHANNON MERCER

"Shannon!"

My team is yelling at me, but I don't care. They slow me down. Usually I don't mind them, but tonight I want to explore alone. As soon as James found a big enough pair of bolt cutters to get us through the fence, I put as much distance between myself and the group as possible.

"Shannon!" James calls again. "Keep your radio on."

I wave him off to let him know I got it as I move deeper into the abandoned Florida theme park. Usually I drive a separate vehicle for these little excursions so I'm not stuck following what the rest of the group wants to do all weekend. I'm not really a *touchy-feely Kumbaya hug it out* sort of guy.

It gives me some measure of peace to know a black rented SUV sits waiting in the parking lot for me, and I'm not at the mercy and whims of the others.

The sun has already set, but there are lights on in the castle. I can't believe no one stole the solar panels when the park closed. That would have been the first thing I looted.

And now I'm questioning everything.

I don't think anyone was using solar panels back when this

place was operational. Sure, I think they existed, but this park was too low budget for such a fancy and green update. They wouldn't have been able to afford them.

So what the fuck?

I use a large machete to hack through the overgrowth of kudzu standing between me and the castle. When I reach the entrance, the drawbridge is down and light spills out. This is very fucking strange.

While researching this place, I learned the castle has a working drawbridge. Or had. Who knows if the crank is rusted out after all these years. Though, I would have thought if the drawbridge was left down there'd be more signs of decay—at least in the entryway.

I move stealthily inside, glancing up at the exposed beams, taking it all in. This place is something else. I make my way through the main floor to a large medieval-style restaurant.

Everything about this is so *off*. I mean, more than normal. You always find weird shit in abandoned theme parks, but I can honestly say I've never come upon a place with lights and warmth... a place that looks lived in.

In my distraction I bump into and knock over a suit of armor. The metal clatters loudly to the floor.

"Oh, sorry." It's a reflex to be polite and apologize, to wear the mask of someone who cares—so people don't suspect what I am. And now I'm apologizing to inanimate objects. *Great, Shannon.*

When I open the door and step inside the restaurant, I freeze as I take in the scene before me. There are two roaring fireplaces—and as if that wasn't a strong enough sign of life—there's a startled couple, covered in a white sheet on a mattress.

Ummm. Okay. Clearly other people explore places like this in different ways from me. I'm about to excuse myself and leave when I realize... I recognize these faces. I know this man. This woman. I've seen them somewhere. I can't recall names or situations at the moment, but at some point my brain catalogued these two and put them in a file to contemplate later.

While I'm busy trying to unpack this mystery, the guy stands and moves in front of the woman. He pulls a gun from his pants, his eyes wild as he stares me down.

Oh. Now I know who this guy is. What a psycho. And that's saying something coming from me.

I pull my own gun. It's already hot, but I bet this guy has to rack the slide first. He seems too jumpy to carry hot.

"Please, just leave us alone," the woman pleads.

Well, that's a plot twist, knowing what I know about these two. But I'm afraid I can't do that now that weapons are involved.

A moment later, he racks the slide, and I fire three into his stomach.

The woman screams, "No!" She momentarily forgets her nudity to press the sheets against his gushing wounds.

My pants tighten uncomfortably, and I'm not sure if it's the thrill of the kill, or the flashes of skin I'm getting from the woman as she franticly tries to stop this loser from bleeding out. He's already dead. I wonder if she realizes that yet.

"Trevor! No! Stay with me, don't go."

"He's gone," I say, as she feels for a pulse.

She turns back to me, as though finally remembering she's not alone. When her eyes meet mine, I have to remind myself to breathe. The world stops moving, and all I see is her.

What is happening right now?

She picks up the gun and aims. Sort of. Her hand shakes so hard, she could empty the entire magazine and not hit me, so I'm not unnecessarily concerned about my safety.

I keep my own gun trained steadily on her. "Do you want to die with your lover? Put the gun on the ground, and slide if over to me."

She hesitates but doesn't put the gun down. "Please, don't hurt me," she whimpers.

I want to do *so* many things to her.

"Put the gun on the ground, and slide it over to me," I repeat.

Finally I see it, the moment she loses hope and realizes she exists now completely at my mercy, even though she still has a weapon in her hand. She and I both know if she tries to shoot me, it won't end well for her.

Finally she lays the gun down and slides it over. I stop it with my boot. And now she's truly mine.

Kill her. You have to kill her. No witnesses. You can't leave a witness, not with others in the park. Follow protocol. Eliminate the problem. Don't let this woman be your first mistake.

Or... I could keep her. I just have to figure out how to get her to come with me without a fight.

1

ELODIE

S*ix months ago.*

AT SOME POINT, right before my memory clicked off, the nightmare fairy must have paid the world a visit. When I opened my eyes, it was twilight, or dawn. I was so disoriented it was hard to tell which. I woke in a pirate ship.

Wait. Let me start over.

It wasn't an *actual* pirate ship, though that might have made more sense to my addled brain. It was part of some theme park ride that had been separated from the rest of the attraction like a wandering child lost from its mother.

The boat was big enough for about six adult tourists, each with a couple of sticky-fingered children in tow. The sides came up around me like a giant cradle. Given that the edges were rusted out, that idea didn't create the serene feelings you might imagine it would. The ship was laid at an angle, almost on one side as if a violent storm had tossed it out of the artificial sea and into the middle of a jungle ride on the other end of the park. The trees around me were thickly overgrown with kudzu vines.

I reached to touch the top of my head, feeling for a bump or cut, but nothing, just smooth forehead and long hair.

I sifted through my mind to recall the last thing that had happened, but I came up blank. I tried to pull a familiar face out of my memory bank, but there was nothing. It was like going to the ATM only to find you'd somehow been wiped out overnight. And the bitch of it was, you couldn't even remember what your balance was *supposed* to be.

I mean I knew stuff—general stuff. Like ATMs and pirate ships and amusement parks in a vague sort of way. I had basic concepts and all the tools with which to create a story of a life, just none of the actual details. It was like nothing had been written yet. I was notes on scraps of paper and pub napkins—weird little observations, images, scenery waiting to be formed into a coherent whole.

The sun sank a few inches lower in the sky, unlocking the mystery of what time of day it was. My head throbbed in echo to my racing heartbeat as if my heart had somehow decided to relocate to my skull. Why couldn't it have been dawn? Everything was easier to cope with in the light. Even though I knew nothing else, somehow I knew that.

Why couldn't I have stayed unconscious just a few more hours? Something—call it a sixth sense or generalized paranoia—told me I didn't want to face what was out there at night.

I squinted into the dark bottom of the ship, looking for an unlikely flashlight. I had no supplies, no flashlight, and I had no idea where in the hell I was or how I got there.

"Hello?" I called out. I was unsure if yelling into the eerily non-fake jungle was a good thing or not but night was fast approaching, and I had a feeling some creepy crawly might eat me if I didn't find more reasonable shelter. And dear God, please let me have been out here with someone.

I closed my eyes and hoped for some Amazon chick who knew how to navigate nature in all its many surly moods to just pop out at me with a giant machete and a friendly smile.

Pounding footsteps darted through undergrowth and brush, moving in my direction.

I shrank into the corner of the ship, unsure if I wanted whatever or whoever to find me now that I'd made my presence known.

"Elodie?"

The voice was male and urgent. Was that me? Elodie? I rolled that word around in my head a bit. *Elodie. Elodie.* I wasn't sure if that sounded right or not. Did I look like an Elodie? I was struck with the sudden disturbing realization that I couldn't remember what I looked like. Was that normal with amnesia? Did I have amnesia? Shit, for all I knew I'd come into the world fully formed in an amusement park pirate ship five minutes ago. It sure felt that way. Or maybe I was an alien sent here on some arcane fact-finding mission. At this point there wasn't a lot I could objectively rule out.

The man burst out of the foliage, breathing hard. "Elodie, thank God you're awake."

I remained frozen in the corner, watching him. There was no internal memory jog, no mental spark. I mean, he didn't look like a serial killer or escaped prisoner or anything, so that was something. Just a regular guy. Athletic. Tan. Good looking, but not absurdly so. Nice voice. If this guy was on my side, I might be okay.

Were there sides here?

His eyes held worry as he approached the edge of the ship. "Do you remember what happened?"

I shook my head. I was afraid to tell him I didn't recognize my own name, didn't know what I looked like, didn't know him.

He might not take that well. If we had some sort of involved relationship, that is. I'm not sure how I knew men could be weird about stuff like that, but somehow at that moment it felt really true.

"I was afraid to move you," he continued, oblivious to my total lack of back story. "I told you not to climb on the ship. It wasn't stable enough."

"I-I'm sorry," I said. My voice croaked, and my throat felt like sandpaper. I felt as if my mouth hadn't formed words for thousands of years.

"Can you stand? We need to get back to the castle."

The castle?

The stranger's eyes narrowed. "Elodie, what do you remember? Be honest. You're safe here."

We must be using different definitions of the word *safe.*

"Well?" he prodded.

"Nothing. I don't remember anything."

"What do you mean you don't remember *anything*? What's the first thing you remember?"

"NOTHING!" I shouted. Did he need flash cards? Anxiety crowded out my ability to think and behave rationally. It felt like bugs were crawling on me. Maybe they were. I smacked at a spot on my arm. It was getting dark fast, and the wildness had clearly overtaken this place. I'm pretty sure I don't like wildness. I thought suddenly that I should start a list of these things as they occurred to me, but I didn't have any paper.

"What do you mean nothing?" he said.

Come on universe. I couldn't be stuck out here with somebody smart?

"I don't know who you are or who I am. I don't remember anything about my life!" It came out a little more dramatic than I'd intended, as if there could be a low key way to deliver this sort of information.

"Is this one of your jokes? Because I can tell you, if it is, it's not funny. I was scared out of my mind when you wouldn't wake up."

"How long was I out?"

"A few hours."

"I t-think I need to go to a hospital."

"That's not an option."

A chill slid down my spine. Maybe this guy *wasn't* on my side. Hell, how did I know he hadn't beaten me over the head with a broken tree branch in the first place?

"Don't look at me like that. I didn't mean it that way. Let's just get back to the castle. We have electricity there. I'll explain it all to you when we get back."

I stared at the hand he offered. "How do I know you won't hurt me?"

He took a deep, measured breath which didn't reassure me at all. "I'm not going to hurt you. I'm your husband. Trevor. Everything is going to be okay."

I flinched when he reached into his back pocket as if he might be going for a weapon. But it was just his wallet. He pulled out a long thin paper and handed it to me. It was deeply creased from being folded and kept for so long. There was barely enough light left to see, but it was a strip of photos from a photo booth. Trevor and a woman.

"She's pretty," I said absently, staring at the blonde girl with brilliant blue eyes.

He laughed. "There's no conceit in your family. You've got it all." Off my confused expression, he continued, "She's you. That was our first date."

"Oh." I handed the strip of pictures back to him, feeling suddenly awkward.

He put them in his wallet and stretched out his hand again. "Elodie? We need to get inside. It's not safe out here after dark."

"But, how do I know that's really me?"

"There's a mirror in the castle. You're going to have to trust me. What's the worst-case scenario?"

"You're a psychopathic killer?" I said, not sure if I was kidding.

He rolled his eyes. "And if that's the case, you're screwed anyway. Now come on. I'll explain everything when we get home."

I FELT SO WEAK, like my legs had forgotten how to work right. Was that the adrenaline and fear? I had to lean against Trevor and half-walk, half-hobble. The castle rose out of the center of the destroyed theme park, shining like a beacon. It was the only building that had electricity. The dilapidated shops and rides along the way lay in ominous shadows as if they might spring to life and attack at any moment. In spite of myself, I clung more tightly to Trevor's hand.

"The castle runs on solar power. It's the only thing here that does, but it's got everything we need for a while," he said.

What had happened to this place? Why were we even here? I was afraid for us to get inside the castle to find out. Whatever it was, it felt like something... apocalyptic.

"Just a little farther. It's safe inside."

After helping me out of the pirate ship, he hadn't let go of my hand, and I hadn't pulled away. I needed help navigating the unpredictable terrain. I was almost afraid to tell him how weak I felt because I didn't need him to think I was dead weight. His hand was warm and solid. It was the only thing that kept *me* solid.

The castle was enormous and the main hub around which all other things had once revolved. The bottom level was some kind of medieval fairy-tale themed ride. Spiral stairs and an elevator on one side led up to the second floor, which had what were once restaurants and a couple of gift shops. Trevor led me up the steps, past the main restaurant, and to another set of stairs. On the third floor were some hotel-type rooms and an office. A final staircase led to the tower, which seemed to be where we were going.

I couldn't get over how weak and wobbly my limbs felt. It was starting to seriously concern me.

I pulled my hand out of his as we reached the final staircase. "Please, just tell me why you can't take me to a hospital."

I knew already. I just didn't want to believe it. I didn't know the details yet, but I knew. It was only morbid curiosity that kept me playing dumb.

He sighed. "I don't know if there *are* any hospitals anymore. Definitely not any close."

"What?" I was getting the hang of this *dumb* thing.

"Just come upstairs. If you really can't remember anything, I think you need to be sitting for what I have to tell you."

The tower was a fancy suite with a large living area and bedroom that were all one large circular room. There was a connected master bathroom off to one side. Or it *had* been fancy at one time. Now it was just as abandoned and broken down as everything else. Trevor gestured toward an overstuffed chair next to a window. I sat, unsure I wanted to hear this.

"You don't remember anything?" he asked again as if still hoping this was all some game to me. I must be wacky that way.

"No."

"But you remember what the world was like *before*, don't you?" The word *before* held more gravity and weight than the rest of his sentence, more gravity than all the other words he'd spoken to me so far.

"Before what?"

"You know about the world in general?" he asked.

"I... I mean, I guess. Sort of. I think."

Trevor seemed skeptical. He sat on the edge of the king-sized bed near my chair. It creaked and dipped under his weight with a great resigned moan of springs.

"Elodie, the world is gone. More or less."

He'd only gotten the first sentence out and already I felt the tears burning behind my eyes. I might not remember my life, but the implications for anybody's life were already surfacing.

"Do you know what a solar flare is?"

"Yes." I didn't know how I knew what a solar flare was, but it was in the box of scattered random awareness like pirate ships, theme parks, and ATMs.

"Okay, there was an enormous solar flare. The last time the world had solar flares this extreme was before such widespread reliance on electricity. This time it knocked out power grids nearly everywhere. Most technology halted. Just-in-time delivery failed."

"What's just-in-time delivery?"

"Almost everything was running in a way where everything that needed to be delivered to various places from fuel to food was shipped and delivered at close to the last minute, so nothing had to be stored long term. Supplies arrived just as the old ones were running out. With trucks and trains and planes, long term storage of staples and essentials seemed unnecessary to people, and it wasn't cost effective. And with cities so large, it gets less and less practical anyway. The point is... stores started running out of things... Hospitals ran out of things. People started panicking and looting, and then people started dying. The economy collapsed practically overnight. It was so fast. You can't believe how fast it was."

I just stared at him, trying to process everything he was telling me. Hadn't I immediately thought something terrible must have happened when I'd woken in a rusted-out pirate ship ride? I mean, that couldn't be a good sign.

"Do you want me to stop?" he asked.

"No." What good would it do to keep things from me?

"Most of the nuclear plants were safely shut down, but a few weren't. So there are some dangerous radiation zones out there. The ones that melted down near coasts and fault lines set off huge earthquakes, followed by tsunamis. The whole world was affected, so there was no one to send aid because everyone was struggling to survive. But with world economies collapsing, money wouldn't have meant much anyway. There are pockets of survivors. We'll be safer if we can find a bigger group, but for right now, we have supplies for a while. The park was well stocked with non-perishables, and even when we get through that, there's enough wildlife around here to eat. The important part is that we have access to plenty of clean water here. That's the trouble with moving on—what to do about water."

"How long ago... when... when did this all happen?"

"A couple of years. Elodie, we're going to be okay. We could stay here for another year or longer, and I'm already making plans on how we'll get out and try to find another group of survivors. Don't worry."

"How did you know all this was here?"

"I didn't. We stumbled on it. We were lucky. There are some chickens that have gone wild living here. I made a make-shift coop for them in one of the kiddie rides. So we have some eggs and meat I don't have to hunt."

No wonder I couldn't remember anything. My brain had probably been waiting for any opportunity to fall and blank out everything, just scrub the slate clean and forget such a nightmare ever could have happened. This couldn't possibly be my life.

"I really need a shower." I felt gross and covered in grime from the humidity outside.

"There's no running water."

Of course there wasn't. The electricity was fooling me into believing I was in some dingy but workable version of civilization.

"But, there's a wide creek that runs under the park; it's where the water from the moat comes from. We don't drink that water. We use a well for drinking, but the creek water is clean enough to bathe in."

The panic began to ease in, graying out the edges of my vision. "I can't do this. I can't live like this!"

"Elodie, you've lived like this for two years. And this is a step up from how it was in the beginning. You were so excited when we found this place. I wish you could remember. It's hard to see you like this again. You were so despondent when we first had to learn how to survive without the convenience and safety we were used to. But things were getting better. You were adjusting. And now..."

He leaned closer, and I flinched to escape as he brushed the side of my cheek in a gesture that was meant to be comforting.

"I-I don't know you."

He sighed and rose from the bed. "I'm all you've got." Before I could determine if there were nefarious undertones or some veiled threat in his words, he said, "I'm going down to the restaurant to make us something to eat."

"Which one?"

"The big one in the middle... The Banquet Hall. It's got the most working equipment. Come down in a few, okay?"

"Okay."

After he'd gone, I closed my eyes, desperately trying to remember something—anything that could help me make any sense of all this. Or wake up. That would be a welcome option as well. I went to the bathroom to turn on the faucet, already having forgotten there was no running water. I stared at my reflection over the sink.

She's pretty.

I was the woman in his wallet, but I wasn't feeling nearly as generous with myself now that I was seeing it live and in person. My clothes were grimy and worn. I brushed back my hair and noticed a dark scar on my temple and wondered what had happened to produce it. I seemed to have a few other scars and wondered if they were injuries I'd sustained while here and how they'd managed to not get infected and kill me.

I looked down at my hand. No wedding band. But why would anyone in some post-apocalyptic wasteland still have a wedding band? We'd probably bartered or sold it early on when we were just getting our bearings, when people still cared about things like that. Or maybe some marauders stole it. I felt like if something apocalyptic had happened that suddenly marauders must have popped up everywhere, and we would actually start using that word to describe them.

Did I have surviving family? Friends? Maybe it was better that I didn't remember anything—I mean, if they hadn't made it. Trevor had said a lot of people died. Why wouldn't my family and friends be with us? Or his family and friends? Wouldn't we have done better in a larger group instead of just the two of us so isolated like this? I had a feeling I was getting the warm-and-fuzzy edited version of events, which was terrifying in itself.

The bathroom had once been luxurious with a giant tub with jets, a walk-in shower built for two on the other end, and an enormous counter with a sink large enough to bathe a fat baby in. Everything had been meant to look as if it were made of gold, but the plating was flecking off, and the whole place smelled like it had been packed up in someone's grandmother's attic for several winters.

The main tower suite was a large open circle with some seating areas, a TV and DVD player, one king-sized bed, and a few windows. It was full dark now, so I couldn't see anything out of the windows. Back when the park was running, it would have no doubt been beautiful all lit up at night. I wondered if any celebrities had stayed in this tower in the middle of the park with their entourage just below in the smaller rooms.

I clicked the button on the TV, not expecting it to work, but a snowy buzz lit up the screen. Of course TV itself wouldn't work. Who would be broadcasting? I looked through the cabinet and found several rows of DVDs. I turned on the DVD player and popped in a romantic comedy. I couldn't believe it worked.

After a few minutes, I clicked it off and left the tower. I looked through the office and the hotel rooms on the floor below. Nothing of interest. Though I don't think I was looking to be entertained. I was looking for comfort, and absent that, distraction.

The gift shop on the second floor unbelievably had some T-shirts. One was in my size. I peeled off the hot, sweaty top I'd been wearing and exchanged it for a gift shop T-shirt. I took one that had been wrapped in plastic. After sitting there exposed to the elements for so long, the ones on the rack weren't much better than what I'd had on.

Trevor was in the main restaurant's kitchen, as promised, heating up food. Something from a can and something from a deep freezer the sun must have kept operational all this time.

I spotted a small handgun lying on the counter near him.

"W-why do you have that?"

Trevor glanced over at the gun and then back at me. "Why wouldn't I have it? We're lucky I have it and that I haven't had to use it. This is a very different world, Elodie. You know that. I have to protect us."

It wasn't as if he'd waved the gun at me like a lunatic. He'd probably had it concealed on him earlier. And it wasn't as if someone as strong as Trevor needed a weapon to harm me, particularly in such isolation, but it still scared me that he had it.

"How come this whole place isn't looted?" I asked, trying to shift the subject away to something safer.

He looked up from a bag of frozen chicken nuggets. "Several of the stores on the main strip were looted. The castle may have been harder to get to when they came through. And the park is a bit off the beaten path. It wasn't a well-known park. So not too many groups would have come through."

The kitchen looked modern, but the main dining room was like a banquet hall in some old castle right out of a fairy tale. There were long banquet tables, which were positioned in a big square, leaving a wide-open space where there must have been some form of entertainment for the diners.

"Those are some big fireplaces out in the dining hall," I said.

Trevor smiled. "Yeah. It's great for when it gets cold out."

We ate in the big, empty banquet hall on two throne-like chairs that I imagined had been set aside for actors playing the king and queen of the castle. Sitting there like royalty dining on food that was anything but royal fare was depressing as hell.

As if I didn't already feel like I was one of the last two remaining humans on the planet.

For some reason it made me think of the story of Adam and Eve in the garden. I couldn't pull out a single personal detail about my life, but somehow an old religious myth was right there perched on the surface of my brain.

The garden was supposed to be some utopian paradise, but I couldn't imagine anything as a paradise that only contained two people. It seemed lonely. No wonder Eve began forming questionable friendships with reptiles.

I picked at the chicken nuggets on my plate.

"Something wrong with it?" Trevor asked.

"Just not very hungry."

He looked concerned as if trying to remember if loss of appetite was related to concussion.

I stared down at the baked beans and chicken on my plate and wondered if I'd ever get my memory back. I wasn't sure I wanted to remember a time that was happier when the world ran like clockwork and no one thought it could ever end. I had a sense of what things had once been like in general, though I couldn't seem to project myself into any of the stories. Maybe that was for the best.

"When are we going to look for more survivors?" I asked, trying to stop thinking about my troubling loss of memory.

"Am I such poor company?"

"That's not what I meant."

I'd seen proof positive that I at least knew him. We had at least, at some point in our history, sat together in a photo booth like we liked each other and gotten photos made. But the number of things he wasn't telling me could no doubt fill libraries. Had we had a rocky relationship? Was there some awful shared trauma he'd been trying not to burden me with? A tragic loss?

Maybe I was the burden. Would it have been easier for him to survive this without me? Did he want to? It didn't seem like this was a fantastic quality of life to aspire to. I wondered if anybody else out there had a life any better. The Amish were probably doing okay. If they hadn't had to fight off hordes of previously comfortable people now without an internet connection.

So many questions. I thought back to the first moments after I'd woken. Trevor hadn't seemed as surprised as I'd expected when I said I'd lost my memory.

It had all happened in a rush, but that part hadn't seemed to ruffle him like it should have. He hadn't even dwelt on it very long. The only part I was sure about was that when he tore through those woods after me, he'd been panicked.

Finally, he answered my earlier question about looking for others. "Let's just give it a little while. We don't know what we'll encounter out there. I don't think we should leave until we absolutely have to."

"But, you said we'd be safer in a group. Shouldn't we at least..."

"Elodie, that's enough!" I flinched, and he quickly softened his tone as if trying to reason with a small child set on ice cream for dinner. "It's not safe. And I don't want you wandering outside the park on your own. We know the park is safe because I test it occasionally with the Geiger counter. I don't want you wandering outside the guaranteed safe zone into a possible radiation pocket. We need to go together."

"O-okay." I didn't even know if that was how radiation worked, but Trevor seemed sure of himself, so I let it go.

I finished my dinner, even though I didn't really want it. But I might get hungry later, and the last thing I wanted to do was annoy this man I didn't remember knowing. I also didn't relish the idea of coming down here alone in the middle of the night foraging for canned goods like an insomniac squirrel. However unsure I might be of Trevor, I liked the idea of being by myself in this big artificial castle even less.

Trevor took the plates and cups back to the kitchen and washed them with some water he must have drawn from the mysterious well. There were several medieval-looking pitchers of it in the industrial-sized fridge, pitchers which waiters and waitresses no doubt had used to refill iced tea. I stayed off to the side out of his way, trying to pick out a memory of anything I had ever personally experienced before today.

When I thought really hard, I got a fuzzy image of a white room and Trevor's face. But then it blurred back into nothing but a bright white visual noise that made me dizzy. I gripped the edge of the stainless steel island for support.

"Are you okay?"

"F-fine. Just a little disoriented still."

Trevor nodded. "Given the spill you took, I'm sure that's quite normal." He left the dishes to drain near the sink and joined me on the other side of the kitchen.

"You can explore the park tomorrow. Just don't climb on any more pirate ships." He gave me a handsome crooked smile that somehow still felt overwhelmingly ominous despite how hard he tried to make it endearing. "Would you like to see the first floor?"

"Sure." What I really wanted to say was 'not really', but I didn't want to piss off the only other person possibly for miles —the only one who knew how to navigate this fresh new hellscape.

On the bottom level, Trevor turned a crank. The drawbridge we'd walked across to get into the castle actually came up, closing us in for the night.

"You can never be too careful," he said.

It had taken a lot of strength for him to turn the crank and raise the drawbridge. There was no way I could do that on my own. It might be easier to lower it, but that was just me guessing because it seemed like letting it down *should* be less strenuous than bringing it back up. I didn't like the idea of him being the one who said whether or not I could leave the castle by a simple display of brute strength.

But that was life now, wasn't it? In a civilized world, there might have been some level of equality, enforced by laws, but mostly enforced by practicality and technology. Now, everything was back to the law of the jungle. And brute strength was king. This wouldn't be a world of happy equality, no matter what type of person Trevor turned out to be.

"I'll show you the castle ride. It's the only one that works."

Right. Because of the solar panels. Everything else in the park was dead, except for the scurrying creatures that had made the husks of rides into dens and nests. I shuddered at that thought, unsure I wanted to explore too deeply even in daylight.

When we reached the entrance to the ride, Trevor flipped a switch. The lights came on, illuminating wooden doors that ostensibly led into the castle ride. A carriage with cracking and peeling gold paint lurched forward and stopped in front of us.

After about half a minute, it moved on and pushed its way through blue wooden doors, beyond which played the creepy music that went with the ride. It was made all the more unnerving by the fact that it didn't play quite right as if the sound came from a record that spun on a warped turntable.

A second creaking carriage emerged from the same darkness the first one had.

"They're on a timer," Trevor said. "It keeps everything evenly spaced while giving the tourists time to get on or off the ride." He spoke as if the park was still in operation, as if a swarm of people would be forming a line to ride this monstrosity at any moment. He held out a hand to me. "My Lady."

"I don't know if I want to..." The whole thing just felt fucked up to me. This isolated half broken down ride that time and the world forgot out in what felt like the middle of nowhere. I felt as if getting in that carriage would edge out the last bits of sanity contained in the universe.

"Come on. It's not like it's a run-down roller coaster. It's perfectly safe. I'll protect you."

It wasn't worth fighting over. I tried to remember what I'd decided about just trying to get along with him and took his hand and got into the carriage. I was barely inside when it pitched forward sending my chicken nuggets rattling around in my stomach.

The music was even more disturbing inside the ride. It was a song about a princess who had been captured and locked inside a castle tower (why did we have to be staying in the tower?) by an evil king who wanted to marry her. But she didn't love him.

At some point in the story/song, there was a witch and some evil magic. Because how could a fairy tale even work without a witch and some evil magic? That part of the story seemed superfluous. The king was villain enough. There was no real need to add any magic, but the flashes and noises probably appealed to the children the ride was intended for—unless it gave them the awful nightmares I was sure it would give me.

Much of the story was the princess crying and hoping some prince she actually liked would come rescue her. The ride was a visual of the contents of the song. It really shouldn't have taken an apocalypse to shut this place down.

The whole thing would have been better without the song. Maybe they could have just played some violins or piano without lyrics instead.

As our carriage moved deeper into the bowels of the ride, I closed my eyes against the eerie animatronic people and the wooden way they moved. It didn't take long for rides like this to fall apart if unattended, unused, and uncared for. A few of the moving characters' eyes were popping out. I imagined without the air conditioning constantly running, the humidity had just squeezed them right out.

Here or there an arm had fallen off. It was macabre. And I swear one of them looked right at me. Yeah, this was super fun.

I looked over to find Trevor watching my reactions. "You thought this was a hoot the first time we were on it," he said.

I shrugged noncommittally, waiting for it to be over.

Finally, the carriage went through a second set of wooden doors. Right before it did, an animatronic court jester jumped out, waved, and laughed like a maniac, asking us to come back soon. Why on earth would we do that? I think my heart stopped for a second when the jester jumped out.

When our carriage came to a stop, I couldn't get out of it fast enough. Trevor followed me and shut the ride off.

"I'm sorry, I thought you'd think it was funny. I thought it would lighten things a bit." He flipped the switch. The lights faded off, and the music ground down into silence.

I wondered about the personal hell of the operator who had to listen to the front end of the song as well as the back end of the song as both sets of doors opened over and over for hours on end. And that creepy court jester. There wouldn't be enough money in the world for me to take that job.

"It's late. We should probably head back upstairs for the night. You can explore the rest of the park tomorrow. You need to exercise and keep your strength up."

I bit my tongue to keep from blurting out the truth about how strange I felt. Had he noticed?

I wanted nothing more than to get out of this dead theme park, but he was right on the practicality of staying. There was clean water here, and it seemed to be a good store of food, and electricity with two large fireplaces to keep warm and plenty of wood to chop down. There were beds and linens. It was survivable. Whereas, we had no idea what awaited us on the outside beyond this tangled oasis.

As we made our way to the tower, I couldn't stop thinking about that stupid ride and the even stupider story. I couldn't shake how much I felt like that princess in the tower, and I knew in a way I can't explain that there were things about our relationship Trevor was keeping from me.

There was a sofa in the tower suite, but only the one bed. It was a room meant for a couple, not a couple and a bunch of kids. Maybe it was the honeymoon suite.

I looked away as Trevor took off his shirt and then his pants. Thankfully he stopped at his boxers. He slid into the bed while I stood awkwardly, my arms wrapped around myself as if to ward off a chill that wouldn't arrive for months yet.

My gaze shifted to the sofa, wondering if I could make that work and how offended he'd be if I did it. Shouldn't he have the decency to take the sofa and offer me the bed? If he was my husband? If he supposedly loved me? Shouldn't he be more concerned about my memory? About my general physical and mental well-being?

He seemed in denial, like he just refused to accept the facts of the situation. Somehow he'd accepted the rest of the world as it was, but me not being able to remember him or our life together was too much. That was his line in the sand.

He turned off the lights. "Elodie... get in the bed."

I kept all of my clothes on and slid in on my side, staying as close to the edge as possible. I closed my eyes trying to get that ride out of my head, trying to get everything that had happened since I'd woken in the pirate ship out of my head. I wanted nothing more than to dream of a world where everything was normal, and all the trucks and trains still arrived on time.

I felt him scoot up behind me. His arm came over my waist like the safety lever on the ride downstairs. His warm lips pressed against my neck.

I tried to squirm away from him. "Please don't. I don't know you."

"Goddammit, Elodie. I'm your husband."

I cringed at his tone. There was no one I could go to for help here. I couldn't stop thinking about the drawbridge that effectively sealed me in with him until he decided to let it down. I was now convinced that I probably couldn't even turn the crank to lower it down by myself. Maybe I was being irrational, but I felt so helpless.

"But I don't remember that," I said. "Please be reasonable. You're a stranger to me. Can't you understand that?"

He stroked my hair and let out a long sigh. I lay there stiffly, just waiting for him to stop touching me. After a few minutes of this, he backed off to his side of the bed.

I sat up against the headboard. Carved golden cherubs stabbed me in the back. I put my pillow between the carvings and me. "Can we talk about this?"

"Talk about what?"

"I don't remember anything about my life, about you, about our life together. And you're acting like I never told you I couldn't remember anything. Like nothing out of the ordinary happened today."

I heard him sit up and silently prayed he wouldn't turn the lights back on.

"I just think it's fucking convenient that you fall and get amnesia of all fucking things right when we were in the middle of a fight."

"So you don't believe me?"

He shrugged. "I just think it's fucking convenient. Do you know how rare and unlikely amnesia is? Especially the kind of full-on memory wipe you seem to be suffering from. On a soap opera, fine. In real life, absolutely not. I just don't buy it."

"Well, I'm sorry you don't *buy* it."

Maybe he just didn't want to believe it. If our positions were reversed and the only person I had to count on in impossible circumstances suddenly didn't remember me or anything that had happened to get us to that point, I'd be pretty upset about it, too. Maybe his anger masked loneliness. Or fear.

"I'm really scared," I said.

"Yeah? Join the club."

"I can't believe my husband would act this way."

"Well, I can't believe my wife would climb around on an unstable pirate ship like a monkey despite how unsafe I told you it was. If you hadn't done that, we wouldn't be in this situation!"

"I'm sorry."

He snorted. "No, you're not. You can't remember doing it, so how can you be sorry? You're just trying to appease me. And I fucking hate that even more. I hate that you're afraid of me."

"I-I'm not afraid of you." I was so glad the lights were out, that the darkness that enveloped us was so total and complete. He would have seen in my eyes that I was lying. I *was* afraid of him.

I was pretty sure by now that he was being honest about

being my husband, but that didn't make him a good guy. Millions of women were married to abusive men. And he seemed to have a short fuse. More than once, I'd already been afraid he'd just grab me and shake me or something.

Even if I couldn't remember him, if he was the kind of man a normal woman would want to be married to, wouldn't I at least feel safe with him? Instinctively? He was definitely good looking. I couldn't imagine it would be too much of a strain to take comfort in those arms going on appearance alone. But something felt so *off* about him.

"Like I said, I'm all you've got. And there's only so long I'm willing to wait for your memory to come back."

"What's that supposed to mean?"

"It means what it means. The only good thing I had in my life was you. The only comfort I had at night was you. And now you're ripping it all away."

What a selfish bastard. He should count himself lucky I'd agreed to marry him to begin with.

I heard him scoot back down on the bed and felt him jerk the covers over his body, ripping them half off me. I didn't say anything else. I was too busy going through the horrifying idea that he'd put a deadline on my memory retrieval, and if everything didn't come back... if I wasn't in love with him, he'd just... take what he felt was owed? We really were back in a pre-civilized world.

"T-Trevor?"

"What?"

"We can't... I mean... I can't get pregnant out here without a hospital. Women died in childbirth before hospitals. They sometimes do even with them. But my odds wouldn't be good without a doctor."

"You won't get pregnant. I got snipped."

"W-why?" Didn't he want kids with me? I mean, don't most

men want kids with their wives? Isn't that part of the dream of normality?

"I just did. I didn't think the world was worth bringing kids into even before it pretty much ended. I'm glad I did it now."

Yeah, I could feel his smugness oozing over to my side and hoped it wasn't contagious.

I scooted down back onto the bed and stared out into the blackness. I jumped when Trevor's hand landed on my waist.

"Relax. I'm not trying anything. I'm sorry for how I've been today. I just can't lose you again."

Again? When had he lost me the first time?

2

I wish I could say the next day felt more hopeful, that the birdsong filling the air awakened a sense of adventure in me, but it didn't. I woke up sore and tired and still feeling weak. I was beginning to wonder if I'd caught some exotic illness out here, a thought made more terrifying by lack of hospitals.

Looking out the window of the tower, I wished it was still night so I couldn't see outside. Much of the park was overgrown with kudzu, the aggressive vines winding and twisting through and around many of the rides and shops.

It crawled over the concrete, determined to let nothing stop it in its quest for total park domination. I had my doubts that this would be a feasible place to stay for another year. Kudzu is like The Blob. The humidity paired with the kudzu almost guaranteed we were in the south.

How did I know that?

Trevor made eggs for breakfast, collected fresh from the chickens roosting in the kiddie rides. There was no milk or orange juice, just water. I had a feeling milk and juice were now rare luxury items as likely to be acquired as a private jet. On the bright side, there was some turkey bacon that had survived in the deep freezer.

"Are you cutting back the kudzu coming our way?" I asked when we sat down in the kitchen to eat. The vines were the most pressing thought on my mind.

Trevor gave me an odd look. "I thought you lost your memory."

"What does that have to do with anything?"

"You were a botanist... before." *Before the world went away.* "When we first got here, the kudzu problem was your first concern."

And it still was, apparently.

"Well? Are you? You have to cut that back. Some of those vines are heading right for the castle and could climb over the wall. If they grow strongly enough to the top, they could cover the solar panels. Then we're fucked even worse."

"I'll take care of it."

"You'd better do it fast. That stuff grows a foot a day. In less than a week it'll reach the base of the castle. We need the freezers to keep working. Speaking of which, how long will this stuff in the freezer last?"

"Maybe another six to eight months if we're lucky. Though I've started hunting and freezing local game already, so once this stuff starts going off, we can just start eating what I'm storing up."

I didn't want to think about being here with him another six to eight months. I didn't want to think about living here for another six to eight days. Even six to eight hours felt awful, like arriving at a menial job you hated, knowing you were trapped for an untenable block of time.

"A-and the canned goods?"

"Those have about another year on them. The challenge is

going to be getting fruits and vegetables when that runs out. We may have to survive mainly on meat and eggs. Maybe some berries. At least you still seem to have your botany knowledge. It'll keep us from eating the wrong berries."

I had the strange feeling that he was happy some of my knowledge survived primarily because he didn't want my amnesia cutting into his berry foraging. What a prince.

"We don't have running water, right?" I asked.

"That's right."

"So where do we... you know?"

Trevor chuckled almost as if he were enjoying this. God, was he that petty that he was still holding some asinine grudge over whatever we'd been fighting about before I fell and lost my memory?

"We go outside, princess."

"Like a bear?"

"Yep."

That sounded fucking terrible. Of all the shitty things so far, this whole *going to the bathroom outdoors* sounded the absolute worst.

"You'll get used to it."

Sure I would. Just like I'd get used to his charming company.

I laughed suddenly at the utter bizarreness of being a plant specialist but being freaked out by too much of the great outdoors.

"What's funny?"

"Nothing." If I told him, I was sure he'd piss all over my tiny inch of mirth. I was convinced I would have to carefully guard any bit of joy I could find, or Trevor might overtake it like the kudzu outside.

After breakfast, Trevor washed the dishes then lowered the drawbridge so I could get out of the castle. He didn't follow me. After I took care of *bear business*, I wandered the park.

Kudzu crept over everything. Statuary was broken with a stone limb here, a random nose there. Strong storms had come through, I could tell from the slant of things, the uprooted bushes and smaller trees, and the way they leaned. I took a closer look at the trees. With the Kudzu and humidity, definitely the south. But there were a few palms as well.

I bent to take a handful of dirt in a spot where the sidewalk had broken apart. The texture was a bit sandy. Could we be near an ocean? Not near enough to smell the salt, but hurricanes definitely could have blown through.

If storms had blown through, how long ago? It must have been before the world ended unless we had the luckiest set of solar panels in the world. And how long had it taken for the well water to be okay again? If it even had been harmed. I wasn't sure about that. I grasped for information just outside my supposed specialty to no avail. What I wouldn't give for an Internet connection and more information right about now.

Trevor hadn't exactly been the most forthcoming tour guide. Hell, I didn't even know what he'd done for a living before the solar flares.

As I moved farther from the castle, I could see shop windows had been broken, and on the main strip at least some looting had taken place. It was easy enough to see the bare walls and shelves through the gaping holes in the glass.

Maybe the drawbridge of the castle had been up when they came, and it hadn't been worth it to try to scale the walls. Maybe that was how Trevor and I had found such a livable environment amongst these modern ruins.

On one wall near an arcade, with what looked like a fortune teller's tent, someone had spray painted something about the fortune teller being dead and her services no longer being needed. It sounded like song lyrics. I was sure it was song lyrics. I strained to try to pick out a memory of the song in my head, a melody, more lyrics, anything, but everything was a blank.

Maybe it was just clever, if not morbid, graffiti. Just because it rhymed, didn't make it a song. Maybe it was some kind of street poetry.

Many of the rides already showed signs of rust. A few of them looked as if they'd been beaten with baseball bats—some hopeless youth taking out aggression at the world for not staying the way it was supposed to, maybe? I wished they'd left the bats so I could take a few swings. It would have been cathartic.

A wooden cut out of a man welcoming people to the park had been painted over so that he looked like a monster—a ghoul or a vampire or a zombie. It was hard to tell which one they had been going for. Covering the sign in black spray paint were the words: "Abandon all hope."

What a cheery place to live. Somehow I couldn't imagine any version of myself that could have ever been excited about this. And if I had been, God, how bad had my living conditions been before we found this place?

As I reached the end of Main Street, the park began to branch into different themed areas. On my right was a giant vampire head, his mouth wide open to form a door. Guests were meant to walk right in between those huge fangs to get to... above his head was a sign that once lit up with individual letters. It said "unhouse". A large F was on the ground near a cluster of wildflowers that grew in abundance throughout the park.

Not my kind of fun. Or "un" as the kids were calling it now.

Just past the fun house, haunted house, and creepy clown-themed rides and stores, were the kiddie rides. The chickens started clucking as I approached. A few of the hens sat on nests, while others pecked at the bugs and worms through large cracks in the sidewalk. A rooster gave me an aggressive stare as if to say he'd peck out my eyeballs to keep his harem intact.

I held up my hands to let him know I had no intentions toward his girls and wondered if such a gesture even translated across species. How had Trevor managed to get the eggs with that rooster lurking about? I backed away slowly until he lost interest in me and went back to eating.

"Oww, Fuck!" I gripped the side of the kiddie ride as a sharp low abdominal cramp hit me. Oh shit. My period. What was I going to do about that? What *had I* been doing about that? I was too embarrassed to bring it up with Trevor. It didn't matter if he was my husband. I didn't know him.

I was relieved at least to have a passingly plausible explanation for my feelings of weakness. Maybe it was just hormones. And I was sure the heat and humidity weren't helping matters.

As I wandered the park, an idea hit me, and I went in search of a ladies' room. I shrieked when a long slinky rodent zipped past me inside the first bathroom I came to. Of course creatures would be nesting in here. But on the wall was just what I expected: one of those machines with feminine hygiene products. Fantastic.

The machines were intact, so unless someone wandering past had a bunch of quarters on them, I might be in luck. I took apart the pipe on one of the sinks and used it to break into the machine. It was a lot more difficult than I expected, especially given how the metal box on the wall was rusting out.

When it finally broke, feminine care products rained out like candy from a piñata. I gathered everything that had spilled out like I had just found a hoard of gold and continued on my way. I stopped in one of the gift shops. Looted. Almost picked clean.

Whoever had been in the park before us must have been guys or the tampons would have already been raided. Despite the shop being savaged, I found a large shopping bag behind the register. I put my bounty from the bathroom machine into the bag then went and collected everything out of the other ladies' rooms. A few of the machines were running low or empty but most were still full.

When I got back, Trevor was in the tower reading a book. "Find anything interesting?" he asked, indicating my bag as if I'd just been out shopping or something.

"More creepy than interesting," I said. I wasn't willing to get into a discussion about my hoarding. I took the bag to the bathroom and stashed it under the sink and locked the bathroom door. I was right, my period had started. I quickly took care of things and went back out into the main suite where Trevor sat with a curious expression on his face.

There was no way I was talking about this directly, but I did need information. What I'd collected would last several months, but I was sure there had to be a storeroom somewhere, probably here in the castle. If it was in the castle, I was set and could worry about what happened when that ran out way in the future.

"Umm, Trevor?"

He looked up from his book. "Yes, dear?"

I wished he wouldn't call me that, but I let it go. "So, I know we don't have running water, but surely if there's a stock room in the castle, we have soap and shampoo at least."

He seemed almost disappointed that I'd figured that out. What an asshole.

"Yeah, there's a stock room on the second floor. Do you want me to go with you?"

"No. I've got it, thanks," I said.

He shrugged and went back to reading.

When I reached the second floor, I found the stock room hidden away at the end of a hallway—something I'd overlooked in my previous exploration because it was so nondescript. I let out a relieved sigh when I discovered the door was unlocked. Inside was a wondrous bounty of little hotel soaps and shampoos, towels, toilet paper, paper towels, cleaning products, and... jackpot... feminine protection. Endless boxes of pads and tampons. It was the happiest I'd been since waking up in that pirate ship. These were things that made me feel halfway civilized.

I didn't bother relocating any of it up to the tower. It was enough that I knew it was there. And with the drawbridge coming up each night, I didn't have to worry someone would wander in and take anything. I was, somehow disturbed Trevor hadn't already shown me this stuff. Wouldn't he realize how important soap and shampoo and all the rest would be to me?

Didn't he care?

I went back up to the tower.

"Did you find what you were looking for?" he asked.

"Yeah. Where'd you get a book?" I asked. I'd been preoccupied before but now that I was thinking about it, I couldn't imagine Trevor had traveled with books while the world was dying. And if he had, he'd probably read it so many times he could have it memorized by now.

"There were a whole bunch of them in the office below us when we got here. We relocated them to the cabinet in the entertainment center. Check the side without the DVDs. You might like some of them. And without your memory, it's all new again."

"Yeah, thrilling. You're such a silver lining kind of guy."

Trevor frowned. "Are you going to be like this forever?"

"Like what?"

"Before you had that stupid fall you were optimistic, acclimating to our life. Things were good."

I wrinkled my nose at that. "They were so good that we had a huge fight before the accident?"

A disturbing thought occurred to me. What if I hadn't fallen at all? What if he'd pushed me? What if he'd tried to kill me during the fight? It would explain why he didn't seem too upset about my memory loss.

Trevor slammed his book shut and stalked out of the suite, leaving me alone in the tower. I was hungry, but I was also exhausted, and I didn't want to run into him again for a while, so I lay down on the bed for a nap.

I woke to find Trevor standing over me with a look I couldn't quite translate into a coherent emotional state. Anticipatory maybe?

"I made you some dinner."

"O-okay." Had he poisoned it? Would this be his second murder attempt? He looked a bit too eager.

I followed him wearily down to the second floor to find that he'd picked wildflowers and lined the tables with them. Emergency candles were lit on the main table where the "king and queen" were supposed to sit.

"Cornish game hens?" I asked, looking at the small birds on the plates, surrounded by vegetables from a can. He must have been holding out on me with the frozen chicken nuggets.

"Actually, it's a couple of the chickens. They were too small and fighting a lot, so I went ahead and slaughtered them."

I shuddered. It must have been before today because when I'd been out by the kiddie rides, I hadn't seen any smaller chickens running around.

He pulled out my chair for me and then disappeared into the kitchen. Music began to play over the sound system. It sounded like what you'd hear at a renaissance fair, but it was probably all that was available here. He returned a little while later with a bottle of wine. Where had that been stashed?

"The manager kept a few bottles in his office. We swore we wouldn't open them except for special occasions."

"And this is a special occasion?"

He shrugged. "Elodie, I don't want to fight. I don't know why this is so hard when you don't even remember what we were fighting about."

"What *were* we fighting about?"

"It's not important."

"No, I want to know. What were we fighting about?"

Trevor looked like he was scraping the bottom of the idea barrel for any convenient lie to feed me. "It's not worth upsetting you."

"Right, because why upset me when our life is so perfect and serene?"

He growled in frustration. "Fine. You asked for it. I got snipped because you kept miscarrying, and it was hurting you every time you lost a baby. So I got the snip so you wouldn't have to keep going through that. We had a stupid argument about something not important that wound back around to that and how you thought I resented you or some other bullshit. As if we'd want a baby now in all this, anyway."

I didn't say anything. I just looked down at my plate and started eating.

~

MONTHS PASSED in the abandoned theme park. It felt like a combination of camping and the aftermath of a zombie apocalypse. Things started to become normal somehow. I started to feel stronger. Whatever may have been wrong with me had seemed to clear up on its own with time. The romantic dinner that night had been a turning point of sorts. It didn't do anything immediately to make me want to get closer to Trevor, but oddly, time did.

The isolation of no other human companionship quickly grew to be too much for me. Feeling or expressing anger or disdain toward him only left me by myself with no one to talk to or seek comfort or reassurance from. Without Trevor, I'd die out here. I didn't think he was going to just up and abandon me, but there is a sort of clinging desperation that begins to take hold when your waking reality is only one other person in the world. It was like Trevor was the only other person still alive on the planet. It probably wasn't true, but it *felt* true.

Suddenly that person begins to seem almost perfect—your soul mate—the only person you could possibly have ever ended up with even in a sea of billions to choose from. We didn't have much real sexual chemistry—or at least there wasn't any on my end. But he was comfortable, like a favorite pair of sneakers.

Little by little the *off* feeling about him started to dissipate, and I began to be convinced that it had only been due to confusion brought on by my fall and the shock of waking into the world as it now was.

His annoying traits receded into the background, and we actually started getting along. I could see glimpses of what I must have seen in him before the collapse. I could even see how we might have ended up together in wedded bliss, a bliss that had seemed unthinkable as even a minor feature of our past when I'd first opened my eyes inside the pirate ship.

The weather turned colder, and we brought our blankets and pillows to set up camp in the grand dining hall of the restaurant where we could use the fireplaces to keep warm at night. It didn't get too incredibly cold, but it got cold enough to be uncomfortable without the added comfort of heat.

Trevor had decided it was safer than running the heating/AC unit year round. He wanted to give the unit a break, he'd said. Because if that thing broke down and he couldn't fix it with what was on hand, we'd be fifteen levels of fucked when summer reached its zenith.

I never questioned why he seemed to do both the hunting

and the cooking, as well as the cleaning up. I asked to help, but he'd push me away, as if he didn't trust my involvement in the process. It created a sort of crushing boredom, and once I'd read all the books in the cabinet, the only thing left to do was fuck—something he seemed quite content with.

We'd begun to do it with the frequency of rabbits—mainly because it kept him happy—but without the procreative results.

Trevor came in loaded down with an armful of firewood and threw a few more logs on the fires. Both fireplaces were lit. They were located in the room such a way that we could set bedding up in the middle and have warmth seemingly from all sides.

"There. That should last us a while."

He joined me on the blankets. We'd created a pillow fort with all the pillows, not only from the tower, but from the guest rooms on the floor below it as well. We'd taken the comforters off the beds so we could make a thick, plush mattress to lie on and cushion against the hard floor.

"Trevor?"

"Hmmm?"

"When will we move on? Look for more people, I mean?" I felt if I spent even one more day here, no matter how much I'd grown to care about him, that I'd lose my fucking mind.

His eyes narrowed, and I was sure the fight was about to start again. He seemed so insecure about the possibility of joining another group of survivors—as if I would only stay with him as long as he was my only option. As if I'd jump on the cock of the first new man who dropped his pants. I didn't understand the depth of his insecurity. There was nothing physically repulsive about Trevor, and he had the one thing most random men out there wouldn't have... built-in birth control. And given the new state of things, that made him the safest man in my world.

Plus there was the months he'd already taken care of me, fed me, kept me safe, kept me from going completely insane. He was dependable. I could count on him. I knew he would protect me from whatever hardships this barren wasteland of a world brought our way.

Though, if I couldn't sustain a pregnancy, maybe birth control wasn't a worry anyway—depending on how early the pregnancies ended. I'd never asked about that. The whole topic seemed like a very sore subject with him, and I didn't want to rile him up. However either of us had once felt about it, not being able to have kids was a blessing now.

Whatever Trevor had planned or wanted to say, he stifled behind a grunt. Then he said, "We need to wait until it's warmer. Not a good idea to leave now."

I couldn't argue with the sensibility of that. It wasn't as if it dropped down into freezing arctic temperatures around here, but depending on traveling conditions, it might be difficult to cope with the cold at night.

Trevor's expression shifted, and his gaze moved languidly over me. I was wrapped loosely in the blankets, wearing only his T-shirt. He pounced on me like a hungry jungle cat, his hands frantically roaming over me while his mouth sought the warm invitation of mine.

He nearly ripped the T-shirt in two as he jerked it over my head and arms, flinging the offending article of clothing far away.

He cupped my face, forcing my eyes to meet his, and asked, "Do you love me, Elodie?"

I still couldn't remember him or anything else from before my fall, but if I were being honest, these long months alone with him... while it hadn't brought back any of the old feelings I couldn't remember, it had brought something new.

"I- I think I do."

There was a loud clatter and a reverberating metal echo as

something hit the ground outside the door. My eyes widened, mirroring his. Our movements stilled. For a moment our breath froze, then in concert it began to move so slowly and quietly in and out of our lungs it was almost painful. I didn't have to ask. Trevor had forgotten to bring up the drawbridge.

I couldn't believe I'd ever resented him doing that at night. It was for my protection—and his—while we slept.

Had some forest creature wandered in, looking for scraps of food and warmth? Or was it a survivor?

Something deep inside me hoped against everything that it was another survivor. Perhaps a group of them. I didn't pause to consider whether such people might be good or bad, only that they were other humans who still existed in the world after months without knowing for sure.

A tall figure dressed in all black filled the doorway. I pulled the sheet up, gripping it tight against my chest. Trevor stood smoothly and moved in front of me. He hadn't managed to fully undress yet. His pants were still on.

He pulled the small handgun out of his pocket. The other man reacted immediately, drawing his own gun so fast it nearly gave me whiplash to watch it unfold. It was a smooth, practiced move. This guy had training. And I wasn't convinced Trevor did.

"Please, just leave us alone," I pleaded.

The stranger didn't even look at me. His eyes were trained on Trevor's as if he could see inside his head to know his next move. Maybe his next several moves.

Trevor wasn't backing down. He racked the slide, but before he could get a shot off, the other man fired several into his stomach.

"No!" I dragged the sheet and scrambled to Trevor's side as he dropped, clutching at him as if to keep his guts from spilling out. I pressed the linen against his wounds, but there was too much blood coming out of him far too quickly. He stared up at me a moment in disbelief, and then his eyes went blank and dead while my tears dripped onto his face.

"Trevor! No! Stay with me, don't go." My hand trembled as I felt for a pulse. There was nothing. Still, I pressed the sheet against his stomach, as if he might come back to life somehow if I could only stop the bleeding.

"He's gone," the man said.

I tried not to think about the fact that I was alone in this castle with the terrifying stranger who'd just shot and killed my husband. My tears fell harder as I wrapped myself in the firm denial that any of this was happening. Maybe he still had a pulse... I just hadn't found the vein. Maybe... maybe...

In a fairy tale, this would be the part where magic and light would swirl around him and he'd get up, revived by the true love and magic that somehow inexplicably existed in my tears. And we'd live happily ever after as the castle sprang to life again. All the kudzu would recede, the graffiti would vanish, and life as I was sure I'd once known it would come rushing back in beautiful full bloom.

But this was a fake fairy tale castle, and my tears weren't magic.

I grabbed Trevor's gun with shaking hands and pointed it up at the stranger from my position on the ground. It felt so foreign to me that even without my memories I was sure this was the first time I'd ever held a gun.

"Do you want to die with your lover?" the stranger asked.

Maybe I did. I couldn't see a reason to go on now after another thing had been taken from me. The world. My memory. My husband and only protector. I'd thought perhaps the stranger might be reluctant to shoot me, but staring into ice blue eyes, I knew he'd pull the trigger without hesitation. And I knew if Trevor hadn't been able to shoot first, my odds were even slimmer.

"Put the gun on the ground and slide it over to me," he said.

"Please don't hurt me." My hands shook so hard, even thinking about aiming properly was pointless.

"Put the gun on the ground and slide it over to me," he repeated. His voice remained steady and calm.

I was sure he would shoot me if I didn't, and I was equally sure I didn't have the resolve to shoot him. And if I shot him, I had no hope of survival. That was it. I was done. I didn't know if I had any hope anyway, but I knew I couldn't survive in the world as it now was without *someone* to help me—ideally a strong male someone. This man and whoever might be traveling with him were my only chance.

I couldn't believe I might have to try to beg and bargain with a complete stranger who'd just killed the only person I could count on. I was struck with the notion that not only did I have to find a way to keep this man from outright killing me, I had to find a way to get him to let me come with him, even if it was the last thing I wanted. I was sure he was strong enough to protect me and help me survive out here. If he wouldn't take me with him, it would be more merciful for him to just go ahead and shoot me, considering the impossibility of the challenges that lay before me without Trevor.

I couldn't even grieve. I had to figure out how to keep going. And I wasn't even sure I wanted to.

I laid the gun down and slid it over. The man stopped it with his boot.

A walkie talkie crackled on. "Shannon. Are you all right? We thought we heard gunfire."

He took the gun from the ground, dropped the magazine and ejected a bullet from the top of Trevor's gun, and put the weapon in his pocket. Then he holstered his own gun. His hands were far too steady after killing a man for my comfort. He raised a finger slowly to his lips to indicate that I must remain quiet. I didn't know what else to do but stifle my crying because I wasn't sure what the others with him were capable of or what he might do to me before they got here if I didn't comply.

Shannon pressed a button on a black plastic device on his shoulder. "Yeah. I'm okay. It was just a wolf. Don't come into the castle unless I call for backup; there could be others. I'm going to check it out."

"Roger that. We'll stay clear. Check in every ten minutes so we know you're safe."

"Will do."

I wrapped the blood-drenched blankets around myself more tightly, struggled to my feet, and got as far back from him as I could. His body still blocked the only easily reachable exit in the room. The fire exits were even farther away, and I didn't think I had much of a chance of getting to them—definitely not while I felt like I was dropping into shock. And he had a gun he'd already shown he was comfortable using on living flesh.

"W-why didn't you tell them I was here?"

"I need to assess the situation first," he said, as if this were some kind of normal response. He eased closer to me, slowly, as if approaching a wounded animal in the forest. "Are you okay?" he asked.

Not the question I'd expected, particularly after our brief standoff. But then, I was a stranger who'd pointed a gun at him —just like Trevor had.

"Of course I'm not okay!" I shouted. "You killed my husband! You fucking savage. The world is gone, and now he's gone."

Immediately, I regretted this outburst. It was so hard to remember I had to appease this person, or I was dead whether he directly killed me or not.

I started to pace. I'd just settled into the new normal. I'd just started to feel like maybe my life wasn't going to be a never-ending nightmare of bare survival. And this man had to come along and murder my husband.

I was sure Trevor wouldn't have shot him. It was just to scare him and make him go away and leave us alone. Obviously, a stranger coming in on his naked wife was a threat he had to address. He had to make sure the man didn't get any ideas in his head. If the other guy had a weapon—which clearly he did—Trevor had to draw first. He had to try to gain the upper hand to protect me.

"What do you mean the world is gone?" Shannon asked. His voice had dropped low and gentle as if he were speaking to a feral cat instead of a person.

I stopped pacing. "What do you mean what do I mean? Weren't you there, too? Aren't you a survivor?"

"A survivor of what? I'm an urban explorer. My friends and I like to check out abandoned theme parks. That man I shot... he was all over the news for months, and so was your picture. Missing doctor. Missing patient. No leads. No family came forward to claim you. It was assumed he kidnapped you. I wouldn't have had to shoot him if he hadn't been about to shoot me. I saw it in his eyes. He wanted me dead, no doubt to keep whatever *this* is, going." He waved a hand around the room on the word *this*.

"W-what? I-I don't understand. What about the solar flares?"

"What solar flares?"

It was like we were speaking two different languages with no translation available between us.

"What do you remember?" he asked finally.

"N-nothing. I had an accident. I-I don't know who I am." I felt so stupid saying that out loud, like it was a failure of my intelligence or the educational system instead of a legitimate medical issue that wasn't my fault.

My head throbbed as I tried to put together what I'd thought was true against what now seemed to be actually true. Shannon's clothes weren't worn or old like someone who'd survived something awful and was wearing the same two or three outfits for months or years. They were new and nice. There was a bit of mud on his boots, but he'd said he was an urban explorer. This was something he did *for fun*. If he wasn't aware of solar flares, they hadn't happened, and the world was still out there.

Oh, God. The world was still out there. All this time I'd been here with some psycho who'd taken me from the hospital... trying to cope with the new normal, and it wasn't normal at all. Possibly just a few miles away, life as everyone had known it had been humming along without a hitch. Just-in-time delivery... still there. Electricity, running water... it was all... still there.

"I-is my name even Elodie?"

Shannon eased still closer to me. "I don't remember. The news stopped running the pictures and story a few months ago. There were some big school shootings, and the news cycle moved on. There were no new leads on your story, I guess, so they never picked it back up."

A sinking dread started to form a knot in the pit of my stomach. "He wasn't my husband." Of course he wasn't my husband. Trevor had lied. About everything.

Shannon shook his head. "The news didn't make it sound that way."

"But there were pictures of us together in his wallet." We must have at least had one date. "He told me the world had ended. And... I believed him."

"Waking up here, no doubt you would. A lot of people don't even think about places like this existing," Shannon said gently.

I started to think back to the way I'd felt about Trevor when I'd first awakened—the giant *fuck no* that had filled my brain at his presence, the big screaming flashing lights that told me this guy was bad news.

I turned away and vomited my dinner on the floor. Then I

turned back to Shannon, embarrassed and ashamed by everything... that I'd been sleeping with my captor that I hadn't even known was my captor, that I was naked and wrapped in a sheet covered in said captor's blood, that I'd just thrown up in front of this stranger whose face held the most horrible pity I could imagine.

"Let's get you cleaned up and go outside. My team has a bunch of supplies, and then—"

"N-no." My lip started to tremble, and I couldn't make it stop. "I can't. I can't stand for them to see me and look at me the way you're looking at me."

"Well we have to report this, get you to the police, get you some help."

I could barely cope with the enormity of the truth as it was. Moments ago, I'd thought I might have to seduce the man who killed my husband in order to keep eating and living in a post-apocalyptic wasteland of a world I wasn't fully sure I wanted to stay in. No part of that was true. And now, suddenly, the idea of facing the police and the media and the world... it was a new horror that was only just now dawning on top of everything else, and I couldn't confront it.

"NO! No police. No." I couldn't imagine the media swarming all over me and then everybody in the country having the look on their face that Shannon had on his. Even if I couldn't see it, I'd know it was happening. Millions of people saying *that poor girl* like a useless prayer.

"But what about your family and friends?"

"You said nobody came forward. They put my picture everywhere, and nobody knows or cares about me enough to have said anything yet."

"But there might still be someone out there. You must have some family out there. Friends. Co-workers. Someone important in your life..."

"NO!" I was screaming now, loud enough that I was afraid

his team might somehow hear me and come running in anyway. I softened my tone, hoping they hadn't heard my outburst and said, "Please, please, I can't do this again. I can't have someone come in and tell me stories about my life I don't remember that I just have to trust and believe are true. I never want to hear another story about my own life that I can't confirm with my own memories. He made me believe..."

"I know."

I shook my head. "You *don't* know. I believed I loved him. I *slept* with him, willingly." As mortifying as it was to say, it wasn't as if this man couldn't figure that out with what he'd been about to walk in on. It was somehow important to me that he know Trevor hadn't thrown me down and had his way with me, that at least I'd wanted, or thought I'd wanted, to be with him.

"I'm sorry," Shannon said.

"I thought we were surviving together in a collapsed world. He took good care of me. I felt *safe* with him. B-but then you show up, and you rip that reality away, and now I'm not a survivor anymore building a life with somebody who loves me. I'm a victim. And he died with me *crying* over losing him. He's won. I can't ever take that victory away from him. I can't trust anybody else to tell me the truth about me. Please just go. Forget you found me. I'll figure something out when the sun comes up. P-please."

By this point, he'd managed to inch his way to within reaching distance of me. "Elodie, the park is dangerous and hard to get in and out of. You have to at least let me help you get out of here, and give you something decent to wear."

I watched warily as he took the pack off his back. He unzipped it and tossed me some pants and a T-shirt. After sizing me up, he gave me a nylon belt that I'm not a hundred percent sure was really meant to hold pants up.

He turned his back to me and waited. I stood there for a

moment, staring at the clothes in my hands, still gripping the bloody sheets around my body.

"I'm not going to look. I promise. Just put some clothes on. I need you to stay here in the present moment, no matter how unpleasant it is. I don't want you to go into shock. Start moving."

I dropped the sheets on the ground and put the clothes on.

"O-okay, you can turn around."

The walkie talkie crackled again. "Shannon. You okay? Where's our check-in?"

"I'm fine. But I think I've come down with a stomach bug. I'm going to head out."

"You sure?"

"Yeah. Where are you guys?"

"We set up clear on the other end of the park near the Ferris wheel. We can't even see the castle from here. Do you want us to come to you?"

"Nah, I'll be fine. Though I did throw up in here so... sorry about that. It's not pleasant."

"Yeah, you sound sorry," the guy on the other end said, laughing. "We might brave it tomorrow. I assume you don't feel well enough to clean up?"

Shannon's voice affected a sick sound, coming out more slow and labored. "No such luck. I might be puking the whole way to the car. You guys okay?"

"Yeah, we feel fine. We'll catch you next trip."

Shannon clicked the walkie talkie off. His gaze went across the room in a calm, assessing way, finally landing on me. "Are you absolutely sure you can't face the world right now?"

I nodded.

"Then here's what will happen. I'm going to dispose of the body, then I will take you out of here. You will stay with me. I will honor your desire to do this at your own pace. For now."

That sounded too much like Trevor's veiled rape threat that first night when I hadn't swooned in his arms immediately.

"What is it?" he asked.

"N-nothing."

Shannon wasn't talking about sex. It wasn't enough that I didn't remember my life; now I had this new screaming vortex of horror to deal with.

3

Once things had been decided, Shannon went into this laser-focused sort of zone—like the whole rest of the world just shut off, and everything turned to auto-pilot. He was suddenly so intense. I sat quietly while he assessed things. I think I imagined if I was very quiet he would forget I was there and leave without me. How hard could it be to get out of the park on my own in the daylight? Even though I'd never ventured to the perimeter, as it was so overgrown and Trevor's warnings had kept me away, I felt certain it couldn't be *that* bad.

Shannon came over to the table where I was sitting like a piece of statuary. He knelt in front of me and pulled a small flashlight from his pocket and shined it into my eyes. He felt the skin on my face with the back of his hand. I wasn't sure what he was looking for. Signs of shock? Were my pupils relevant in that? I didn't know. Ask me something about plants.

"Is there a big drain somewhere in the floor of the kitchen?" he asked. "Most industrial kitchens have one somewhere."

"I-I don't know. I think so. Why?"

"Trust me, you don't want to know." He picked up Trevor's

body and carried him back into the kitchen.

I stayed still and quiet where I was for half an hour—maybe longer—wondering if I was in shock. I must be, right? Everything felt like it had gone into slow motion. Dimly, in the back of my mind I felt I should be doing something... I should leave... get out of here. But I couldn't quite figure out why that was so. My brain didn't seem able to process what was going on. Everything felt foggy and surreal. Finally, I got up and went into the kitchen to see what Shannon was doing.

He was right. I didn't want to know.

He'd found the drain in the floor and had bound Trevor's body to a long metal food prep table. He'd propped it up with some heavy crates so the body was upside down at an angle. Shannon had slit his throat, and the blood was flowing out of Trevor straight into the giant drain.

My hand went to my mouth. I thought I was going to be sick again. I was sure of it.

"Oh---Oh God."

"I told you you didn't want to know," Shannon said, not looking up from his work.

"Oh God."

"If you're going to vomit again, do it back out in the main room."

I just stared at him. For some reason, I don't know what I thought was going to happen when he said he was getting rid of the body. I just... I expected maybe he would bury it in the woods or something. I mean... it's understandable. I thought this was just some new awful unpleasantness he would deal with for both our sakes.

But this... this wasn't someone who'd never killed a person before. This was someone who had a... a *method* for body disposal. How many people did you have to kill to develop a method? They couldn't *all* be self defense.

On the counter, he'd lined up all the pitchers of water from the fridge. For clean-up most likely. There were also about twenty gallons of purified water on the counter that Trevor must have had hidden somewhere. That must have been our *well water.* It reminded me briefly that Trevor was the only person here who had hurt me so far. But then off to the side I noticed big thick plastic sheeting and a wicked sharp saw... Oh... God.

Shannon finally glanced up. "I found that in the freezer. The plastic makes sense, but I have no idea why Trevor had a saw in there. I was sure I'd find something useful in the castle, it's a big place, but... the angels are smiling down tonight."

Or the demons were smiling up.

"Do something useful and bring me that sheet with all the blood on it from the other room," he said.

But I stood there, frozen. My hands started to shake again, and the tremor seemed to move through my whole body.

"H-how do you know to do all this?"

"That's classified."

I was sure he was some sort of ex-military. The way he moved. The way he talked. The calculating precision of every movement that showed signs of training well beyond that of a police officer but too regimented for a garden variety psychopath.

But that didn't explain how he knew so much about getting rid of bodies. That couldn't be standard military procedure.

"You think I'm a monster," he said. He didn't seem to be very bothered by the possibility.

I didn't respond, but I was sure the truth was easily readable in my eyes.

"I've never killed an innocent. Are you innocent, Elodie?"

"Y-yes."

"Then you have nothing to worry about. Now go get the sheets."

Unsure what else to do, I started toward the door. His voice stopped me.

"And Elodie? Don't make me chase you."

I should have run, I know I should have, but I was so scared I couldn't think straight. I didn't know if I could trust he didn't kill innocents, but if I ran from him would I stop being innocent in his eyes? Would it justify killing me too? He clearly knew his way around places like this. I knew he could find me. I knew he could outrun me. Then he would chop me up into little pieces just like he was about to do with Trevor.

I tried to blank my mind of everything but the immediate task in front of me and went into the other room to get the sheets. When I returned, the body had been drained and he was moving it onto the plastic.

Shannon arranged the body and then took the sheet from me. He squeezed the blood out down the drain in the floor. "Now go put that in one of the fireplaces to burn."

I shook my head. "Please... I-I can't..."

"Sure you can. You couldn't survive what's happened to you out here if you weren't strong. I need you to keep moving."

But still I stood staring at the bloody sheet he held out to me like it was nothing. All of this was nothing to him.

"Why do you need to drain and cut him up to bury him?"

"I'm not burying him."

"Why? No one would find him out here."

Shannon just stared at me, his eyes frigid blue ice. "No. I don't do loose ends."

I got the terrified feeling that he was beginning to see me as a loose end and I started to cry again. He ignored my tears and stood up, cleaning his hands in one of the pitchers of water. "Come with me," he said.

"W-why?"

"Because I don't trust you. You look like you've changed your mind about things. Have you changed your mind? Because now is a bad time for that. We are past the point of return. I'm destroying evidence. That looks bad. You're in this with me for the long haul. I chose to help you on your terms because, against all my training and better judgment, I feel sorry for you and the fucked-up shit you've been put through. But now that means I need to know I can trust you before you're allowed to be a free range human again."

That didn't sound good. So I was effectively a hostage now? Why hadn't I just let him call the police and get me help? But how could I have known what he was? How could anyone expect... this?

"Let's go," he said.

I couldn't move. What if this guy was a million times worse than Trevor? Whatever he'd gone through to develop into a person who could do something like this had to have shut off the tap of at least part of his humanity. Even if he'd shown some in being willing to help me, it was such a small gesture compared to what I'd witnessed from him since.

"Just leave me. P-please. I swear I won't say anything. How could it benefit me to talk about this?" I sure as shit didn't want the attention it would bring.

Shannon's expression closed off, and suddenly it was like any pity he'd felt for me had been sucked away into another dimension somewhere or maybe down that big drain with all the blood. He took a coil of rope out of his bag and advanced on me. I turned and ran, my self-preservation instincts finally coming to my aid. But he was far too fast for me.

He grabbed my arm and hauled me over to a chair in the banquet room.

"Sit," he ordered.

I sat. "Please... I don't know what I did wrong. A-are you going to kill me, too?"

"No. I'm not killing you but I can't have you running."

I sat there miserably while he tied me up. Why had I thought even for a second this guy could be any better than

Trevor when all evidence had pointed to the opposite? I'd just been so desperate for anything safe to hold onto that I was making up imaginary saviors where they obviously didn't exist.

Once he'd secured me, he disappeared back into the kitchen. He came out with the bloody sheet and tossed it on the fire, then he was gone again. He went to another part of the castle, then finally came back with a wheelbarrow and shovel. I have no idea where he'd found that, but he was right, the castle was big and contained all sorts of useful things. He propped the shovel next to the fireplace and took the wheelbarrow back with him into the other room.

It was a long time before he came back out. When he did, he had Trevor in small pieces in the plastic inside the wheelbarrow. He tossed the pieces on the flames of the fireplace he hadn't used yet, then he took the plastic and returned to the kitchen once again.

He didn't seem remotely distressed by any of this, and I became increasingly convinced he planned to kill me next, but now that I was tied up there was nothing for me to do but cry and wish somehow I could have made a different choice. I kept reviewing everything in my head from the moment he'd shown up, trying to think how and when I could have truly escaped. Would he have let me go if he hadn't started the process of getting rid of the body? If I didn't know what he was?

He took the plastic back into the kitchen and was gone another maybe five minutes before he returned. The plastic was clean now. He'd obviously rinsed the blood off down the drain. He folded the plastic neatly and set it next to the fireplace. Why?

I tried to think of it all as a puzzle. I tried not to think about what I was really witnessing or the horrifying smells of burning flesh coming from the fireplace that contained pieces of Trevor.

Shannon went back into the kitchen again—I guess for further clean up—while I tried not to gag from the smell of burning flesh and equally tried not to think that it could be me in those flames next. My lip trembled as I worked to keep my crying quiet. I was sure he was just one minor annoyance away from deciding I wasn't worth sparing.

Finally he came back with another pitcher of water, some soap, and some rags. I watched as he scrubbed up the blood on the floor from the initial shooting. He went back to the kitchen for a moment, then returned with wrung out rags that he tossed in the fire with the sheet he'd tossed in earlier. The fire smoldered a bit from the dampness still in the cloth, but quickly recovered.

I glanced over at the other fire that was still eating Trevor and I somehow found the courage to speak. Maybe if I got him to talk to me he wouldn't see me as just more evidence to dispose of.

"Wasn't there any bleach?" I asked.

"There might have been, but it leaves too strong a smell. If my friends come in the room, they'd wonder why one room in an abandoned theme park castle smells like bleach and is ridiculously clean. It's why I left the vomit. It works in our favor. They aren't going to clean it up. They're going to stay away and out of this room because they're pansies. By the time another random group of people comes exploring, nobody will know what it was or that anything of note ever happened in here."

"But that smell... where you burnt him... that's a lot worse than vomit. They'll smell it."

"I guarantee you they've never smelled anything like that. They'll take one look, get one small smell, and flee without analyzing it too deeply. People notice what they want to and everything else gets filtered away and buried."

"O-okay... but... the fire won't burn him all the way... there will still be bones." I said this like I'd somehow figured out something he didn't know. But of course that was crazy, all things considered.

"I have a contact at a crematorium. He can incinerate the rest. I just wanted the body unrecognizable. I trust my contact, but you can never be too careful, and I would prefer he not recognize this guy. Too many questions with it being such a high profile case."

I cringed when Shannon came over and sat next to me at one of the tables. He brushed a long strand of hair out of my eyes.

"Don't be afraid of me, Elodie."

"H-how can I not? After what you just did... and how calmly you did it."

He sighed and stared at me for a good long time while I tried to perfect the art of invisibility. Finally he said, "Okay, I'll play your game. Hypothetically I just leave you. What's your next move?"

"I-I wait until day, and then I get out of the park."

"How?"

"I don't know. It can't be that hard."

He looked skeptical, but he let the logistics slide. "And then what?"

"I-I don't know."

"Do you have any money?"

"No. I mean... not on me. I don't remember if I have any in general." Was I the type of person who saved? Had I been in the position to save? If I was a botanist, did that mean I still had student debts, or did botany pay pretty well? How could I know how fast kudzu grows but not know how much botany pays? Maybe Trevor had lied about my job. Maybe I had just been fixated on kudzu in my former life, and somehow it slipped through the cracks of my amnesia.

I blinked a few times, realizing Shannon was still speaking to me.

"Where do you live? Where do you bank? How will you get into your bank accounts? What do you plan to do when that runs dry? If you don't want to have to deal with the police or the media or anyone else, how do you plan to live under the radar and get money to survive long term?"

He just kept hitting me so fast with all these questions. Questions he knew I couldn't answer. Finally, I shouted, "Why are you doing this?"

"I'm just trying to show you that the anonymity and safety from scrutiny that you asked for isn't available going on your own. Even if I didn't have to worry about the fact that you just watched me kill a guy and dispose of the body, it's not feasible for you to do this alone. And you know it."

"M-maybe I'll just go to the police."

Shannon laughed. "Not now, you're not. Do you recall begging me not to make you do that? I'm not hanging out to dry because you can't make up your mind. I'm sorry for what you've been through, and I know you're terrified, but honey, you're coming with me."

"Maybe I'll scream. Maybe your friends are wandering around and will hear me. Whatever you do to me, they'll still know what you are. Is it worth blowing your cover?"

He stared me down in that way wild predators do when defending territory and space, and I instinctively flinched. If I hadn't been bound to a chair, I would have taken a step back. I'm not sure where my sudden insane bravery had come from.

"You don't want to challenge me. I'm only a few degrees removed from the psycho you just spent the last however many months with."

A few degrees in which direction? Trevor ruined my life, but he hadn't beaten me or killed me. God, that sounded like some Stockholm Syndrome right there. He'd basically fucking raped me and held me captive living like a wild animal in Tetanus Land.

"I thought you didn't kill innocents."

"I didn't say I would kill you. Now, are you coming with me

when I go?" He asked like I had a choice. He'd already made it clear I didn't. I didn't blame him for not wanting to risk his freedom for a total stranger. In his position with his strength and abilities, I might have been on the same path to ambiguous felony he was on.

"I don't know who I can trust. And you just killed someone," I said, deflated.

"You know that was self defense. And as much as you don't like the implications, you know I know what I'm doing. Do you believe I'd also know if someone was going to shoot me? That was his only option because there was no way he could let a witness leave either."

If this guy really wanted to hurt me, he could take me out like he had Trevor. He wouldn't even have to use his gun. It would be quiet and easy. A quick snap of my neck—a little crunch of bone to oblivion.

It didn't seem plausible that with no plan or intention to, he'd interrupt his weekend fun time to kidnap a woman he'd randomly stumbled upon. But then, what Trevor had done seemed even weirder when you thought about it. How long had he thought he'd get away with it? How long could he have put me off about looking for other survivors? Where was he getting the money to survive without his job at the hospital? Wouldn't he get tired of living like this? But then there were long periods he was gone. I thought he'd been hunting. Maybe not.

Suddenly, remembering all those gallons of purified water in the kitchen, I realized he'd probably stocked the deep freezer ahead of time with stuff he'd bought from the grocery store. I was such an idiot.

I jumped when Shannon put a hand on my knee.

"Elodie. I will not hurt you. I'm sorry I'm scaring you, but I trust you as much as you trust me right now. Not at all. You're putting me in a bad position. My training screams *eliminate the problem.* I'm not going to do that, but you *are* coming with me."

I found myself nodding before I realized I had. The stress of being in this position of not only not remembering anything and having the world pulled out from under me, but being in this limbo with someone so dangerous had me making choices I was sure I would otherwise never make.

He untied me and put the rope back into his bag. "Now, come help me put out these fires. It'll help if you can stay busy."

I nodded and followed him to the fireplace.

He handed me the small shovel and said, "Just keep scooping the ashes on top until the fire goes out. And then do the other one. I'm going to look for something to store the body in. Can I trust you not to run? I don't want to chase you."

I nodded again and focused on putting out the fires. When he left I tried not to think about running because he was right about all that stuff he said. I couldn't make it on my own with no memories without involving the police. And if I involved the police, well... Shannon would never let that happen. He'd die before he'd let me get out of this park to implicate him.

Right around the time I'd finally gotten the fires out, Shannon returned, practically gleeful and giddy with two large rolling pieces of metal luggage. "Look what I found in the lost and found."

He took the shovel from me and scooped out Trevor's charred remains and put them in the wheelbarrow. Then he went back to the kitchen. When Shannon returned several minutes later, he was empty-handed.

"Where's Trevor?"

"In the freezer. He needs to cool a bit before I can pack him in the luggage. I think he's in small enough pieces to fit."

As fucked-up as that statement was, by this point it was hard to work up a lot of shock and distress after I'd been immersed in this macabre process for hours now. And he was right, putting out the fire had helped settle my nerves a bit.

"Do you have shoes?" he asked.

"Y-yes."

"Let's go get them."

I found myself anxious again, moving with him up tight staircases and up to the tower. We were isolated and alone anyway, but before we'd been in a much larger space. Shannon had this really strange sort of energy. On the one hand, he was terrifying. But on the other, a solid, stable calm emanated from him, and for small bits of time, I could imagine that if I could somehow trust him, I could start to feel truly safe again.

He waited just outside the door while I put my shoes on, then we went back downstairs. Neither of us spoke while we waited for Trevor to get cool enough to transport. Finally Shannon took the plastic and luggage and went back to the kitchen. I followed him and watched while he moved Trevor out of the deep freezer and into the luggage. With the plastic in there, too, he just barely fit.

Shannon did a final sweep to check everything, and then he led me out of the castle. I got the feeling he was taking me purposefully in a different direction than he otherwise would have and then doubled back to avoid his traveling companions.

He was right; it was dangerous getting out of here. His group had hacked their way through some of the thickly growing bushes around the perimeter and had cut through a fence. It made me wonder how Trevor had gotten in and how he'd gotten me in. There must have been some other easier entrance at another part of the park that Shannon and his group didn't know about.

We came out in a nearly deserted parking lot. The street lamps were all out, and the pavement was cracked and full of pot holes. Just looking at the physical state of the parking lot, it was possible to imagine the apocalypse really had happened, but Shannon led me to a shiny black SUV and pressed a button on his keys to unlock it. I got inside while he put the luggage containing Trevor in the trunk.

I was still half-convinced he'd drive me to a remote location and kill me. Even though all reason and common sense said he could have just as easily done this back at the castle. There was no reason to drag it out, to take me through the park, risking one of his buddies catching him in the act. But what if he wanted me for *other reasons*?

I mentally rolled my eyes at myself. There was that vanity and conceit again that Trevor had mentioned. Shannon was plenty good looking enough to get his own dates without having to resort to kidnapping. And though I knew he was some type of predator, I wasn't sure his elevator even went up to the sex floor. Not once had he looked at me that way. Could it be possible that his intentions really were noble?

"How far are we going?" I asked as the SUV pulled onto the road.

"This is a rental car. My friends and I flew to get here, but I can't get you on a plane. We'll have to drive." He plugged coordinates into a GPS in the dash. "Twelve hours to our destination. But we're going to stop and stay somewhere. It's getting late, and I'm too tired to drive straight through."

I clasped my hands on my lap and tried not to think about sharing a motel room with him. When we reached the interstate, I started to cry

"Are you hungry?" he asked, ignoring the tears. He just didn't seem to respond to crying.

In a way, I was glad he ignored it. I didn't want to explain what it was I was crying about. As scared as I was of everything right now, that wasn't what triggered the waterworks.

"It really is all still here. I can't believe it." Big semi-trucks zoomed past us on the interstate. Bright city lights framed one side of the road. I could see an uncountable number of restaurants and hotels, and suddenly it occurred to me I would be able to take real showers. And use a toilet like a civilized human.

"Elodie? Food? Do you want me to stop and get you some?"

He was being so nice, but then Trevor had been nice... kind of. Once I'd started cooperating with the insane world he'd invented, once I'd known all the triggers that made him angry and worked to skirt around them.

"C-can I have a burger and some fries?"

He nodded and took the exit off the interstate. We went through the drive-through, and about fifteen minutes later, we were back in motion.

"There's a rest stop ten miles up the road. We'll stop there to eat."

"Okay."

At the rest stop, we ate quietly. It was the best thing I'd ever had. As far as I knew. And soda. Holy shit. Soda, my new friend. I'd spent months drinking what I'd considered to be possibly questionable water—which Trevor had really just bought at the store with everything else. He couldn't have pretended the park had some never ending supply of other beverages?

I was sure I must look like a pig, the way I was eating. But Shannon was busy with his own burger and fries. He seemed okay with silence. If we got down to it, Shannon seemed strangely calm and okay with just about everything. What the hell did he do for a living? Black ops? Contract killer? Did he torture people?

He seemed uncomfortably at home with other people's suffering. So much so that I was shocked he'd had it in him to give any kind of shit about my outcome at all. And I wondered idly if he'd worked past that and was now suddenly over giving any kind of shit about it.

Trevor was the type who'd always had to be talking, and everything out of his mouth had been either baiting me for a fight or had seemed like a weird attempt at gaining my approval. Shannon didn't seem to give a fuck what I approved of.

When we were finished, he went to throw out the trash. When he came back, he said, "Use the bathroom now if you need to. I'm not stopping again until I'm ready to stop for the night."

I got out of the SUV, and he followed me up to the ladies' room. He went inside and had a look around. I don't know what or who he was looking for. I'm not sure if he had some paranoia that made him check the safety of every space before using it or if he thought there might be some other person in there, and I might ask for help.

Whatever he was looking for, when he was satisfied with what he saw—or didn't see—he went outside to wait.

I can't describe the luxury and meaning of an actual bathroom. I'd spent long periods of time back in the park just standing in the suite's bathroom, wishing flushing toilets and hot showers were still a thing. And now they were. It was like Christmas. I flushed every toilet. I turned on every faucet.

I know that's extremely strange, but it was like I couldn't quite believe these were real things that functioned, and I had to test them all out just to make sure the world still worked. It was like... if every sink and toilet worked, grocery stores and malls still existed. That's just the leap my brain made. Even seeing all the lights off the interstate and going through a drive-thru, I still felt the need to test the reality of every modern convenience I came upon. Just to be sure.

When I got outside, Shannon gave me another of those assessing cold stares. He'd obviously heard all the flushing and running water. Before I knew what was happening, he'd swiftly spun me around and pressed me against the brick wall outside. He patted me down.

"Okay, let's go," he said after a moment.

"W-what was that about?"

"Making sure you didn't make a weapon or have a cell phone."

"Make a weapon out of what?" And as if some dinky rest stop bathroom weapon was going to have any effect against someone like him. I wasn't that suicidal.

"You were in there a while, and then there was all the flushing and faucets. I thought you might be masking some activity you didn't want me to know about like making a weapon or calling for help."

The more he worried I was going to kill him or call for help, the more I worried that maybe I really needed to be considering those options.

He kept a brisk pace back to the SUV while I stumbled along—like I'd just learned to walk last week—trying to keep up with him.

"Where the hell would I have gotten a cell phone?" I asked when I reached the passenger door, already out of breath. As if Trevor would have let me have one. Yeah, we had electricity. We could have kept one charged, but that would have completely defeated his end-of-the-world charade.

"There could have been one in the tower when we went up for shoes. I should have gone in with you and watched, but you were already so skittish, and I was more concerned with getting you out of the park undetected."

"In the reality I was living in, cell phones no longer functioned, and even if they did, the cell phone companies would have all collapsed, preventing service from being provided. And the battery would have died anyway. So, no, I didn't have a cell phone."

"Right," he said, looking almost human in his momentary embarrassment. "I can't believe how elaborate his scam was."

The way he said it, it seemed like some part of him respected or was impressed with the effort. Like professional admiration or something.

The SUV beeped and unlocked, and I got into the passenger side still a little shaken from the way Shannon had just flipped to that laser-focused place again. It was the same place he'd gone to when he was cutting Trevor up into small, barely recognizable pieces, and ideally I wanted him to spend as little time in that place while he was around me as possible.

More driving in silence while I stared out the window.

By this point, I was seriously contemplating trying to find a phone or make a weapon. How could I not? He kept putting the ideas in my head. If he'd just act like a normal person for five minutes, I might not be so paranoid.

What was I doing? I should have let him call the shooting in —back when it still looked like self-defense instead of like he was trying to cover crime tracks. Maybe I should have just let the police get involved and deal with the fall out and awfulness of being plastered all over the news some more and trying to cope with memory loss in the spotlight. Was my choice going to end up being... go to the police or die? Framed that way, I'd made the most foolish of all possible choices.

I'd just been so overwhelmed and didn't want to go to the police or doctors or face a million questions and poking and prodding. I was terrified someone would finally come forward claiming to be someone close to me—someone else who might spin lies about my life that I had no choice but to go along with. I hadn't thought about what asking Shannon not to make me face the world meant would happen next. Nor had I realized how quickly he'd spring into action and start hacking up a body like it was nothing. I mean... who did that?

What did they say about snakes? They're more scared of you than you are of them? Shannon seemed in that category, like something had rattled him out of whatever in his world passed for comfortable. Now that it had happened, he saw me as a potential threat. And the last thing I wanted was for someone like Shannon to see me as a threat. So I sat very still and silent, hoping in another of his laser-focus moments, he'd somehow forget my existence so I could slip away quietly.

4

He drove a few hours before stopping at a run-down motel off a small, barely marked exit. Half of the neon-lit vacancy sign was burned out, but the point still got across.

I swear every single thing Shannon did was like the lead-up to the climax of a horror movie. Nothing was normal. It was all weird or paranoid or terrifying. I wasn't sure I wanted Shannon to continue being my tour guide for life outside the park. During the drive, he hadn't made conversation, and he hadn't turned on the radio. And though, by the second hour on the road, I'd desperately wanted to turn on the radio, I didn't make a move for it because I had no idea what he'd do in response.

He'd taken me through a drive-thru where I could have screamed for help but didn't, then he'd treated me like a criminal at the rest stop. I just didn't know what to expect from him. And I wasn't sure knowing would be better anyway. It was Trevor all over again, just in slightly different packaging and without a colorful apocalyptic back story.

Shannon turned in his seat toward me. The clock on the dash said 10:48. This probably wasn't a place that kept a front desk person all night. There was no doubt a bored clerk inside ready to go home, annoyed we'd just pulled up.

"I'm going in to get us a room. I'm locking you in the car. Do not make any kind of scene. Do you see that kid in there?"

I looked through the window he pointed at. A skinny college-aged guy stood behind the front desk, watching the clock and sending a look of derision our way. It was exactly the type of person I'd expected to see.

I nodded.

"Even if you make a scene, you have no way of knowing that kid wants to get involved in this. Not everybody is a hero. Most people aren't. And I'm really good at reading people. He isn't a hero. Are we understanding each other?"

If Shannon was so good at reading people, why didn't he know I wouldn't rat him out for killing Trevor? Though in honesty, I wasn't even sure I wouldn't have said something to the police, so maybe his radar was right on the money. Despite saving me, Shannon had crumbled apart my entire frame for the world. As terrible as it had been, it was far worse to know I'd suffered for months for no purpose and that everything I thought I knew of the world was a lie. There was a part of me that was angry with Shannon for throwing me into more chaos and for changing the lens I'd been viewing my life through.

He snapped his fingers in front of my face. "Elodie. Do we have an understanding?"

"Yes."

He unbuckled his seat belt and started to open the car door.

"Shannon?"

"Yeah?"

"If you really don't plan to hurt me, why are you acting like this?"

"Just protecting myself. You're an unknown risk still. You're too traumatized and flighty to trust."

He was right about that, but still.

"You're freaking me out. Can't you just act normal?"

"I wouldn't know where to start." Shannon got out and locked me in and went inside to get a room.

Five minutes later he had a key. It was one of the old-fashioned keys attached to a red plastic ring where the room number was half worn away.

He drove us around to the back of the motel, parking the car where the license plate was pointed toward the room instead of where anyone driving by could see it. It was these little details that kept reminding me how deep in shit I was now. I didn't know exactly what this guy was a pro at, but I knew he was a pro.

I got out and followed him inside. There was only one queen-sized bed.

"Why didn't you get a double room?" There were only two other guests staying around the front side of the motel and none here at the back. They would have rooms left with two beds. If he didn't have bad intentions why hadn't he gotten me my own bed?

Shannon sighed. "One bed, you're my wife or girlfriend. Two beds, and you're an unknown variable. Two beds invites questions of who you are to me that makes someone remember me beyond the few minutes it took to check in. It's never good to create questions in people's minds. If you want to be a ghost, you have to learn that now."

I hadn't said I never wanted to re-integrate into the normal world. Just not right now. I still hoped I would regain my memory and then at least have some sense of solid ground underneath me before having to deal with nosy curiosity.

I tried to remind myself that this guy actually had friends, that he explored abandoned theme parks for fun. What had he called himself? An urban explorer? That sounded like some hipster nonsense. I couldn't even imagine how that Shannon meshed with this one.

Once inside, I used the bathroom then came back out to the main area. The place was a bit run down, but clean. Well, clean enough. I didn't have a black light to shine on the walls, and I probably didn't want one. Sometimes a place just looking clean was enough.

Shannon put the chain on the door and scooted a chair underneath it like he thought we were going to be under siege any minute. Yet none of his movement was frantic. It was all calm and calculated, and once again, I thought he was going to kill me.

"Lie down on the bed."

"W-what?" Or rape me.

"We're going to sleep."

I wasn't convinced by his explanation, but he'd kind of blocked me in here. And I'd gone along with most of the steps along the way. Suddenly something flashed into my head. It was like a memory, but I wasn't sure if it was anything attached to my life personally or just some random bit of general knowledge my brain had held onto. *Don't let them take you to a second location. Fight like hell to avoid it.*

I kept telling myself this was my fault somehow. I never should have asked him not to involve the cops. But if Shannon was really bad, he could have done whatever he'd wanted anyway. As if he would have called for real help if he were evil. Who was I kidding? This guy had clearly done evil things. Me not being a target of it... yet... didn't change that basic truth.

"Elodie, I'm tired. I want to get on the road early tomorrow. My house is much nicer than this. You'll have your own room there."

Room or basement? Or garden shed?

He started to look impatient. I didn't want to escalate things, so I lay down. For better or worse, this was where I was now, and there was no real way out of it that didn't escalate into violence. I had a very strong feeling that if I fought him too hard, that thing in his brain would click on again and he'd decide I was too much trouble.

Shannon undid the nylon holding my borrowed pants in place and ripped it out of the belt loops. Before I could process what he was doing, he had my hands over my head and tied to the headboard. He could have used the rope in his bag, but I got the feeling he wanted to move into and own my space.

The headboard was older and solidly well-made with slats to run rope through. Maybe Shannon was just super lucky. Or maybe he'd done this before. Though I was sure, even without such a convenient way to tie me down, he would have easily figured something else out with whatever the room had offered him instead.

"Please, don't do this." I was crying and blubbering, and right on the cusp of a panic attack. And despite my best efforts not to become too much trouble for him to keep dealing with, I struggled, however vainly. But it was nothing to him and didn't slow him down more than a few seconds in his goal.

Once I was secured, Shannon shut off the lights, kicked off his boots, and lay down on the other side of the bed, turning his back to me.

"Go to sleep. Things won't seem as bad in the morning."

Shannon was a man who obviously knew how to create trauma but didn't know the first thing about undoing it. Nearly everything he'd said or done from the moment we'd met had triggered one fear or another. He'd kept me on a razor's edge of anxiety, but somehow I didn't think it had been intentional.

Even so, it was well past the point when Shannon's breath deepened in sleep before I could find my own fitful peace for the night.

~

THE NEXT MORNING, I had that experience where you wake up in a new place and forget how you got there. Except for me, this was a bit more upsetting, seeing as the last time it happened, no memories came back to fill in the spaces.

I felt my hands tied, panicked, and screamed.

Shannon rolled over faster than I thought a human could move. His hand clamped over my mouth so hard I was sure there would be a red hand mark when he removed it.

"What the hell do you think you're doing?" he hissed.

I whimpered behind his hand.

"If you scream again, so help me..."

I shook my head frantically. What good would that do me? It wasn't as if I'd planned to scream in the first place.

He pulled his hand away slowly.

"I forgot where I was, and my arms are asleep, and I freaked out. I-I'm sorry."

The sun streamed into the room around the edges of the curtains. Shannon untied the nylon around my wrists and rubbed them until the pins and needles sensation faded. It was the first time I'd gotten a really good look at him.

The castle had been dark except for the fireplace the previous night, and it had of course been dark outside. It wasn't as if he'd been a total visual mystery to me. But there were details you could only fully catch in the light of day—like the fact that he had the longest, most beautiful dark eyelashes I'd ever seen on a man. But somehow they didn't make him seem less scary or any less masculine.

"What?" he said.

"N-nothing."

He got up and left the nylon belt or rope or whatever the hell it was meant to be used for—it was fucking versatile—lying on the bed beside me.

"If you want a shower, now is the time."

God, yes, I wanted a shower. I hadn't had a real shower in

months, and even worse was the fact that I couldn't remember it when I actually had.

I was in there a lot longer than he preferred. Probably fifteen or twenty minutes. Until the water ran cold. It was just such a lovely novelty having hot water pouring over me.

Shannon banged on the bathroom door. "Let's go."

He probably thought I'd climbed out the bathroom window. There was no bathroom window, but I'm sure it didn't prevent him from imagining some way I could still do it. Or maybe he thought I was fashioning a weapon out of the sink pipe.

I was just turning off the water and pulling back the shower curtain to get out when he kicked the door in. I jerked the curtain around me.

"We need to get on the road," he said as if he hadn't kicked the door down. Just a normal day with Shannon. I wondered what his friends thought of him or if they were just as bad. Maybe they were all just like him: highly paranoid and shady.

Shannon retreated back into the bedroom, and I got out, dried off, and put the clothes he'd given me at the castle back on. He didn't say another word about either my long shower or busting in on me like that. Every time he had an opportunity and I thought he was going to pounce on me and just... take... nothing happened. I was becoming increasingly convinced that I was right about Shannon not prioritizing sex.

In a way, that scared me more. I felt sure it was some deeper sign of sociopathy or something. Like he got all his thrills from the big death instead of the little one.

We got back in the SUV, Shannon turned in the key, and we were on the road again. I wondered what he'd used for ID when he'd gotten the room? Had he used his real information, or did he have fake IDs? Or had he talked his way out of it, using the kid's desire to leave work against him?

Shannon stopped a couple of times for gas, a couple of

times for food, and gave me a few more bathroom breaks. He watched me like a hawk at each location.

I was about to go crazy without the radio or human speech. You'd think I would have gotten used to it with all the time with only Trevor, but there were the chickens. And birds. And sometimes deer would wander into the park. A few times I sat so statue-still that they'd come up to me. But it had taken weeks. It had been a game to see how close one would come. I think six feet from me was my record. And then a stupid crow had sent it running.

And there had been music in the castle. Ren Fair music, but still. And at least Trevor spoke to me.

I could probably manage to fit most of my conversation with Shannon since leaving the castle onto the back of a napkin.

He'd had to make a detour to the airport where his car was parked and drop off the rental SUV. He carefully kept me out of view of cameras without making it look too odd, then we got into his car and continued.

His real car was a shiny black four-door Cadillac that looked like something you'd drive the president around in. The license plate said, Georgia. I half expected to ride in the back with a glass divider between us, but he put me in the front with him. There was no glass divider.

I could have screamed for help in the airport rental place, and I'm pretty sure he wouldn't have been able to stop me. But there was that luggage with Trevor in it that we were dragging around. What if I got help but then they decided I'd been an accomplice? There was also an insane part of me that trusted Shannon, despite all reasonable evidence that I shouldn't. There was still a part of me that wanted to crawl inside his cold dead silence to escape the scrutiny of the world.

Shannon was a man of utility. He packed the most practical, versatile things. He drove the most unobtrusive car. He spoke the fewest words necessary to get his point across. When we got to his house, I knew it was his because the inside matched everything else I knew about him.

A little cold. Very minimalist. Clean. Regimented. It was a big, nice house in an equally nice neighborhood. It wasn't flagrantly lavish, but it screamed either upper middle class or, *I've got a fuckton of money, but I don't need you to know about it.* Considering all the illicit jobs I'd imagined him holding during our endless trip, I was leaning toward the latter.

As soon as we crossed the threshold, the security system blared at us. Shannon turned it off, locked the doors, then turned it right back on again. Message sent. Nobody went in or out of this house without him knowing about it, and it was going to be locked up tighter than Fort Knox at all times.

Inside, everything was gray and black and white. The only splash of color was some red here and there. The color of blood. I wondered if he realized how much of his internal state he broadcast just with his decorating choices?

"Stay. I'm going to put my stuff up."

Anybody else would have tossed his bags beside the door and handled it later. We'd been driving all day, and he was obviously tired. But in Shannon's world, it seemed everything had a place, and nothing ever deviated from where it was supposed to be.

He took his bag upstairs while I stood in the living area glancing around awkwardly. A bright red photo album caught my eye from the coffee table. To give myself something to do, I sat on the sofa and flipped through the album. It was filled with pictures of abandoned amusement parks. Decapitated mermaid heads and fins and creepy peeling clowns abounded. There were broken down wooden roller coasters that looked to be rotting and seemed held up only by vines. One rather sad image showed a couple of paddle boats abandoned in the middle of a lake.

What was it about these places that drew Shannon? They were so empty. Maybe it felt familiar. He wasn't in any of the photos, making it clear he'd been the photographer. But there were almost never other people in any of the photos either. Occasionally there was a stray leg or arm, even the side of a face and body as someone walked through the frame—no doubt his fellow urban explorers. But people in the photos were clearly accidental, never intentional. People weren't what Shannon was interested in.

He'd traveled all over the world for this hobby. Not only were there several photos of signs in foreign languages but Shannon had put labels on each one of where it had been taken. As I worked through the book I saw he'd been to Canada, Spain, Italy, Korea, Japan, China, Vietnam, Russia. He seemed to have been everywhere, capturing all the strange, wacky, and creepy of these theme parks.

There *was* one photo with people in it. It was a picture of a cluster of found photos of smiling employees from a South Korean park. It was telling that Shannon needed to be this many degrees separated from real people to take a picture of them.

Despite the emptiness in these park images and my fears that it reflected far too much of Shannon himself, something about this hobby made him seem more human to me.

I took my time perusing the album, sure Shannon wouldn't mind, but he was upstairs for quite a while, so finally I got up and went to explore the kitchen. Unlike the photo album, I was pretty sure my going through all his cabinets and drawers would annoy him, but I was curious.

There was nothing unusual in the kitchen. I didn't find any heads or fingers in the freezer. Much to my relief.

I ended up standing in front of the sink with the faucet on, staring at the water as it came out, like it was the most interesting thing I could have ever discovered.

I could have been standing in that state for five minutes, ten minutes? An hour? Hell, I don't know. Time melded together, and all that existed for a while was moving water.

The only thing that broke the spell was Shannon's hand pressing down firmly on the handle, making the water abruptly stop. "If you're this fascinated with running water, you could have a future as a plumber," he said.

He took me to an office on the first floor and sat me down behind a desk in front of a laptop. A browser window was open with several tabs to clothing stores.

"Do you know your sizes?" he asked.

"I... yes, I saw the tags in the clothes I wore there." At the park.

"Good." He indicated the chair. "Fill some shopping carts."

"I-I don't understand."

"Well you aren't wearing my clothes. And you aren't going naked. What were you planning to wear?"

I hadn't thought about that. I hadn't thought about much of anything. It was all too hard and overwhelming. It would have been bad enough trying to reintegrate into the world and get my life back if Trevor had held me captive like he had with my memories intact. But without anything solid to rely on, it was even worse. I was just surviving minute to minute and trying desperately not to think about anything, trying to make the inside of my mind as empty and silent as my surroundings had been most of the trip with Shannon.

Maybe I'd been lying to myself about going crazy from the silence. I was really going crazy from how relieved I was to have it. Running water *and* silence. The motherfucking lottery.

"Shop." He sat in a chair next to mine so he could watch me. I barely had time to marvel at the continued existence of the Internet.

"I-I don't know what to get or how much. How will I pay you back?"

"I don't need you to pay me back. I need you to look like a normal person in my house and not a kidnap victim. Decide on a new hair color and style also. I've got to get stuff for that. And we'll get you colored contacts. No high heels. Every picture they showed of you on the news was in something nice enough to wear heels. People probably imagine you a little taller than you are. Flats only."

I looked through the sites he'd picked out. It was all nice stuff. "So I'm going to leave the house and see other people?" I asked.

"At some point."

"You aren't worried I'll say something? I thought that was the whole reason you didn't give me a choice about coming with you?"

"I said you couldn't be free range. I didn't say you'd never see other people. You saw what happened at the castle. Do I seem in any way traumatized by it?"

I shook my head. I'd tried and failed multiple times during the trip to his house to not think about how matter-of-factly Trevor's killing and disposal had been carried out.

"I don't mind a body count. Don't put me in a situation to make one or to make you part of it, and you have nothing to worry about. Deal?"

Sure. Nothing to worry about. But I nodded quickly and went back to looking at the sites.

Something else occurred to me suddenly. The ever-looming feminine protection quandary. "I... I need some... some toiletries," I mumbled. That was the most tactful way I could put it.

Shannon studied me for a moment. "You mean tampons." Off my shocked expression he said, "Don't look so surprised. I was raised by a woman, not by wolves. My dad went on a lot of tampon runs when I was growing up. I'll take care of it. Just write down anything that will help me out in that department.

They have a lot of options out there—probably a lot more now than when I was a kid." He opened a drawer and took out a notepad and pen and put it beside me on the desk.

"Thank you." I was so ridiculously grateful that not only had I not had to explain to him what I meant, but that he hadn't made me feel awkward or dirty. It was so strange—yet in hindsight made so much weird sense—that I'd hidden the entire thing from Trevor, unwilling to bring it up under almost any circumstance, yet, I'd somehow been able to tell Shannon, however subtly. Why did I trust this guy when there seemed no rational reason for me to?

"Shannon?"

"Yeah?"

"Why did you bring me home with you? Why didn't you just kill me back there?" Probably not the best question to ask a guy like this, but I had to know what had been going through his head. Why not just keep things neat and tidy if he didn't mind such ugliness?

"I don't know."

It was a far less comforting answer than I'd been hoping for. I had a feeling that the amount of emotion and empathy I'd seen on his face when he'd discovered me with Trevor was about the most he'd ever shown. Somehow, despite knowing he'd been traveling with others that night, I imagined him as a person who lived completely alone.

But I was wrong about that. A fluffy white cat sauntered into the room. She jumped up on Shannon's lap and started to purr, giving me a disdainful glare as if to say, *Bitch, no way am I sharing him with you.* I worried the cat might scratch my eyes out while I slept.

"What's her name?"

Shannon just stared at me for a moment, completely baffled. "She doesn't have one."

"How can you have a cat without a name? Is she new?"

"No." He stroked the back of her neck, and she pressed harder against his hand. "I've had her for a long time."

"How old is she?"

"I don't know. We could cut her open and count the rings."

I wasn't sure if he was serious.

I couldn't believe it didn't occur to him just how fucking weird it was to have a pet in your house that you chose not to give a name to.

"If she doesn't have a name, then what do you call her?"

"I don't need to call her anything. She comes to me on her own when she's ready. We communicate just fine. She doesn't have a name for me." The words were almost defensive, but he didn't sound defensive when he delivered them. It was more like he was just rattling off a list of logical facts that should be obvious to any thinking person.

The cat probably *did* have a name for him... it was just some version of a meow that didn't translate straight to English.

"I thought sociopaths killed small animals." I don't know why I felt the need to say that. It was out of my mouth before I could stop it. It seemed unwise now that it was out there—like making unappreciated commentary on someone's handicap.

He gave me a dark look. "You watch too much TV."

"I don't remember ever watching TV." Except the movies at the castle. He must have forgotten the amnesiac trapped in a theme park for months situation.

"You must have watched it at some point. Where else would you get your ideas about sociopaths? The abnormal psychology fairy?"

Had he just made a joke? Possibly his second in the space of a couple of minutes? It was so odd even thinking about him making a joke. I swear his face just had that one expression. I wasn't sure how he got on in life without every single person near him clearing a big wide path in terror. I thought sociopaths were supposed to be outwardly charming. He was really attractive, but I wasn't sure I'd call him in any way charming.

"There are plenty of low-level sociopaths in the world who get a lot of evil accomplished with very little feeling involved. More than you'd care to know about have wives, kids, dogs. For most, those things are camouflage."

"Is your cat camouflage?"

Shannon shrugged. "Not a lot of things make me feel things. When they do, I don't let them go."

I'd made him feel something.

I couldn't bring myself to ask more. He already seemed like he'd hit his human interaction quota for the day, and more frightening than making him feel something where he wouldn't let me go, was not making him feel something so he would. I was sure with Shannon, letting someone go was pretty much final.

When I was finished shopping, he ushered me out of the office and locked the door.

"I have to finish cleaning up. I'm going to lock you in for a while."

"I... um... finish cleaning up?"

Shannon looked at me like I was a mental patient. "The body?"

"Oh." I'd somehow almost forgotten about Trevor's charred remains. "Okay."

"I'll get your... toiletries while I'm out."

When I was alone, I finally had time and space to think. I searched the house. Nothing weird anywhere. There were a few locked doors, including what I thought was probably Shannon's bedroom on the second floor. There was no land line phone anywhere in the house, and no computer outside the now-locked office.

The white cat followed me from room to room yowling in an irritated fashion like she was going to tell on me for checking things out. But everything looked *normal.* So normal, in fact, that for a moment I could pretend that Shannon was just a regular nice guy and that all the nasty business with Trevor had never happened.

But it *had* happened. Intellectually I knew I should be searching for a way to escape, but I couldn't bring myself to believe that a man who wanted me dead would have just spent so much money buying me new clothes.

5

Eventually, we settled into something resembling a routine. I finally stopped fearing that he'd throw me down and take my imagined virtue, or that he'd kill or otherwise harm me. Shannon treated me like I was his roommate—his deadbeat mooch of a roommate who didn't pay rent. I actually started to feel guilty about it. I was wearing clothes he'd bought, using his water and electricity, eating his food, invading his space. And so far he hadn't asked for anything in return.

But still I felt like it was coming. I expected any day now to see some version of an invoice slipped under my door with a demand for immediate payment.

This invasion was clearly uncomfortable for him—like my existence interrupted the flow of his space, like I'd thrown off the *feng shui* or something. But he didn't comment on it. He didn't act like he was going to get rid of me. The cat followed him everywhere, shooting me dirty looks whenever she passed by. If anybody was planning my demise, it was that freaky nameless cat.

So far, despite Shannon's promise, I hadn't left the house

yet, even though my hair had been short and black for two weeks now instead of its previous long blonde. My eyes were now chocolate brown instead of blue. Or they would be if I ever left the house and wore the contacts. They mainly just sat in their case. A part of me doubted I'd even remember to put them in if and when he ever let me venture outside.

When I looked in the mirror, I felt like even more of a stranger to myself, as if a new wave of amnesia would come along and drag me under its empty dark water, erasing everything before I'd met Shannon.

He left during the day sometimes. Not every day, but most days. And it wasn't a set schedule like he was going to the nine-to-five grind. Sometimes he was gone when I woke. Sometimes I was sure he left in the middle of the night. Sometimes he left around noon. There was no set schedule, no rhyme or reason. I'd asked once or twice where he went, and he would say, "to the gym".

I think he probably did go to the gym sometimes. Sometimes he was dressed for it. And there was a gym bag that often left with him. Being as paranoid as he seemed to be about everything, it wouldn't surprise me if he constantly varied his routine, working out at bizarre hours to throw *whoever* off this trail.

Why would a man need to be that paranoid if he wasn't doing something wrong or dangerous? But then, I don't think I'd ever believed Shannon was a nice guy with a normal job. He was dangerous like a wild animal was dangerous. Whatever it was that had come along and civilized humanity so we could function properly in groups, had bypassed him. He was his own law.

One evening at dinner, Shannon dropped an orange manila envelope on the table in front of me.

"What's this?"

"It's you."

I stared at it. "What do you mean?" But I knew what he meant. I was just stalling.

"Open it." He slid a silver letter opener across the table.

I stopped it with the edge of my hand and slit the envelope open. Inside was a dossier. On me. There was also a DVD. A shiver traveled down my spine. He'd been out there stalking my information. I wasn't sure if this felt like a kindness or a threat. I couldn't bring myself to read the details just yet.

"Where did you get all this? H-how did you get all this? How do I know this is the truth? You could be lying like Trevor."

Shannon shrugged as if it didn't matter to him one way or the other what I believed. "I could be. It's up to you whether you want to believe what's in there. But it's a narrative that doesn't include the end of the world. Do what you want with it. I need to make some calls."

He got up and put his plate and glass in the sink and ran some water over them. Then he went to his office down the hall and closed the door.

I put the papers back inside the envelope without reading them and took them upstairs to my room. I slid the envelope under my mattress. I wasn't ready for more stories about me. Even though I had a strong feeling these were the stories that were true. Now that I held it in my hands I was afraid to know that truth.

What kind of a misfit hermit had I been if no one had called the hospital or police to claim me? Maybe I was afraid to see a bunch of wasted time staring back at me—no accomplishments to speak of. Nothing the world cared about. As long as I didn't know, I could pretend I'd had a meaningful impact, even though I knew that couldn't be true. If it were true, someone would have called. Someone besides Trevor would have missed me.

When I went back downstairs, the office door was still shut.

I eased up to the door and pressed my ear against it. I could hear Shannon on the phone. Just barely. He didn't have a land line, just what he called a *burner*. It was a simple black pre-paid cell phone. He routinely disposed of them and bought new ones.

"I told you I've been busy... I got a new pet. I needed to get her housebroken and acclimated... of course another cat... you know I can't have a dog with my travel schedule..." Why did I think I was the cat in this scenario? Shannon could be lying about how long he'd had the white cat, but she was far too territorial to be new. "... No, the money's not the problem. It's our agreed rate. You said it wasn't dire, so I took you at your word. But I'm ready now. It'll be done within the week. Be out of town next Thursday with people who can account for your whereabouts."

When the call ended, I practically flew to the living room couch, and sat there trying to look like I hadn't just heard what I was nearly a hundred percent certain was a discussion about killing someone.

Shannon came out and looked at me for a long moment. Then his gaze shifted to the dining room table. "Elodie?"

"S-sorry." I got up and quickly took my plate and glass to the sink and put it in the warm water. I don't know why I got so freaked out whenever that tone came to his voice. Actually, I did know why. It's just that he'd never done anything personally to me to illicit this fear.

Shannon was so fastidious. I was sure he would just *snap* if something was left sitting out... if a towel was left crumpled on the counter... if a box of crackers fell over on its side. It wasn't like he'd ever harmed me for leaving anything out. He'd never hit me or yelled at me or smashed or thrown things. It was just... this disappointed tone like you get with a kid who eats an unauthorized cookie before dinner. I hated doing something wrong in his house—especially given how much he provided for me without asking for anything in return. I felt like my behavior had to be... perfect—to somehow compensate for what an inconvenience I must be.

I also felt like I had to somehow make him trust me so I could be a *free range human* again. I liked the comfort of his home, but it felt like a clock was running. At some point, he'd get bored with the novelty of another person taking up space like the white cat. He had to believe I could be trusted or... I didn't want to think about the *or* right now.

"I'm tired," he said. "I'm going up to bed. I'm having a party tomorrow night, and I'll need you to stay in your room until it's over."

"O-okay." The next day was Sunday. Was he killing someone tomorrow? Or was he really having a party? Aside from his supposed urban exploring friends, Shannon didn't strike me as a super social guy. What kind of a party could he be having?

"Shannon?"

He stopped at the bottom of the staircase. "Yeah?"

I was afraid I might make him mad, but I pressed on with my question anyway. "We disguised my appearance. The media has forgotten about me. Why can't I go to the party?"

He offered me a kind smile, which I swear he must have stood in front of the mirror for hours practicing because it didn't look right on his face. "It's not your kind of party. Trust me. I'll take you out next weekend if you want. I'm sorry I haven't been a better host. Oh, and I've got to be out of town a few days next week. Business."

Then he drifted up the stairs. Moments later, I heard his door click shut.

I'd tried to sneak into his office early on, but he kept the door locked at all times when he wasn't in there. And I wasn't foolish enough to think it would be any different tonight. There were a few other doors in the house he kept locked all the time as well. But he pretended as if those doors didn't exist, and I wasn't dumb enough to let him know I was aware that they did.

I sat on the sofa and looked around, at a loss for what to do. It was only nine o'clock and felt way too early for sleep. The cat sat on a chair opposite from me, glaring, plotting.

I went back up to my room and took the envelope from under the mattress. There was no way I would be able to sleep with my life lying a few inches underneath me. I came back downstairs with it and dumped the contents out on the coffee table.

The DVD was in a clear plastic freezer bag and just said "Cache" on it. I set it aside for the moment and turned to the information Shannon had somehow acquired about me.

"Elodie Rosen. Age: 28. Graduate student of Botany at University of Washington."

Washington state was on the other side of the country. Did Trevor live and work there? Had he taken me all the way across the country, or had I gone to where he was? Maybe spring break or something.

But why had nobody called? The story must have made national news if Shannon heard about it, unless he'd been traveling in the area. For business. Maybe I'd been wrapped up in my studies and had no close friends. But no family either? Didn't my professors give a shit about me? Or did they think someone else would come forward?

I looked back to the list. It didn't appear that I'd had a job. I'd mostly kept to myself. But according to Shannon's search, I didn't have student loans, either. Had I inherited a lot of money? Surely I had to have money. And nobody was speaking up for me?

People really *didn't* like to get involved in things. It was just like what Shannon said. I could have screamed my head off, and that kid at the motel might have pretended he couldn't hear me—anything to not get involved. What was wrong with people?

I scanned further down the paper. "Fluent in French. Spent several semesters in Paris as an undergrad." Maybe someone in France gave a shit about me.

I glanced back at the DVD and slid it out of the plastic. I put it in the player and settled back on the sofa. It was a French film. It must have been a version of the film made specifically for a French audience because there were no subtitles or dubbing.

But I understood all the dialogue.

I wasn't sure if Shannon had chosen a creepy foreboding movie on purpose or if it was just difficult to find a French film that didn't fit that mold, but I nearly leaped off the sofa when Shannon came down the stairs during an intense scene. It didn't help that he moved as stealthily as the cat did.

He went to the kitchen for a glass of milk and then came back out into the living area. He wore pale gray pajama pants that showcased his tan and no shirt. The white cat jumped down off the chair and took the opportunity to weave in and out of his legs, leaving her scent on him. She stared at me pointedly while she did it. As if I were going to rush over there and fight for cuddle privileges with perhaps the least cuddly person in the world.

"Est-ce que tu t'es rendu à l'histoire du chien dans la scène du dîner?" Shannon said.

"Ne me gâche pas tout." Even though I knew I understood French, it still shocked me when I spoke it. Or did it shock me that Shannon spoke it? Maybe he'd just learned the one phrase. But his accent and enunciation were impeccable.

"Interesting," he said. "Have you read all of the file yet?"

"Not yet. I wanted to watch the DVD, and then I got sucked in."

He nodded. "It's a good film. You should read the rest of the file. I think this confirms a theory I had."

"And what theory was that?" I asked, trying not to look too eager.

"You've clearly got retrograde amnesia, but your skills and general knowledge seem to be intact, just not specific autobiographical memories. That's generally how it works. So you'll find you know things but you won't know how you know them. Like with the French."

"Do you think I'll ever get my memories back?"

Shannon shrugged. "I'm not a doctor. But I did a lot of research on the condition when I was collecting information. Realistically, probably not. If you've gone this long with memory loss this severe, you're probably stuck with it. Anything's possible, but this isn't a movie."

A part of me had been living in fear of memory recall. I'm not sure why. I'd also equally been harboring the fear that my memories wouldn't come back but someone else would show up claiming to be a husband or a friend or a relative and feed me bullshit stories that weren't real, or else feed me real stories that still smelled like bullshit. I worried that over time I would hear stories about myself so much that I would start to believe them and start to imagine them. Maybe I would even reconstruct them in my mind and think they were true memories.

If there was little hope for recovery, I was glad Shannon had spared me the police and media circus. Surely someone real or fake would have shown up claiming to know all about me, and then it would just be Trevor all over again, only without the apocalyptic backdrop.

"Why didn't anybody call about me?"

"I don't know. Maybe someone did. But the authorities only wanted family—someone who could legally take responsibility for you. You know how the hospitals are. They weren't going to just send you home with any random person who knew you for five minutes in some vague capacity."

I looked back down at the papers. Shannon had discovered my mom was a single mother who had me young and had died from complications of the flu a few years ago.

"If I was raised by a single mother, how did I live without a job and have no student debt?"

"That's where it gets interesting. You have or had a mysterious benefactor. I think it's your father. I think he set you up for life to avoid a scandal. That makes him a powerful politician or someone famous whose brand would be damaged by an illegitimate child. Whoever it was is as much of a professional as me because the trail runs cold."

"He didn't call when my face was all over TV, though. Did he not recognize me?"

"Oh, I'm sure he recognized you, and equally sure he considered his problems over, with the woman he knocked up dead and the inconvenient child he didn't want no longer a problem."

I wondered if I'd known who my father was before the amnesia.

"Do you remember anything from your childhood at all?" Shannon asked.

"I... I'm not sure." Honestly, at this point I wasn't even sure what a memory felt like. At least not an old one. The whole concept seemed too wispy to nail down into anything solid. I did occasionally get a few images, bits of conversation and activity. It could be from my childhood. It definitely wasn't anything recent.

"The farther back the memory loss goes, the more serious the case. Recent memories are lost first."

So even if I remembered stuff from my childhood, it didn't mean I'd remember everything or anything else.

"How much money do I have?"

"A lot," Shannon said. "More than me. And I'm certainly not uncomfortable."

I stared at him for a good long moment, wondering if he'd idly thought of killing me and draining my bank accounts. Surely, if he could find out this much about me, he could find out how to gain access to my money once I was out of the way. Why hadn't Trevor done that?

But I think I knew. Those photos he kept in his wallet told me everything. I had to have dated him and then rejected him. And what he'd wanted more than my money was to force a relationship with me. When I woke without my memory, maybe he'd thought if he could just isolate me enough, make me depend on him enough... he might have a chance with me.

It sounded crazy-vain for me to think this way, but he'd obviously been obsessed. What else would explain the lies he'd concocted? In his fantasy, I was his wife and depended solely on him for everything. And he'd found a way to make it happen. I don't think he cared even a little bit about my money, or maybe he'd been planning for us to live off it indefinitely. Maybe that was how he was getting by just fine and stocking the deep freezer without his job at the hospital.

"If you know how much money I have, does that mean you've been in my accounts somehow?" I didn't even want to think about how he might have accomplished this, but I had every confidence Shannon was capable of figuring it out.

He gave me one of his patented calm, assessing looks. "I have."

"Had there been recent withdrawals?"

His eyes widened as if surprised I wasn't a complete idiot. "I'm impressed. Yes, Trevor gained access to your accounts. He had your cards and PIN numbers. I used them to get in. He'd been leeching off your money."

"How much did he take?" I didn't even know how much I had. More than Shannon. But what did that even mean? I had no idea how much Shannon had, but I was sure he had a lot more than it appeared to the casual passerby.

"Not as much as I would expect. I think he was just living off you since he fled his job."

I wondered even more now about what Trevor's end game had been. Surely he hadn't thought we could live in an abandoned theme park forever. And even if we could temporarily, he'd been a fugitive, so it wasn't as if he'd roamed freely without fear. Was there a second improbable location he'd planned for us? How would he have kept the ruse going? Or was he deluded enough to think he could win my love and then confess the truth to me, and we'd go off somewhere happily into the sunset? Was that why he'd tried to confirm that I loved him the night Shannon shot him? Had he thought he could move us to the confession and the next phase of his plan?

But... I had money. At least that was something.

"So I can pay you back now. For all the clothes and food and everything."

"I don't need your money," Shannon said.

"I didn't say you needed it. I just... you should be compensated for... for everything."

"I don't *want* your money."

Shannon took his empty glass to the kitchen and went back upstairs. The cat followed him and then yowled when he shut her out of the bedroom.

However much he might be attached to the animal, it didn't extend to bedroom privileges. She sulked back down the stairs, gave me a look of pure evil as if it were my fault he'd locked her out, then curled up on the chair she'd been in before.

"Mrrrawr?" she said.

I might be going crazy but I was half-convinced she wanted to finish watching the movie. Maybe the white cat understood French, too.

THE FOLLOWING NIGHT, we had dinner early. Shannon brought home Chinese take-out. At five minutes til six, he took my box of food away from me, closed it, and calmly placed it in the fridge.

"What?" I was only halfway finished.

"It's almost six."

"So?"

"So, my guests will be arriving any minute. They're very punctual. You have to go to your room."

"But..."

"You can finish dinner when they leave." Shannon never allowed food out of the kitchen for any reason. He'd said something about attracting bugs—as if bugs got together and conspired to find the houses where people ate in more than one room.

"I still don't understand why I can't just..."

Shannon loomed over me and pointed upstairs.

"Okay! When will the party be over?"

"I don't know. Late. Go. Don't come out of your room. And keep your door locked."

What the hell?

But I didn't fight him on it. I went upstairs as instructed and locked my door. I heard people come in, but I didn't hear any growing noise or loud music. It seemed pretty quiet for a party. What the hell was going on down there? Were they playing Scrabble? Was it a hit man mixer? Very low key. Cocktails. Discussion of strategy—like best body disposal techniques—while Schubert played in the background.

By nine o'clock, Shannon hadn't come up to tell me I was free to go downstairs, and I was getting hungry again. I'd only had half my dinner after all. Finally, I just decided fuck it. I was hungry, and whatever was happening downstairs, it couldn't be worse than all the things I was imagining might be going on.

I unlocked the door and took a peek down the hallway. Nobody up here. Except the white cat. She sat just outside my door giving me that look again. Was she my guard cat? Would she report to Shannon that I'd been bad? I kind of wanted to kick her down the stairs. I was convinced she was the most disagreeable animal in the world with everyone except for Shannon. And I think he liked that about her.

As I started toward the stairs, she began a loud howling meow as if she were in heat. It sounded like she was sending out her own emergency broadcast signal.

"Will you shut up?" I hissed back at her. This cat definitely wanted me dead.

The main level was silent as well. Some party. Maybe they'd relocated to somebody else's house, and Shannon hadn't bothered to tell me—or he'd forgotten about me. I still couldn't fathom what he'd even do at a party besides brood near the punch bowl. He just didn't seem like the social butterfly sort. As time had passed, it seemed increasingly ludicrous that he had friends to explore abandoned theme parks with, let alone to throw parties for.

I went to the kitchen and heated the rest of my *lo mein* and chicken and vegetables and sat at the table. As I ate, I kind of faintly heard—but really more felt—the throbbing of music below me. The sound vibrated against my bare feet.

So Shannon had a basement. I suppose I should be grateful I hadn't been locked in it. I couldn't believe it hadn't occurred to me that one of those locked doors might lead to a basement level, which made it all the more suspicious that the door remained locked all the time.

I finished my food and put the cartons in the trash. I'd planned to go back to my room, but I went down the hallway on the main level instead. One of the mystery doors was cracked a fraction of an inch, the music drifting ever so slightly up and out to my ears.

The temptation was just too great. I had to know what the hell happened at a party this man would host. As soon as I took a peek down the stairs, I discovered I was wrong about yet another thing. Shannon's elevator *did* go up to the sex floor.

The deviant sex floor.

The basement was a big finished space like an open floor plan apartment. It stretched fully from one end of the house to the other, creating a complete underground level.

There were maybe thirty or more people downstairs, every single one of them naked. There was no pretense of lingerie or underwear for either the men or the women. But the freaky part about the whole thing was that they all wore masks. Not masquerade masks that just covered your eyes, and not those creepy white masks that made you look like a mannequin, either.

No, these were the kind of masks you'd wear for Halloween. Maybe it was a costume party, though I was pretty sure it wasn't Halloween. There were gorilla masks and monster masks and wolf masks and alien masks—even a few freaky cartoon character masks that were way age inappropriate given the circumstances down here. The only requirement seemed to be that the mask had to be full coverage, not one that only hid half the head or face.

The only thing not going on at the party was oral sex—for obvious mask-related reasons. The guests partner-swapped so fast it nearly gave me whiplash. I couldn't even begin to guess which one was Shannon. Or was he hiding somewhere watching it all and not participating?

The rule of the night seemed to be that anyone could fuck anyone—no holds barred—because no one resisted. No one said no, no matter how many people they were passed around to. And the whole thing was utterly and completely anonymous.

Except for the masks, it was what I imagined an ancient Roman orgy might be like. I thought it must have been the case that if you decided to play at all, you were committed to whatever happened. The idea of complicated consent and negotiations seemed unlikely somehow. It was the same here. It didn't seem a single person was willing to take no for an answer. If you came downstairs, well, you came downstairs.

The floor was a dark shiny hardwood. Expensive black leather sex furniture was interspersed throughout the large space as well as a few beds for those who preferred more comfort. There was spanking and whipping going on in the middle of the large space and a few women and one man being led around on leashes. There were three different couples fucking on one bed, and more lined against the walls like an assembly line of depravity.

I turned to go back upstairs, but a hand ensnared my wrist. "Where do you think you're going, lovely? You aren't following the dress code. I think we need to punish you for that." The voice didn't belong to Shannon.

I tried to pull away, still thinking I could reason my way out of this. "Let me go. I have to go back upstairs."

"Shannon didn't tell us he had a girlfriend. Do you just let your boyfriend fuck whoever he wants? That's generous. Does he allow you the same freedoms? I can't imagine him being so gracious with you." His hand moved to the button on my jeans.

I tried to ease out of the situation again, but he wasn't having it. Even though I couldn't see his eyes, I somehow knew he planned to take *Shannon's girlfriend* right here on the carpeted stairs. I looked back again at the orgy going on only a few yards away, still wondering which one was Shannon. Had he spotted me yet?

I wanted to scream for help, but I was both afraid someone

might recognize me even with my new look and even more afraid to draw Shannon's attention. Maybe I could stand to just let this guy do his thing and then slip back upstairs. It wasn't as if Shannon hadn't told me to stay in my room and keep my door locked. Even as I did it, I couldn't believe I was trying to rationalize the situation—as if it would be my fault this guy couldn't process the word *no*.

The stranger shoved me down on the black carpeted stairs and stripped me down so fast I couldn't believe it had already happened. My clothes lay in a chaotic pile near my feet. I had barely enough time to try to wrap my head around anything that was going on and whether or not I thought I could handle it better than the alternatives.

His heavy weight settled on top of me, and I freaked out and screamed. I couldn't just let it happen. Shannon was going to kill me for breaking his rules and coming down here, but I'd rather Shannon kill me than this guy fuck me. I had such messed-up priorities.

Nobody paid attention to my cries. Maybe they thought my scream was role play. Or maybe they didn't care. Or maybe they were locked into their own fantasies at the moment and didn't feel like dealing with someone else's traumatic reality. After all, that wasn't part of the fantasy orgy package. I was sure they'd all been given an intense list of rules and that they all knew coming down those stairs was consent... to anything with anyone. But the only rule I'd been issued was to stay away.

While I processed these thoughts and tried not to think about what was about to happen, the stranger was ripped off me. A second later, a guy in a gorilla mask had him by the throat against the wall. "Did she look like someone here for you to play with?" Shannon shouted.

"N-no."

"She's *off-limits*!" He turned back to the rest of the guests, most of whom were slowly coming out of the orgy fog to notice the commotion. "Everybody get the fuck out! Party's over!"

I pressed my clothes against me and slowly backed up the stairs.

"Not you!" Shannon said, eyes blazing with fury from behind the mask.

I froze where I was. He'd never yelled. I'd never heard him yell before tonight. He was calm and methodical. I hadn't been totally sure he had the emotional range to yell. But tonight there was a new and very different energy about him.

Suddenly I was overwhelmed with the reality of naked Shannon. To say he was sculpted was an understatement. I'd had some vague idea of what he must look like under his utilitarian black clothing, but the briefly flitting imagination didn't do it justice. I looked away from his quite substantial erection, my face flaming.

Most of the guests scrambled to get their clothes and get out of the basement. A few lingered—trying to finish up as if they couldn't make their own orgasms at home. Like it was worth risking a bullet to the head or a snapped neck, two things I was sure Shannon was more than capable of delivering.

He physically broke up a few sexual encounters, herded them all up the stairs, and shut and locked the basement door, leaving me down below.

When everyone was gone, the door unlocked and Shannon came back down, only slightly calmer. He still wore the gorilla mask. The white cat was on his heels looking smug, like she couldn't wait to watch this unfold.

I should have taken the opportunity alone to put clothes on. They were in my hands. I was just so freaked out by everything. Maybe it was shock. It felt eerily like the night I first met him all over again. I backed away from him, still clutching my clothes to me like I'd done with the sheet the night in the castle.

Shannon continued to advance. The music still blared. He turned it off, and silence poured like water into each space that had once contained sound.

When he spoke, his voice was dead calm, which was about a thousand times more scary than the yelling of only minutes before. "I thought I told you to stay in your room."

"I'm s-sorry." I couldn't keep my eyes from straying over him. He was still naked, and hard. I didn't want to think about what part of this was exciting him. If he was a normal person with any sense of decency and morality, seeing some other guy almost violate me wouldn't have him worked up this way.

"T-take the mask off." I continued to back up until I ran out of space to retreat. He sounded so inhuman, his voice warped behind the rubber.

"No." He said the word slowly as if pausing to taste it first before giving me his decision. "It makes you uncomfortable, doesn't it?"

"Yes." I knew there wasn't a lot in those eyes, not usually. But I still wanted to be able to see them. Because as inhuman as Shannon might be, he was infinitely more human than a rubber gorilla mask.

"You broke my rules. I've been very good to you. I've protected you and kept you safe. Except for the night we met, I've kept all the darker business of my life away from you, including this. You are the one who opened the box, my little Pandora. Now we can't close it. All the evil inside can never go back in. It's in the air now. Can you smell it?"

What I smelled was sex and alcohol.

He ripped the clothes out of my hands and dropped them on the floor. "Do you know how much I've had to rearrange my life for you? My schedule? My routine? All so I wouldn't have to kill you? I've asked myself... Why, Shannon? Why even bother? I knew why, but I wanted to keep you pure and untainted by all the dark things that crawl around inside me.

But now you've seen too much of it, though not nearly the worst of it. You know what? Fuck it. I kill people, Elodie. For a living. But I bet you already knew that, didn't you? You're smart. Maybe too smart."

I thought I'd known, but hearing it out loud was a whole other thing. There was a part of me that had thought it was pure invention, my imagination running wild, my mind playing tricks on me.

"Shannon, please stop."

He was never letting me go now. Not only had I seen his freaky little sex party, but we couldn't pretend anymore that I was ignorant about how he financed his life.

He wanted it that way... for me to know... to be sure that I knew how he made his living so he could justify keeping me locked up in his house. I didn't know why he wanted to keep me here, but I knew that he did. The way he'd acted just now with that other man wasn't the indifference I'd thought I mostly inspired in him.

"Do you know what else?" he prodded, just gaining steam. "I really *like* my job. A lot. You can't believe how much job satisfaction I have. It's a shame guidance counselors in school aren't allowed to suggest this career path. Robbing young minds of their callings, I say. But hey, more fun for me."

"You're drunk," I said.

He laughed. "No. I haven't had a drop. This is all me, baby."

"You're no better than Trevor." In fact, Shannon was probably worse.

"In general, you're right, but where you're concerned..." He took a step back and released a heavy sigh. "You might still be right."

He hadn't lied to me. At least not overtly, not that I was aware of. Maybe he lied by omission, but everybody did that, and in truth, he owed me nothing. He hadn't kept me prisoner in an abandoned theme park, thinking the entire world had ended and almost everyone in it had died. But he'd kept me prisoner in a nice house. Was it that much different?

I had begun to think of my life in two chunks of time: the theme park captivity and the monochromatic minimalist house captivity. The world may as well have ended for all I'd seen of it during both imprisonments.

When Trevor took me, and my face was splashed all over the news, he'd ended the world for me. Shannon was keeping the same cycle going. Though I couldn't imagine any reality in which everything wouldn't be completely fucked. The moment some part of my brain had shut down and locked up all my memories was when things had gone to shit. Because from that point there was no option of heaven, just different circles of hell.

My eyes kept straying downward unable to stop looking at Shannon in all his glory. He just chuckled.

God, why was I so attracted to him? On the looks scale, both Shannon and Trevor were very appealing—certainly neither of them looked like the monsters they were. But from the first moment I'd seen Trevor in the pirate ship, there had been an active revulsion. It was only desperation and fear and isolation and the need to survive that had brought me around to finally sleeping with him, then to convincing myself I actually loved him.

But Shannon? I'd been trying to pretend I wasn't attracted from the beginning because our story didn't start with the fuzzy lie that he was my loving husband. I'd known what he was. I'd known the moment he started chopping up my fake husband and throwing him in the flames.

With Trevor I'd had to force myself to feel things; with Shannon I'd had to force myself not to. Think of him as a big brother. Think of him as a sexless bodyguard. Think of him as a distant guardian angel. But God, whatever you do, don't think of him as a potential lover.

It had been easy before tonight. He hadn't tried to take anything from me. There had been no overtures, no innuendos. I'd had safety and warmth in my own room. I'd had food and shelter and running water. I'd had someone who didn't demand anything from me at all. I'd been convinced he was this asexual being, that the hunt and the kill were all that mattered to him. That the only way he interfaced with a human body was by destroying it and chopping it into pieces.

And now, that one safety had been ripped away because Shannon was the worst possible man for me to want or fall for. He might be a much more sexual being than I initially thought, but whatever kernel of an emotion the cat made him feel or I made him feel… I knew it was continents away from love. It was the barest glowing ember, ready to die at any moment. And what happened when the ember smoldered out? All bets were off, right? Then what would keep him from disposing of me when I became too inconvenient? What kept him from it now?

"I've tried to keep you at a distance," he said, echoing my own thoughts back to me. "You make me feel normal. Like a real person. When I saw you in the castle, I felt this warmth I didn't know was possible. I felt something like that but with less intensity with the cat. But never before with another person. I have these idiots around me who think they're my friends who can't see behind the mask. But it's all surface shit with them. They don't notice because they're just that shallow. I can't give you what you probably deserve, but for my own self-preservation, I can't let you go, either. I thought if I thought of you like another pet in the house it would be fine, I could keep you compartmentalized. And now… I can't anymore."

This was the most Shannon had talked to me in the weeks I'd been living here. Normally it was a perfunctory robot sentence here or there, nothing of much depth or value. I tried to determine if he was being honest or just belatedly turning on some sociopathic charm to chase his own selfish impulses. But that stupid gorilla mask was still between us.

"Please take the mask off."

He ripped it off and tossed it on the floor, then his hands went back to pressing against the wall, framing either side of me.

"W-what are you going to do with me now?" It must be a special talent of mine to always ask the most wrong questions—things I didn't really want the answers to.

"Everything."

From the way he looked at me and the way his gaze shifted to the sex furniture, it was clear what *everything* meant. Whatever had allowed him to treat me like his roommate or kid sister had vacated the building. In its place was something wild and hungry that might devour us both if given half a chance.

"Why can't we just go back to how things were? I'm sorry I left my room. I'll pretend I never saw any of this."

His hand started in my hair, then trailed down my face and along all my contours. A tremor ran through me, chasing his hand down the length of me as if each cell in my body stood in line, waiting its turn to show appropriate fear of him.

"Elodie, what was it like living in that theme park?"

I didn't like to think about any of that. It was a testament to how awful it had been that this set-up with Shannon occasionally made me forget I was technically still somebody's prisoner. On a visceral level, I still thought I'd been saved instead of just captured again.

"Hopeless. Awful. Boring. Dead."

"Did he light you up?"

"No." Trevor had been mostly nice enough once I'd figured out which buttons tripped what, but I'd only ever gotten to the point where I could cope with it. I'd thought of fucking him as my *wifely duty*—some comfort I owed him. A transaction to pay for the food and shelter he provided me. I'd felt too guilty to take away the last shred of his wife from him. And the whole time he'd been taking from me. Everything. But somehow Shannon's everything and Trevor's were solar systems apart.

"Do I light you up?" he asked.

"It doesn't matter. I can't do this again." *I can't fuck another monster who holds my life in his hands.*

Shannon's mouth found the pulse point of my throat. He sucked gently on the skin—enough to make me gasp, not enough to mark me.

"What if I made you? Would you cry? Would you fight me?"

"You'd like that, wouldn't you?"

He pulled back and stared at me for a full minute before he answered. "I don't know. I don't know how I feel about your pain yet."

Yet.

He was so bizarrely honest. But that didn't help anything. It didn't make Shannon more feasible. Given my limited experiences with men on this side of the wasteland that was my lost memory, it was easy to assume all men were monsters. I'd yet to have an experience to contradict that notion—even though I felt like I knew in the vague way I knew about ATMs and pirates that not every man was this way. Somewhere out there was someone who was kind and considerate and smart. Someone who would let me be a part of a world where I wasn't the freak show or... *that poor girl.* Someone who would love me in a way that was safe and in a way I didn't have to work myself up to wanting.

If only I didn't want Shannon so much.

"You're going to play all my games, Elodie. And you're going to love every minute of it. I'm tired of you being a toy I can't play with. I'm ready to take you out of the box."

"What if I'm not ready?" I desperately sought to turn this into another veiled threat like Trevor's. As if the idea of being in Shannon's bed could distress me half as much.

His hand dipped between my legs. He smirked as he raised a finger to his mouth and licked off my juices. "Oh, you're ready."

I thought he was going to throw me down and fuck me in the basement—now filthy from other people's trysts—but instead, he scooped me up and carried me up the stairs. On the main level, he set me on my feet.

"Go to my room and wait for me. You have a punishment coming for your earlier disobedience."

I'm sure my mouth hung open like a fish, as if I couldn't believe he'd really just said that to me. Despite everything I knew of Shannon, despite the orgy I'd witnessed and almost been recruited into, somehow this one utterance almost unhinged me.

I wanted to run for the door, despite my lack of clothing. But not only was the security system armed, I knew now from observing him, that it wasn't a one-way system. The door wouldn't open for anyone going in or out without the code. And I didn't know it.

But I didn't try to run. I went upstairs just like I'd gone upstairs earlier. I passed my room and went to his at the end of the hall. His room was another forbidden room. He'd never stated it outright. It wasn't always locked, but I felt like lightning would come out of the ceiling and strike me down if I were to go snooping around in there.

His room was the same exercise in restrained minimalism as the rest of the house. Utilitarian was the best word I had for it. There was an attached master bathroom and a balcony—which were the only big differences from my room. And then there was the normal bedroom furniture one would expect. Nothing freaky or kinky or serial-killer like. No hooks hanging from the ceiling. No blood splattered on walls.

His bed was a standard king-sized four-poster. The frame and posts were a sleek, shiny steel. Given what I'd seen in the basement, I imagined that could be of some use to Shannon's proclivities, but someone who didn't know anything about them wouldn't think it odd. It fit into the clean, simple lines of the room.

He didn't have a bunch of knickknacks lying around, or framed art on the walls. It was just a crisp bare emptiness. Utterly peaceful. Much like my own room. But I'd expected that much from the guest room. I wasn't sure I'd expected it fully from Shannon's.

The balcony door was oddly unarmed at the moment. So I went outside. It was the first bit of fresh air I'd gotten in weeks. From here I could yell and possibly have some hope of someone hearing me. I could see other houses. They were a bit of a distance off, but technically in the same neighborhood. Within screaming distance. Surely this option for escape hadn't been available to me all this time. Had it?

As fucked up as it was, I think I'd wanted to stay cocooned in Shannon's house. As long as I felt safe, I didn't want to escape. And up until this point, despite logic, I'd felt safe. Whatever he did out in the larger world, I just thought I was in a separate category somehow. He didn't skin and cut up his cat, so I thought he might not do it to me, either.

I'd always thought I'd want to go outside eventually and interact with the three-dimensional world of people, places, and things, but I'd been content to remain shielded for a while, secretly hoping my memory would return first, so when I did venture out, I didn't feel like an alien from another planet.

"Thinking of jumping?" Shannon whispered in my ear. He'd been like a ghost, silent as mist wafting through walls.

"N-no."

He threaded his fingers through mine and guided me back inside. There was a coil of rope and a paddle on the bed.

"First I'm going to paddle you for coming downstairs and

interrupting my party. Then I'm going to tie you up and fuck you."

I wanted to protest, maybe negotiate my way down to a light spanking and missionary sex with the lights off. Give me the illusion of love and caring. But the way his face lit up when he spoke and thought about doing these things to me... I'd never seen him look more like a real human being before.

There was no coldness in his expression now. It was all warmth like the sun. It was the closest we'd gotten to that first night when he'd felt pity for me. At the time that emotion from him had been awful. In hindsight, knowing more about him, I realized what a rare gift it was—to make him feel something like that. To make him feel anything.

He was still aroused, and I couldn't help the way my eyes continued to stray over him. But when I finally was able to tear my gaze away from his erection, I saw that he was equally captivated by me. His gaze roved over me, soaking in each detail he'd denied himself all these weeks starting when he'd turned his back on me in the castle so I could dress.

"If you wanted me, why didn't you take me at the castle?" I asked.

"I *did* take you."

I rolled my eyes. "You know what I mean. Why didn't you just fuck me there? Why did you turn around to give me privacy to put clothes on? You could have done whatever you wanted then."

"I didn't know what I wanted."

"Oh."

"And if I'd fucked you then, you wouldn't have wanted it. You would have been too scared and upset. You were still processing the death of the man you thought was your husband. You would have screamed and fought me. No way would I have been able to get you to come with me peacefully out of the park. I would have had to kill you."

It was good to know Shannon wasn't impulsive. But then, I'd already known that. Absent necessity, he didn't do anything without a plan and probably a thick dossier on whoever the plan involved.

Shannon stepped over to his closet and pulled out a pair of freshly pressed jeans. Yes, he ironed his jeans. I feel like that should be in a list of psychopath traits somewhere: doesn't name his cat, irons his jeans. He pulled the jeans on and zipped them.

I raised a brow. He fucked with his clothes on?

"I like the power imbalance: you nude and helpless, me at least partly dressed. I could go outside right now without calling any odd attention and without putting another stitch of clothing on." His gaze moved over me again. "You, not so much."

He sat at the foot of the bed and dragged the paddle up next to his thigh. "Elodie?"

I still didn't know how we'd gotten here, from basic safety and food and shelter and polite indifference to... this.

"Shannon?"

"Yeah?"

"What if I hadn't come down to the party? Would this still be happening?"

"Probably not."

"So then, aren't you glad I interrupted your party?" I asked hopefully, thinking it might buy me some... something.

He smiled, a real smile that made me forget everything he was and everything he wasn't. "Yes, I'm glad you interrupted."

"So why punish me?"

The smile remained on his face, but it twisted somehow as the rest of his face seemed to fall into shadow. "Try negotiating with me again, and you'll get more. Do you want more?"

I shook my head quickly, already certain that I didn't, even without any experience to base that feeling upon.

So this was how it was going to be? I'd fantasized about Shannon, but my fantasies had never been like this. Though realistically, I didn't know what kind of sex I expected Shannon to be into. Once I'd decided he wasn't into it at all, I could think about any silly romantic thing I wanted. If it wasn't happening ever at all anyway, why worry about what he'd *realistically* do? Who cared? Realism wasn't required to come.

I'd been using him to erase Trevor from the first night inside Shannon's minimalist sanctuary. Each orgasm brought on by vague sexual thoughts of him made Trevor fade a little more into the background, first into a nameless face in a crowd, then into a shadow, then into a ghost. Until he was mostly gone except for when I had a bad dream about the park. I didn't bother Shannon with those. I was sure he didn't care about any post traumatic whatever I had going on.

"Elodie. Now."

I glanced back at the balcony door, trying to decide if I should run out there and scream my head off. But I didn't want to.

"What if you lose control and kill me?"

"I'm not a Halloween monster. I don't get red tunnel vision and think *kill kill kill*. I'm always in control of myself. But this continued discussion is adding to your punishment."

When it became clear that I couldn't bring myself to go to him, he stood, and brought the paddle with him.

"Okay, then."

With every step forward he took, I took a mirroring step back. Like some dark tango. When we got close enough to the wall, he grabbed my wrist and twisted my body to face it.

"Ow, ow, ow."

"Relax," he said, as if it were possible with the way he'd wrenched my arm behind me. Maybe he'd once been a cop. Or military and cop. Or military police. I could imagine Shannon cuffing a criminal. Easily.

When I stopped struggling, he released his grip on my wrist. He kept one hand on the back of my neck, holding me in place against the wall while the other brought the paddle down across my ass and thighs several times in quick, hard succession. The sound rang out like a hollow gong in the echoing empty minimalism of the room.

Tears streamed down my face at the intense burning sting. "Shannon, please. Please, stop." It hurt. It *really* hurt. But I think my fear was that, despite everything he assured me, he would lose control. I was afraid he'd just beat me to death. I was afraid he liked this too much.

The paddle came down against my skin once more, even harder, so hard it briefly knocked the wind out of me. He kept his grip on the back of my neck.

I pressed my hands flat against the wall on either side of me, bracing myself, seeking anything to hold onto. I tried to focus on the texture of the light gray wallpaper rippling beneath my fingertips in elegant, sophisticated patterns. I took slow, measured breaths. I did everything I could to live inside those breaths and nowhere else.

"Beg me again. Beg me not to hurt you." His voice was low and guttural, not even human.

"Please, you're scaring me. Please don't hurt me."

"Apologize for your behavior. And be specific."

"I'm sorry I disobeyed you and went downstairs. I'm sorry I left my room. Please," I sobbed.

"If I tell you not to do something again, are you going to go ahead and do it anyway?" he asked.

"No."

"No, *Sir*," he said.

"N-no, Sir."

When he flung the paddle away, it made a soft thud against the carpet, such a seemingly harmless sound. Heat rose off my flesh as if I were burning up from the inside. But despite this fact, and despite my terror, I felt a hard, steady pulsing throb between my legs, and I was sure if my hand were to stray to the apex between my thighs, that I would be very wet. Embarrassingly so.

Shannon pressed himself to my back and cradled me against the wall for several minutes, his breath and heartbeat keeping time with my own. I didn't speak. I didn't know what to say. I couldn't say no man had ever done this to me before. Perhaps they had. How could I know? Trevor hadn't. Trevor's tastes had always run strictly vanilla, without so much as a stray rainbow sprinkle to be found. It was all lights out and missionary with Trevor—nothing too threatening.

I had never really gotten off with him, but at times, there had been a comfort in warm body grinding against warm body, of embraces under down comforters near a warm roaring fire. I hadn't wanted to fuck up the tiny bit of *not terrible* that had defined my life in the park.

I don't think I'd ever once thought that I *needed* Trevor to fuck me—as if he were the only source of water that could put out my flame. It had never been so dramatic as that. But standing shoved against the wall with Shannon's rough jeans pressing against my heated raw flesh, I thought I would climb out of my own skin if he didn't put his dick inside me.

I would never say this out loud. I was still waiting for a man who wasn't a monster to bust in and rescue me off to a clean suburban politeness where everything was safe and smelled like lemons.

And yet every raw nerve ending screamed for Shannon to possess me and keep me forever, and now that he'd paddled me and I'd reacted as I had, I suspected in the darkest well of my being that I didn't *do polite sex*. I couldn't say it was Trevor's sociopathy that had kept me from being excited by him. Because Shannon was a sociopath, too.

He sighed against my hair. "It's exactly what I was afraid of."

"What?"

But I knew.

"I like your pain and fear."

I tensed beneath him, but inexplicably the excitement between my legs didn't fade away.

6

Shannon released me and began to pace, lost somewhere inside his own head for the moment. I just stood there, except now I was facing him. I leaned against the wall, memorizing the pattern of the wallpaper pressed against my bare flesh. I'd lost the will somehow to feel self-conscious about my nudity. He'd drunk it up like peach tea on a hot summer day, so it seemed weird to be self-conscious after all that appreciative ogling. There was no question he was attracted.

Or that I was, no matter how desperately I'd tried to ward those impulses away.

"Go to your room," he said, refusing to look me in the eyes.

"Why? I thought..."

He took a long, deep breath as if he were one of those toys that had to be wound up before it could express itself. "Until very recently, the only person in the world I cared even a little bit about was myself. I can fake empathy pretty well under the right circumstances. Most people don't notice because most of their empathy is just as fake. Everybody's wrapped up in their own shit, so maybe we're all just pretending, and it's not just me."

He stopped and seemed lost inside that thought for a moment. Finally, he managed to untangle himself from it to continue. "I don't trust myself with you if I like hurting you... given the other things I like."

As if he had to spell that out for me. He thought murdering people was fun. He thought hurting me was fun. He loved it when I cried and begged him, so exactly how little would it take for him to cross over to the thrill of killing me?

If I was a smart woman, if I had any brains inside my head at all, I would have done what he asked. You'd think without memory to take up much space in my brain that I'd have more room for deeper cognitive reasoning.

But instead, I went to the bed and picked up the rope, then I went back to Shannon and pressed it into his hand. *This* was insane. I was insane. My captivity with Trevor must have broken me. In a sense I'd been born in captivity. I didn't remember a time I had ever been free. Now I needed the ropes and the cage to feel safe—even when I knew I was anything but.

Shannon's hand closed over mine and the rope as he looked hard into my eyes. "If you cross this line with me, we aren't going back."

"Is it going to end in my grisly murder?"

"I hope not."

I believed he meant it. But how could I know? He was so good at faking everything.

"I thought you weren't a Halloween monster. I thought you were always in control."

"I'm going on past performance. I might be wrong."

And I might never get my memory back. I might always live in this gaping void, this endless eternal twilight, this space where lost souls wandered and moaned in hallways in the dead of night.

He seemed to consider the point we'd reached for a moment, as if he could rewind the night to before I'd walked in on the orgy, as if we could go back to the happy roommate illusion we'd been living in.

There was no time for me to change my mind, as if I could bring myself to. I was terrified of him and what he was capable of, and yet I needed him to fuck me more than I'd needed anything since I woke in the pirate ship.

He tossed me on the bed and began tying my hands to the headboard much like he'd done in the motel room that night. I still couldn't believe I'd handed him the rope. But in only a few moments he'd created a gnawing hunger inside me that I knew only his cock could satiate. I needed him inside me like I needed air.

I was certain that no amount of touching myself in the darkened room down the hallway would ever calm the desire he'd ignited. I needed to be perched on the knife-edge of living and dying. I needed to be so swept up in the present moment that I had no time to worry about the giant pieces of nothing inside my head or the giant pieces of lies Trevor had put there.

This was the only space and place in which I could be free of all of it.

Shannon spent a good ten minutes securing me to the bed frame, spread out before him like a buffet he would no doubt take his time with. Briefly, a panic settled over me, some primal deep thing... maybe something attached to a memory. I didn't know. Because whatever it was refused to crystallize into a fully formed vision or thought.

"Elodie," he said calmly, his hand pressing gently over my belly, stilling my movement.

I looked up sharply, trying to shake off the weird feeling. "Yes, Sir?"

"Do you want me to fuck you?"

"Yes, Sir."

"Then this is the way it happens. Or not at all. Do you understand?"

"Yes, Sir."

He didn't have to sell me on this. Really, he didn't. If he wanted to sweetly make love to me in what I assumed was the standard normal way, I would have probably found it unappealing in general, judging from what had just happened and the way I'd reacted to it. Despite my wild attraction to Shannon, I had a sneaking suspicion that much of that attraction was this dark sexual layer that I may not have seen consciously, but somewhere, deep inside my mind, in the places untouched by the amnesia, I'd recognized... something.

I might not have my memories, but I still knew in a very basic way what I liked because what I liked was formed and reaffirmed each moment I existed. I didn't need decades of remembered history behind me to tell me grapes were delicious or sunsets were pretty or that I liked sex mixed up with a little bit of danger—or a lot, depending on an outside observer's tolerance for risk. It seemed apparent that my tolerance for it was endless, despite this brief moment of visceral fear.

"I'll leave your feet free as long as you don't try to kick me. If you kick me, things will get ugly. Do you understand?"

I nodded quickly. I wasn't sure what all that entailed for someone like Shannon in this particular situation, but I was one hundred percent sure I didn't want to find out.

Instead of stripping off his jeans, he sat beside me, his hip settling into the groove of mine, the scratchy denim rough against my skin. He leaned over me and tweaked my nipple hard between his thumb and finger.

"Ow!"

He merely smiled in return. Unlike over by the wall, I could actually see his face now and how much he liked every drop of pain he delivered. My self-preservation finally kicked in, and there was nothing I wanted more than to get away from him.

I wanted to go back to the moment in the castle, the moment when he was going to call his friends and the police and get me some help. I closed my eyes and tried to remember it, the smell of burning flesh from the fireplace, the smell of Trevor's blood. The smell of my fear.

Shannon was right. This was too dangerous, this fire I played with. He wasn't some regular guy who liked a little slap and tickle with silk scarves. I twisted away, jerking hopelessly at the ropes.

"Let me go. I changed my mind."

He looked angry. His hand moved up to wrap around my throat and he squeezed...just enough. Just enough to let me know the danger I was in, how completely I was at his mercy.

"Why?" he practically growled at me.

"I'm scared."

"I know. I *like* it. I like it so much that I never want it to end. So if you're worried I'll just snap and kill you or do serious damage, you can put those fears aside. I would never do anything to endanger my ability to do this again and again."

"It's too dangerous."

Shannon's eyes narrowed until all I could see were slits of pure evil. How could I have trusted this man? What was broken in me that I thought Shannon could give me safety?

He took his hand off my throat, and a whimper escaped my mouth. The second it was gone, I wanted him to put his hand right back where it had been. But it wasn't safe.

"You gave me the rope. I was going to take the high road."

"I know."

"I told you if we crossed this line we weren't going back."

"I know. I'm sorry." I was so fucking stupid. It was like giving a bottle of whiskey to an alcoholic or asking a junkie to hold some heroin and syringes for a few days.

"No," he ground out. "I told you not to come downstairs, but you came down anyway. I was going to let you go back to your room, and you put the rope in my hands. Do you want me to fuck you, Elodie? Don't lie. I can't abide liars."

I wanted to say no, but if I lied to him, he would see right through me, and God help me if I ever betrayed him.

"Yes."

"Do you want me to make sweet romantic love to you that we both know is a lie?"

I shook my head. The thought made the bile come up in my throat. It was too much like the sham with Trevor.

"Good. Because I don't make love. You know you're mine, right? You were mine the moment I laid eyes on you in the castle."

My pulse fluttered harder in my throat.

"Answer me, Elodie."

"Yes, Sir."

"Now, I'm going to fuck you, and I'm going to do it my way. Unless you are in genuine distress you will not speak another word until I've come inside you. Are we clear?"

"Yes, Sir." There was a small crazy voice inside me that said if death was the possible price for having his hands on me, then let it come.

I closed my eyes and jumped into the gaping chasm where Shannon had already set up a life of comfortable darkness.

He didn't remove his jeans, just undid them. My hips surged upwards as he drove into me, his fingers digging hard into my hips. Somehow I knew he wanted to flip me over onto my stomach, but the intricate knotwork he'd made wouldn't allow for such spontaneity mid-game.

"Shannon, please, the ropes hurt."

He fucked me harder causing them to pull and chafe even more. "Good. Cry for me."

My eyes were still closed, and the tears slid from the corners of them, down my cheeks, and onto the sheets. The ropes dug and burned into my wrists like a branding iron, but I wasn't crying because of that. I cried because despite the overwhelming relief of Shannon's body moving inside of mine, of all the tiny nerve endings he awakened with this relentless friction, I was convinced I was going to die.

What if, at the last moment, the known killer in bed with me decided killing me *was* better than fucking me after all?

A moment later, I felt a warm tongue on the side of my face, licking up my tears as I cried them. It startled me enough to make me open my eyes.

When Shannon pulled back to look at me, that intense expression was back. It was the look that made me wonder for brief seconds at a time how I could ever fear him. That was the look of a man who wanted me to live forever. Just so he could keep doing this.

That final thrust made me gasp, and pushed me right up to the edge of my own pleasure.

After a few beats, he pulled out of me. I was going to let it go. Even without completion, even with the moments of abject terror, it was far and away better sex than the droopy display with Trevor had ever been. But Shannon knew I hadn't come, and he wasn't having it.

He still straddled me, one hand gripped my throat, forcing me to look at him. The other snaked between my legs, stroking me in a slow, steady rhythm until my release came, causing a scream to tear out of me like nothing I'd ever heard. At least not in my known memory.

We stared silently at each other for several minutes. Somehow I knew he'd fucked a lot of women, but whatever emotion he felt now, it was new. It was mine. His face was filled with the same awe as a baby discovering his own hands for the first time.

Shannon untied my wrists and pressed a kiss against the

rope-burned skin. He got up and retreated to the bathroom then came back with a tube of something and some gauze and medical tape.

The way he rubbed the cream into my wrists and wrapped them, it was obvious he'd never done this for someone else before. It must be so baffling trying to heal when what you most craved was to do harm. Like a lion nurturing an injured gazelle back to health.

Finally, he finished. He put the supplies up along with the rope and paddle. Everything in its place. Then he got back into the bed with me and pulled the covers up around us.

"Shannon?"

"Yeah?"

I wasn't sure if my next question was wise. It might be sensitive. It might make him angry. But I had this burning desire to try to understand him, to find some kernel of something human and sympathetic that I could use to justify my growing attraction to someone who did terrible things to others, and would be doing another brand of terrible things to me. Admittedly things I'd probably like, but I still didn't want to think too hard about that.

"Were you abused as a kid?" I asked, all the while wondering if maybe *I* had been abused as a kid. Never mind what was wrong with Shannon. What was wrong with *me*?

"Why would you ask such a thing? I have zero appropriate social skills, and even I know that's out of line."

"I'm s-sorry, I'm just trying to understand what made you like this." If I could understand what made him like this, maybe I could figure out what made *me* like this. Because I thought I probably wasn't a sociopath, but Shannon and I seemed like two sides of the same coin. He was the perfect predator; I was the perfect prey. I was the fucked-up prey that wanted to be ensnared.

He seemed to be trying to decide how much he was prepared to tell me. At least he didn't appear angry.

"No," he said after another moment's thought. "I wasn't abused. That's not why I kill people. I didn't kill small animals when I was young or burn the wings off of flies. My parents are good people. They raised me in a good environment and taught me good morals. They loved me. I'm sure they still do. I know whatever it is that they feel toward me, it's something real, even if I couldn't understand it or feel it myself. I knew even when I was young that there was something very wrong with me—at least by the general population's standards. I don't know how I knew, but I knew I had to keep it a secret, so I pretended the best I could and did what the others around me did. But I never felt the things they claimed to feel. And I wasn't even sure if they were lying or not. I just wanted so much to fit in and be like the other kids."

"But how could you become this way if something bad didn't happen to you?" I'd wanted to uncover something in his history that would make me understand so I could say, *Ah, that must be it. So much pain almost had to turn him into a monster.* Then I could feel pity for him. I could be this light of salvation. Maybe I could heal him. And even if I couldn't, I could claim that my motives were virtuous. I could pretend I didn't just like to stand a little too close to the fire.

"It's not all nurture, Elodie. There are predators in this world, and I'm one of them. There's nothing I can do to change that."

"Would you if you could?"

"I don't know."

I wasn't sure how long he was going to put up with this probing, but I wanted to find out as much as I could while he tolerated my questioning. I had no way to know that anything he told me was true, but given everything else I'd experienced, I knew that sometimes a story was all you needed—something that made sense. And I desperately wanted to find a way to make sense of who Shannon was and how he got to be that way.

"W-when did you kill for the first time?" I asked.

"Not until the military. I couldn't afford college, and my parents couldn't afford it either. Instead of taking on debt I might never get out of, I decided to join the armed forces. I wasn't scared of anything, so I thought I might be useful. Turned out I was right. They test you in all sorts of ways, and they're always watching, trying to figure you out. I fit a certain profile. I was a tool they could use. A weapon. I could be put to use doing the less savory jobs that most other soldiers can't handle or can't justify, the things most private citizens would be horrified by but which still must be done to keep us free and safe."

I waited, wondering if he would say more. He seemed to be weighing whether he should or not. Finally, he did.

"The first time I killed someone, I felt... something. It was this rush and this sense of joy. Before that moment everything had felt dull and dead, but in the kill, I came alive. When I got out of the service, college was forgotten. I started taking lucrative contracts in the private sector and never looked back."

The way Shannon described taking a human life was not unlike how a normal person might describe the experience of eating a really good hamburger or going on an amazing trip to Europe.

"If I hadn't begged you not to make me face the police and you hadn't had to dispose of Trevor's body, would you have let me go?"

"I don't know."

"Because I made you feel something?"

"Yes. You made me feel pity. I've never felt pity for another living soul, not ever. It's a fucking awful feeling, but it's a part of the set of experiences I don't have and which make it impossible for me to relate to people in any real way. But the idea of killing you... I didn't get a rush from it."

Lucky for me.

"What about the cat?"

"I feel a sort of detached affection for her. But before you came along, it was the strongest emotion toward another living being I'd ever felt that didn't involve that being's death."

"Why are you telling me all this now?" Just because I asked, didn't mean he had any obligation to answer, and I was kind of surprised he was going along with my questioning in the first place.

"I no longer have anything left to lose because I've decided I'm never letting you go."

I'd suspected as much, and he'd said something close to this before, but the word *never* hadn't entered into it. There was a finality and stubborn resolve to that *never* that caused the tightness inside me to finally relax. Because I believed him. He wasn't letting me go. And he wasn't going to kill me—at least not tonight. And whatever else he was planning to do... he was probably right that I'd like it because apparently I was a freak like that. Like him in my own twisted way. Yet another reason to not want to remember my past.

I closed my eyes and against all reasonable common sense, fell asleep in the only arms that felt safe to me.

~

When I woke, I was back in my room down the hall. Shannon must have carried me back once I'd fallen asleep. The clock on the nightstand read *ten o'clock,* and sun was streaming in through the windows. How had I slept so late? I must have been out eleven hours at least. I rolled over, stretching, startled to find Shannon leaning against the door frame watching me.

"You'll want your own room for sleep. You'll need a space that is yours to process your experiences."

Even though he'd been decent to me up to this point, somehow everything he said managed to sound terrifying with about thirty layers of meaning tucked inside them, half of which I was sure I would never fully unravel until it was far too late.

There was an abrupt buzzing sound, and he retrieved a shiny red phone from his pocket. It wasn't a burner like the one I normally saw him talk on. It seemed quite nice and expensive, definitely not the kind of phone you ditched in a nondescript undisclosed location every two weeks.

"Mom, hi."

I could hear an animated female voice on the other end of the call.

"I know. I've been working," Shannon said. "I know. I know. I'm free tonight."

The woman on the other end squealed. An obvious sign of approval. But then something that sounded like nagging started.

"I found someone," Shannon said, interrupting her tirade.

Utter pin drop silence on the other end for nearly a full minute. Then there were more animated questions I couldn't decipher from across the room.

"We'll see," Shannon said, noncommittally. "I'll see you tonight."

He put his phone back in his pocket and regarded me with something like amusement. "How would you like to meet my parents? You'll be playing the role of my girlfriend."

"What am I really?" Words like *girlfriend* seemed way outside the scope of anything that had or would go on between us. Still, I wanted to know how he defined *this*.

"You're mine," he said, as if that clarified everything.

"Your what?"

"Just mine."

Since Shannon was perfectly comfortable killing a person, he must be equally untroubled by owning one.

"And when you get tired of playing house?" These questions and concerns had been in the background since we'd first arrived. But now that things had escalated between us to a mockery of coupledom, I was even more concerned about how these things ended with a contract killer. Surely it couldn't be a nice ending. And this couldn't last forever.

"I haven't gotten tired of the cat."

This statement was absolutely insane to me but seemed reasonable to him. How could he compare me to a fucking house pet? Oh, right, because I was just another type of pet to him.

"How long have you had the cat?" I asked.

"Seven or eight years."

He'd managed to care for a cat for that long? Sure, they didn't require a lot of maintenance, but he had to make sure she was fed and got her shots. And she seemed healthy and well taken care of—spoiled even. He fed her a super fancy brand of cat food that was probably better quality than most kids got at school. You could put it on a plate and feed it to a kid, and they'd probably think they were eating food meant for people.

So maybe there was some credence to his view on this. From your average person, such an unusual assurance wouldn't mean much to me, but maybe he really wouldn't get bored. If I could make him feel something without having to die at his hands first, then maybe he wanted to keep that feeling going. If it had only been me and the white cat who'd been able to elicit anything close to a human emotion from him, we were both far too rare to be casually discarded.

I hoped.

"How did you get the cat?" Somehow I couldn't imagine him sauntering up to a pet shop or searching the classifieds.

What situation could have possibly moved him to acquire an animal companion?

He smiled, remembering back. "I was on a job. I had a contract for her owner. She was skin and bones, barely being fed or properly cared for and little more than a kitten. She was so dirty that I thought she was gray at first. When I killed him, I think she actually smiled at me. She kept following me around, meowing at me as I cleaned up. For some reason, I couldn't bring myself to leave her behind, so I brought her home with me."

I wasn't sure what kind of story I'd been expecting. I guess something a little more pedestrian. I shuddered, thinking it was like she was some kind of trophy from a kill. Like me after Trevor in the castle.

An awkward silence descended between us, then he said, "So dinner with my parents?"

I couldn't believe he was taking me out of the house. And I was very curious. I was convinced his parents must somehow be evil, and maybe Shannon was in denial about it or was simply lying. It wasn't as if lying would give him an attack of guilt. Though his lack of shame also made honesty much easier for him than the average person. If he could control certain parameters, he could tell me anything without caring what I thought about it.

"There will be ground rules, of course," he said. "You will not at any point give them any indication that you are the girl who went missing or anything about how you truly came to be with me. Let me handle the details of how we met when they ask. Nor will you seek their help to escape me. Don't put me in a position to do something I'd rather not do. I'm sure you don't want blood on your hands."

I stared at him, not even sure how to process that statement. "You'd kill your parents if I tried to get help?"

"I'm sure it wouldn't give me pleasure."

Oh *that* made it better. How could he speak so casually about killing the supposedly wonderful people who raised him?

"I'm not like you. You know this. Don't assume I'll be held back by the things that repulse normal people, and plan your own actions accordingly. It's likely you'd be far more traumatized by the event than I would. Just know I will go to any lengths to protect my secrets."

"And what would theoretically happen to me if I was this stupid?" I wanted to know the worst case scenario with Shannon as he saw it currently.

"Let's just say it would be a very long time before I took you out of the house again. You'd be an indoor kitty."

In truth, I had no intention of saying a single thing. Where the hell would I go? In the time I'd been in Shannon's house, I had not once developed some burning desire to have my photo plastered all over the news and have strangers in my face trying to convince me of our history together, or having everyone I met from this moment on look at me with condescending pity.

I was sure that if I were to be able to go through all that, I would additionally be able to access my money at least and put together a reasonably non-horrible life. But I had no anchor. I would always be "that girl who doesn't remember anything, poor thing."

Aside from the initial moment in the castle where Shannon had felt the spark of pity that no doubt saved my life, he hadn't acted like what had happened to me was any big deal. That might sound cold and horrible, but he hadn't handled me with kid gloves. There were some bizarre benefits to spending time with a man who lacked empathy. I was sure that if I'd been with any other person, I would have spiraled down further and further into post-traumatic stress as all the well-meaning concern made life more and more impossible to cope with. I would have no doubt mirrored and aped the reactions those around me expected.

Sometimes all a person needed was to be treated like they were normal. At a certain point sympathy and empathy become another version of aggression.

"Elodie? Are you going to dinner?"

"I have a choice?"

"About this? Yes."

"I'll go, but what will I tell them about who I am?"

"Make something up, but keep it as close to the truth about what you know about yourself as possible. It'll be easier to remember. You should make up a different last name if it comes up, and I wouldn't tell them the university you attended. Pick another one, on the other end of the country, preferably."

"Do I have to wear the brown contacts? Don't I look different enough without them?"

My hair was much shorter and darker. And while I didn't wear makeup with just us in the house, Shannon had bought me some. The colors I would wear would be far different than what would have worked with long blonde hair.

"What is your objection to the contacts?"

"Discomfort. Not wanting to touch my eye. And what if we forget them sometime? Or I might forget to take them out. I have to clean them. A lot of things."

"What about a pair of non-prescription glasses?"

"Okay."

"Good. I'll handle it while I'm out running errands today. Finish up your leftovers for lunch so I can get it out of my fridge. I don't want the kitchen smelling like *lo mein* for the rest of the week."

I had thought we might discuss the previous night, or that he might give me some indication of how he saw our relationship progressing. I don't mean that I thought we'd pick out rings or discuss babies, just that I thought surely he might give me some indication of his plans for me. In reality, it seemed he only planned to let me see a few feet of the road ahead of me at any given time. Whether he'd privately planned any farther than that remained a mystery.

~

AT SIX-THIRTY, we sat in Shannon's car in front of his parents' house. They lived in a really nice—almost posh—upper middle class neighborhood in a generously sized red brick two-story with large white columns in the front.

"I thought you said your parents couldn't afford to send you to college," I said, sure I'd caught him in a lie. Not that it would matter in the grand scheme, but somehow I was disappointed he'd lie to me about something so trivial. I'd thought that because it would be easier to be honest for someone with little to no guilt, that he *would* be. Bad assumption on my part.

"They couldn't. This isn't the house I grew up in. We were firmly middle class. I had everything I needed and a lot of things I wanted, but college was still outside of our budget, and I didn't have the kind of grades for a scholarship. But that was twenty years ago. In that time, my father's small business has grown and his investments have paid off."

"Oh," was all I could manage, ashamed for thinking he'd lied about his family. Though I was sure he couldn't care less whether I thought he'd been lying or not. He might be a demanding control freak, but it didn't seem as though anything had the power to make him defensive.

Shannon got out of the car and came around to my side, opening the door for me with a smooth and polished flourish. If we'd been on a real date and I didn't know the truth about him, I would have believed his act. In one hand, he held an expensive bouquet of pink roses he'd picked up for his mother from the florist on the way. The perfect gentleman.

On the front porch, he rang the bell while I straightened my skirt and my hair and pushed the glasses up the bridge of my nose. I wasn't sure I would ever get used to these things and thought maybe I should have opted for the contacts after all.

"Stop fidgeting," Shannon said as the door opened.

"Shannon!" His mom swept him up in a hug and pulled him into the house. I stepped in behind them and closed the door, shutting out the frigid air outside. She seemed to be about early sixties and was slim and polished in a smart red pantsuit. She had chestnut colored hair swept back into a bun and bright green eyes. "Frank! Frank! They're here!" She called out behind her, a rich, southern twang wrapping around her words like velvet.

I realized suddenly that Shannon didn't have an accent. Had he worked to rid himself of it? I couldn't imagine someone wanting to hire a killer who sounded like a lead singer in a country band. There was no reason Shannon should seem less deadly with a twang or drawl, but somehow it didn't fit.

His mother was far more animated and friendly than her polished presentation might suggest.

By this point, we were in the foyer, easing our way into the belly of the house. "Here, let me take your coats," she said.

"Millie, for God's sake, I live in the same house you do," Frank said, a similar, though more brusque accent flowing from his own mouth. Frank looked like an older version of Shannon, if Shannon were to stop working out and gain about thirty pounds, go gray, and take up pipe smoking. He was similarly dressed to his wife in a nice understated navy suit and a tie. They looked as if they were about to attend church.

I wondered if he dressed this way for his work or if Millie had made him put something nice on for dinner.

"Oh, are these for me?" Millie asked, gushing at the roses and inhaling the fragrance wafting off the pale pink blooms. "You didn't have to bring me flowers."

"Let me put them in some water for you." Shannon deftly escaped to the kitchen with the roses and an empty vase he grabbed off a side table on his way.

Millie turned her attention to me. "And you must be the girl. My rude son didn't even tell me your name!"

I could tell by her tone, that she didn't really believe Shannon to be rude at all. It was just the good-natured ribbing that happened in families. These people were not what I'd expected. At the very least, I'd expected them to be cold and distant. Frank was a bit reserved, but not cold.

"I'm Elodie."

"Well, that's a lovely name. Shannon hasn't ever brought a girl home before," she said, leading me toward the living room. "And I've been dying to show off his baby pictures."

"Mother, I will kill you," Shannon called out from the kitchen.

For a moment I was actually terrified for her, but then I realized Shannon was just playing the role of embarrassed son. He had no intention of killing her for showing me baby pictures. I doubted he cared one way or the other about me seeing the photos. It was just part of the mask, the play he starred in where he was like everyone else.

"Oh, nonsense," she shouted back toward the kitchen. "You wouldn't hurt a fly."

Could they really not see the cold dark spot inside their son? Were they that blind? Frank wasn't as animated as Millie, but even he seemed excited to see his son and to learn he'd brought a girl home. I imagined they were both marking time in their head, planning imaginary weddings and buying imaginary baby outfits for the grandchildren that I surely would dutifully deliver for them.

In the living room, Frank retreated to a brown leather chair in the corner out of the way, while Millie led me to the couch. She pulled out a big family photo album stuffed to near exploding with pictures. On the red leather cover in gold lettering, it read, "Mercer Family Memories."

"All the gory details are in here," Millie said, winking at me.

I could tell she'd been waiting years to show some poor woman the story of Shannon's early years in pictures. Though I was also certain I knew far more gory details than his mother would ever be privy to. I couldn't imagine how much it would break her heart to know the truth. Even if I were desperate, I wouldn't have had the will to tell his parents or seek their help. I doubted they'd believe me anyway.

Then I was inundated with photos of practically every mundane second of Shannon's life. If these images were to be believed, he really did have a near-perfect childhood. I suddenly wished I had photos of my own childhood, but I doubted they'd be like this—judging from my dossier, at least.

In the photo album were the obligatory splashing naked baby in the bathtub pictures, the eating solid foods for the first time pictures, some funny pictures of him in a giant wooden bowl that made him seem freakishly tiny by comparison, the bumbling toddler years, birthday party pictures, and Christmas after Christmas.

Shannon seemed so sweet and adorable as a baby and toddler. As he grew through the photographs, he became a bit more stoic and detached.

"He gets all that seriousness from his father," Millie said.

I glanced at Frank and wondered if he was secretly a sociopath, too. Were Millie and Shannon just his camouflage? Did this run in families? Shannon seemed to believe he'd been born this way, so where had it come from? Certainly not from Millie unless she was the world's best actress.

And yet I was sure if Frank were a predator, Shannon would have easily been able to spot it. And Frank would have just as easily spotted the traits in his son. No, Frank would be as horrified as his wife to learn what his son was.

"Did Shannon tell you he served our country in the military?" Frank asked, beaming and animated for the first time of the evening.

I wasn't sure what Shannon wanted me to say, but this must be a safe enough topic. I was sure his parents had no idea what exactly he'd been doing in the military, but they seemed so proud of him and their vague notion of their son the soldier fighting to protect our freedoms. Over the fireplace mantel was a large framed photo of Shannon in his formal dress uniform.

Even though I knew it was foolish to feel anything for someone like Shannon, I couldn't help it. Seeing him like that, my heart leaped up into my throat. There was something about a man in uniform.

Shannon appeared in the doorway then. "Mom, I put your flowers on the table in the foyer."

"Thank you, dear. Dinner's ready if everyone would like to come into the dining room," Millie said.

She'd made a roast in a creamy gravy and mashed potatoes and green beans and a salad. And she'd pushed something called *sweet tea* on me with extreme insistence.

"Those beans are from Millie's garden out back," Frank said as he took his seat at the head of the table. "She canned a whole mess of them. Shannon, you and Elodie need to take a few jars back with you."

"Oh yes, you really have to," Millie said. Then she turned to me. "Have you ever had green beans from the garden, Elodie?"

I felt frozen, my blood turning cold in my veins all of a sudden. I'd been about to automatically say 'No, Ma'am, I haven't', when it occurred to me that perhaps I had. I just didn't remember if I had. It was moments like this I'd been dreading: everything rolling along just fine until some small innocuous thing reminded me of how different I was. Everyone at the table watched expectantly, waiting for my answer.

"No, Ma'am, I haven't," I went ahead and said. It may or may not be true, but from my perspective it was true enough for the moment.

"So," Millie said, "How did you two meet?"

I was happy to let Shannon field this one.

"At an amusement park."

I nearly choked on my green beans, which were as wonderful as advertised. She'd added some kind of oil to them and sugar, which made the flavors pop.

"Oh?" Millie said. "An operational one, or one of the ones you and your friends like to explore?"

"It was operational. We were both there alone on a special lovebirds discount day and we pretended to be a couple to get the discount. Then we spent the day together in the park. By the time they started shooting off fireworks that night, I was smitten."

Millie sighed. "I love that story."

I loved it, too. Too bad it wasn't true. But somehow I doubted, *I killed the man she was with in an abandoned amusement park castle, disposed of the body, and basically kidnapped her, and now she can never leave me*, would be as charming.

The rest of dinner was as delicious as it looked. Shannon's mom was quite the cook, which was hard to believe, given how fit she was. But I had a feeling she'd made this dinner special for Shannon and that these were some of his favorite foods.

I was grateful I didn't have to talk much about myself. Millie and Frank asked the polite questions about what I did for a living and where I'd gone to school. I took Shannon's advice and stuck to script, deviating only in the places that might give me away, though I was sure I looked nothing like the photos of me that had made the news network rounds months ago. And how many people would remember anyway? At best, I would look vaguely familiar. They'd be sure they'd seen me somewhere, but couldn't quite remember where.

I still found it hard to believe Shannon had recognized me

and Trevor immediately in the castle. But Shannon had probably been trained to notice details in a way most hadn't. And then there was the endless perceptiveness that had been required in his childhood just to survive it with his mask of normality intact.

After dinner, Millie brought out coffee and a chocolate silk pie. I wasn't sure I had room for it, but she insisted.

"So, how serious is it?" Millie asked, aiming her question directly at Shannon.

She was certainly a nice woman, but I was sure Shannon could have brought in a bag lady off the street and Millie would have been equally excited that her nice boy had finally found someone.

"Mom," Shannon hedged.

"I mean it. I want to help plan a wedding. I want to dance at my son's wedding. I want grandchildren! How much longer will I have to wait for all that?"

I wondered if I could in fact have children. Trevor had said I couldn't but that was probably all part of his elaborate lie. Had he really gotten the snip? Maybe the reason he wouldn't let me handle the food was he'd been slipping birth control into it.

"Can't you just be happy I'm seeing someone?" Shannon asked, clearly uncomfortable with the turn the conversation had taken.

Millie switched her attention to me. "Elodie, would you marry him if he asked you to?"

"I... um..." I didn't know what Shannon wanted me to say. I was pretty sure if he wanted to continue this charade to coddle his mother's fantasies that I wouldn't have much choice in the matter.

"Mom, don't put her on the spot. You're making her uncomfortable. We haven't discussed the subject. This is still new. I promise if we do, you'll be the first person to hear about it."

After that, the rest of dessert and coffee went smoothly.

Frank let Millie carry most of the conversation. When everyone was finished eating, I was surprised to see him collect the dinner plates and take them to the kitchen. From the beginning, he'd struck me as the kind of guy that went to watch football immediately after dinner, leaving the women to clean up after the meal they'd cooked.

"I've never met a man who loves washing dishes, but Frank does. He also does his own laundry. Did I get a keeper or what?" she asked.

How these two people's genes had mingled to create Shannon was probably one of the universe's strangest mysteries.

We didn't linger long after dinner, Shannon made an excuse, saying he had to get some work done. I wondered what his family thought he did for a living now that he was out of the military.

"Well, that was bracing," I said as Shannon started the car.

"They mean well. You did good in there."

I knew there could still be some secret abuse that I wasn't aware of. But from what I'd seen, they really did seem to love Shannon. They were proud of him, almost achingly so, and believed him to be a good man, a hero even. And in some twisted sense, I knew that was true, both for me and for the country at large.

"What are you thinking?" Shannon asked.

I stared out the window at the nice houses with well-manicured lawns, not unlike the neighborhood Shannon lived in, though it was a bit of a drive to get to his parents' house since they lived in Savannah, while his house was in a smaller town nearby. "I just don't understand how you could have been raised by people like that and be what you are."

Shannon frowned. "It's not as if they made no difference. In a different environment I would have turned out far worse."

"What's worse than being a killer?" For a moment, I almost

thought I'd wounded him somehow and felt guilty for it. Then I wondered if he was just manipulating my emotions. Didn't sociopaths do that?

"I'm not out slaughtering innocents, Elodie. The world is better off without the people I've killed. The people I kill deserve to die, and I enjoy killing them. It's win-win for everybody who matters."

There it was. Everybody who matters. For now, his family mattered enough that he wouldn't slaughter them unless pushed into a corner. And the white cat mattered. And I mattered. For now, for whatever reason, I might matter enough that he'd be unwilling to kill me in almost any scenario, but I wasn't sure how secure being in the *everybody who matters* circle really was. I wanted to believe it was secure, because God knew I needed *something* secure. Even if it was amoral.

7

When we got home, Shannon fed the white cat then took me to the basement. He'd cleaned up down here. It was so clean the place nearly sparkled and seemed new. The dark brown hardwood floors were especially shiny and nice as if he'd spent hours down here polishing them to a high finish.

Off my confused expression at the state of the space, Shannon said, "Sometimes I can't sleep. When I can't sleep, I clean."

That explained a lot about why his house was so irritatingly shiny all the time. I wondered how bad his insomnia was and if he'd given me my own room because of it.

"Why don't you sleep?" I asked.

He shrugged. "My mind stays busy. Planning jobs, thinking of possible things that can go wrong and planning for those contingencies."

"Oh." So, not guilt, then. I'd thought perhaps that subconsciously at least he might have some guilt. Somehow I'd convinced myself that deep deep down his work was eating him up inside as well as the fact that I was more or less his hostage. I really wasn't fully sure on that point. I had felt—up until the other night at least—like his house guest. Now I wasn't sure what I was beyond... *his* in all the finality such a proclamation implied.

Shannon crossed the expansive space and sat in a large black leather chair across the room. From this vantage point, he silently and unnervingly watched me. Unconsciously, my fingers strayed to my hair to fix imaginary flyaways. I licked my lips. I became paranoid something was on my face from dinner. I straightened my clothes and shifted my weight.

"What are you doing?" I asked, finally unable to stand the silence any longer.

"I'm studying."

This went on for another several minutes. After a while, I couldn't take it anymore and sat on the floor.

"Did I tell you you could sit?" he asked.

"N-no, Sir." I said, remembering what he'd asked me to call him when we were like this. I quickly stood back up.

"When we are down here, you make no independent decisions. Your only decision is whether or not to obey my orders immediately."

I didn't have to ask what would happen if I didn't. Looking around the basement, I realized this place was even more of an outfitted dungeon than I'd thought. He must have kept some things put away during the party, because now that everything was out on display, I noticed there was some extra bondage furniture I hadn't noticed the other night.

There was also a big box of toys and implements that hung from shining silver hooks in the exposed brick wall that hadn't been there during the party. The recessed lights in the ceiling cast bright spotlights on everything. I stood inside the pool of one of those lights. There was an empty unobstructed path between me and Shannon. Was he waiting for me to come to him?

I was about to ask what he wanted from me when he spoke again.

"Are you ready to begin, Elodie?"

I swallowed around the lump in my throat. "Y-yes, Sir."

He stood and went around behind the chair and retrieved a couple of decorated bags that had clearly come from nice stores. He crossed the room, set the bags down at my feet, then went back to the other end of the room and resumed his reclining.

"Put the lingerie on. You can use the furniture if you need to sit for part of it."

By this point, the contents of the bag weren't surprising, though the quality was. Inside one bag was the most supple black leather lingerie: a mini-skirt with slits up the side, and a corset of the same color with material that didn't cover the breasts. Inside the second bag were thigh-high shiny black heeled boots with laces that looked at though they would take ages to get on.

Shannon watched from across the room, his expression indiscernible. "I would like you to consider this performance art, Elodie. Entertain me."

I started to remove the glasses.

"No. Leave those on. I like the way they look on you."

I left them and slowly took off the shoes and dress I'd worn to his parents' house. Music began to drift through the space from the speakers located near the ceiling at the four corners of the room. When I looked back at Shannon, there was a tiny black remote in his hand. The music was hard to describe—sort of an electric drumbeat with other lighter instruments layered on top.

Almost as if it possessed me, I began to move to it, forgetting to be self-conscious. He'd seen everything already anyway, what was a little strip tease? My panties and bra joined the pile, and then I began to dress in the lingerie as slowly and provocatively as I'd taken the other clothing off.

I was right, lacing up the boots took a small eternity. And I had to sit on a spanking bench to get it accomplished. The bench was just a few feet to the left of where I'd stood previously and had another spotlight shining on it.

I started to get up, but Shannon's voice stopped me.

"Spread your legs and show me your cunt. Look me in the eyes while you do it."

The last part was the hardest part. He held my gaze for nearly a full minute—I counted the seconds, my breath unconsciously held the entire time—and then his gaze dropped to the flesh I'd exposed between my legs.

"Stroke yourself. Feel how wet you are."

My fingers moved between my legs, rubbing circles over my clit in light butterfly touches.

"Keep your eyes on mine," he said.

I was almost to the edge of my orgasm when he said, "Stop. Now, walk over to me."

I started to walk carefully across the floor, afraid of damaging it.

"No," Shannon said. "I want to hear the heels strike the floor and echo along the walls. You have to walk with purpose for that to happen. Go back and start again."

I went back to the spotlight I'd been standing under and hesitated.

"Well?"

"Sir, I can't. These heels will mess up the floor if I walk any harder. It'll put little dents in it."

Shannon smiled broadly. "And you're afraid if you put dents in my floor, I'll punish you."

I nodded.

"You're right about the dents and the punishment. Now walk. I want to hear it."

He wanted me to walk across the floor in such a way that ensured I would damage it and invite retribution. So I walked, exactly as he'd asked, across the polished wood to him. When I reached his side, he got out of the chair.

"Don't move. I need to inspect the damage." He walked slowly across the floor and then slowly back, studying and counting and recounting the dents my high-heeled boots had made in his beautiful floor.

"Twenty-eight," he said finally. "I counted twice." He shook his head as if disappointed. "Whatever will I do with you for putting twenty-eight dents in my floor? So many thrilling possibilities."

He moved in close to me, his lips brushing my ear. "I think we both know what kind of girl you are, don't we?"

Yes, I think we did both know. I could feel the excitement dripping down my thighs as much from the thrill of hurting his floor and knowing what it would mean as from the almost-orgasm. Shannon parted my legs with one hand, slipping a finger inside me. "My filthy little whore." His voice was practically a growl. "Go get on the bed."

I crossed to the bed, walking as carefully as I could so I wouldn't put any more dents in the floor.

"Not that bed," he said. "The bondage bed."

I turned toward where he pointed. The bondage bed was an elevated table-like piece of furniture covered in black leather. There were various shiny rings around it as well as a shiny silver pole affixed to each corner, allowing a wide variety of bondage options.

"On your stomach," Shannon said when I reached it.

I climbed onto the table and lay on my stomach. He came up behind me and spread my legs and arms out wide. He produced leather cuffs from the box and put them around my wrists and my ankles over the boots. Then he connected them to rings at the edges of the bed. He carefully unhooked the back of the corset and opened it so that my back was bare. Then he flipped the skirt up so he could get a clear view of my ass.

"You like being exposed this way, don't you, you little slut?"

"Yes, Sir." I didn't even think I was lying. I did like it. I liked the way the cool air flowed over my skin and then how just as quickly it heated again from his eyes on me.

He took a blindfold from the box and covered my eyes. I heard him going back and forth across the floor and wasn't sure if he was collecting items he planned to use on me or if he was just pacing. There was a deliberate, measured sense about his movements that suggested the latter.

"Elodie... Elodie... Elodie..." he said it in a slow sing-song voice, dragging out the syllables. The way he said my name sent ice cold fear shooting through my veins and a trail of goosebumps moving down my spine.

Finally, he stopped beside me, his lips again brushing my ear. "Elodie, I tried so hard to be a good boy where you are concerned. But then you had to come down into the basement. I wonder, did you think the other night was all I planned to do with you?"

"No... No, Sir."

"Are you going to cry for me like a good girl? It will make me so happy if you cry for me."

"Y-yes, Sir."

I heard something light thud gently on the table next to me, and I flinched. Shannon just chuckled in response. "You're terrified of me." He didn't say it like he was displeased about that fact.

Somehow I had faith that whatever happened in here wouldn't permanently damage me, that even if I couldn't trust in some sense of humanity in him, I could trust that he wanted to keep doing this enough to be careful with me. And I knew from the length of time he'd had the white cat that Shannon was capable of caring for fragile living things.

I gasped as his hands slid under my breasts. He stroked them for a moment, and then something hard and metal closed around each nipple.

"Ow!"

"Just wait until they come off," he said, chuckling.

He walked away for a moment, rummaging in the box, then returned. He pressed what felt like a rubber ball, about the size of his fist, between my legs. Then he secured it to me with straps which he wrapped around my body and buckled in place.

A humming vibration began.

Before I had time to enjoy that, he dragged something that felt like several long leather cords gently across my back.

"Twenty-eight dents in my floor," he said. Then I heard and felt him climb up on the table with me.

I jerked in my bonds when his warm tongue stroked from the base of my spine all the way up between my shoulder blades. A moment later, the flogger came down hard across my back.

"One," he said with the kind of satisfaction I was sure only killing normally gave him.

It was clear he intended to lash me twenty-eight times for the damage he'd insisted I cause to his floor. I gasped after each stinging blow, but I didn't beg him to stop. I knew it wouldn't do any good, and a fucked-up side of me that I was sure had done this before didn't want him to.

After the tenth lash he said, "Where are those tears, Elodie? Don't disappoint me now."

I could only imagine what disappointing him could mean, so I stopped trying to be brave and strong and tough and I let each strip of leather cord coax the tears and pain out of me until I was crying so hard I wasn't sure if I would be able to stop.

"Good girl," he said.

When he was finished, and I had a stripe across my back for each little mark I'd put on his floor, he put the flogger down and started to caress me. First he ran his fingertips over my back where I could feel the tender flesh welting up. Then he moved a hand between my legs and pressed it over the vibrating ball I'd almost forgotten about. He pushed it against me, then released the pressure and rolled it around on my rapidly moistening skin. He used the vibrating ball to massage me until I came in a cry more forceful than anything that had come before.

After the pleasure had run its course, he turned the ball off and unbuckled the straps and took it off me, then I felt him enter me from behind. He was rigidly hard, my tears having the same effect on him and his anatomy that they'd had the night before. He drove into me in a kind of frenzy for several minutes while the music in the room blanketed us in drumbeats and some exotic wind instrument.

When he came, his weight fell heavy against me for a moment. Then he rolled off me. The blindfold came off then, and I could see he lay next to me, his eyes locked with mine, staring intently. I would have looked away except that I couldn't turn my head easily the way I was bound. He brushed my hair out of my eyes.

A few moments passed like this, and then his hands moved to my breasts again, and he removed the clamps. The pain was as exquisite as promised.

"Fuck, Shannon!" I shouted.

He struck my ass with his palm. "Sir," he corrected.

But I couldn't imagine screaming "Fuck, Sir!" at him would have been much better.

He moved behind me again and massaged a soothing gel into my back, then he refastened my corset and pulled my skirt down. He uncuffed me and then he carried me upstairs to my bedroom and put me to bed.

~

THAT NIGHT, I had another nightmare. Only this time it was different. It wasn't the park. It was a memory from before the park. I was studying for my Master's degree in Botany at the University of Washington. I was in the biology lab, my professor standing behind me. He was far too close for my comfort, as if he didn't believe in the concept of personal bubbles.

His hands slid under my shirt, and then underneath my bra to stroke my nipples. He wasn't even subtle. He had no shame about the brazen act at all. He acted as if he were entitled to this, but he wasn't. This wasn't a repeat occurrence. It was something new. And the boldness of the act shocked me.

I pulled away, trying to shift out of his grasp, trying to pretend what was happening wasn't happening. I wasn't into Professor Stevens. Not that way. I respected his mind. I'd been thrilled to get to study with him, but this had not been a part of the course work I'd signed on for.

He smelled of scotch and cheap cigar smoke as he leaned in close to my ear. "Elodie, come on now, we all know what kind of girl you are."

From the moment he'd walked in on a private sex party a few of the students had thrown together at one of the frat houses—one I'd been at—I'd been his number one target. Because certainly if I liked to be tied up and whipped and fucked by half a dozen frat boys, I must have no morals at all. I must have no limits. There must exist no man that I could legitimately say *no* to. How could I even have that right anymore when I'd said *yes* so many times?

If I said no, then I was just being selfish and terrible because, of course, I was *that kind of girl*. In my grandmother's generation *that kind of girl* had been as tame as a woman who would blow her own husband. In my mother's it had been the girl who'd slept with a couple of different men before marriage. In my generation it was the freaky ones. That bold, open freakiness made unsavory men believe that it was all up for grabs and that the word *no*, simply wasn't allowed if you were *that kind of girl.*

"Stop it!" I said more firmly, pushing his hands away. This man had the power to halt my degree in its tracks. He could fail me, and then the only way I'd have a hope of salvaging my future was if I reported him. But wouldn't that be convenient? It would be my word against his, and with the stakes involved, he could just say I was trying to get a grade I hadn't earned by threatening his career.

And since *that party* had become common knowledge all over the school, I'd be treated like the whore who cried wolf.

"Don't worry, no one will walk in on us," he said. As if that were the problem rather than his abuse of position and the general grossness of this whole thing. He wasn't even some sexy youngish professor. He was old enough to be my father and short and balding and not exactly fit. How could he pretend surprise that I didn't want him or this? Some men only accepted *no* from a woman who kept her pussy under total lock and key. Because why should a few men get to have fun with you but not all of them? Forget the fact that the frat guys I'd fucked had looked like underwear models and had been my age. Nope. One dick gets in, they all get in.

I used every bit of mental power I possessed to... *WAKE UP, wake up right now, Elodie! Wake up!*

My heart beat wildly as I bolted upright in bed, taking in the darkness of my room in Shannon's house. It was safe and quiet. I didn't even question why I felt safe in Shannon's house. I did. And that was that.

I wasn't sure if I remembered everything about my past or not. But I remembered enough. I wondered if the earlier escalation of the games with Shannon had triggered the unlocking of my most powerful and vivid memory before the accident. I was beyond grateful that I'd woken before having to live it over again. My professor had taken me to a *second location*. Because of course he had. No wonder that idea had pulsed through my mind randomly even before my memory had returned.

The campus had been largely shut down for the holidays. And because I didn't have anything in the way of family to go home to, I'd stayed behind in the lab to catch up on some extra work. It had seemed baffling to me at the time why he'd chosen to switch venues. At least until we'd gotten to his house.

He hadn't killed me, obviously, but he may as well have. Because he liked the kink, too. And if he liked the kink, and I liked the kink, well then what was the problem? Fuck my agency. I was *that kind of girl, goddammit!* When he'd finally let me go the next day, swearing up and down that if I told anyone, nobody would believe a word out of my filthy whore mouth, I'd packed my shit up and left. At least everyone was away for the holidays, and I wouldn't have to answer any uncomfortable questions.

I'd left my schooling in the dust, afraid to even try to transfer somewhere else, afraid his vengeance would follow me. I'd moved to Florida and just lived off the money my biological father—who I still didn't know—had given me. He'd been generous. He'd set me up for life. He'd even paid for school above and on top of the money he'd dropped into an account for me.

I had thought at the time if only I knew who he was, maybe he would have done something about the professor so I could finish my education, but I was sure he wouldn't want to get entangled in my frat house sex scandal—not if he couldn't even handle the shame of having fathered me in the first place.

In Florida, I'd met Trevor. On paper, he'd looked great. Good-looking successful doctor. But something had felt *wrong* about him early on. I'd been trying to forget about what happened at school. I didn't want to think there was something broken or wrong about me now—something I couldn't get back. When I ended things with Trevor, not long after they began, he started to stalk me. I hadn't gotten a restraining order because, hell, what good would that do? It would just piss him off more, and it wasn't as if that piece of paper was a magical shield that could protect me.

The most fucked-up part of all of it was that the accident that landed me in the hospital involved Trevor chasing me in a car like the crazed lunatic he clearly was. And then, I'd been entrusted to his care in the hospital because no one had known any better.

Trevor's car hadn't been involved in the accident. I'd gone off the road. And beyond that, everything was a blank. The brief flash of him in the white room must have been when I'd woken in the hospital and hadn't remembered anything. That must have been when he'd put his plan in motion.

I'd never fallen in that pirate ship. Trevor must have carefully placed me there and waited for me to wake up into the sinister reality he'd manufactured for us. All those scars... they'd been fresher than I'd wanted to admit when I'd first caught my reflection in a mirror. Probably injuries I'd sustained in the crash. And that strange weakness when I'd woken up in the ship... it was probably from the coma and not using any of my muscles for however long I'd been out. I was sure someone had moved my arms and legs to try to keep atrophy at bay, but I still would have needed physical therapy. No wonder I'd felt so weak and helpless and confused when I'd woken in the forest.

I scooted back down under the covers and tried to close my eyes again. I'd had nightmares before at Shannon's house, and I'd gone back to sleep. But somehow I knew this was different. Before, I'd been a broken glass object held together by the glue of my lack of memory. But now there was no glue. I wanted to go back to before, when all my mind held were missing, gaping holes of lost stories. I wanted the blank slate again. It was safe and comforting.

When I closed my eyes now, all I could see was that night with Professor Stevens in his house, tied down to a bed in his basement... his belt tearing through belt loops and then leaving red welts across my bared flesh. No wonder the first night when Shannon had tied me to his bed had caused that sense of panic I couldn't quite nail down. It was as if a whisper of the memory was already working its way through, trying to protect me from a repeat experience.

In some ways, I was grateful things had moved forward with Shannon before I was in possession of my memories. After, I'm not sure I would have had the courage for it.

I got up and slipped out of the room. Down the hall, the white cat lay just outside Shannon's door. She hissed at me as I got close. I couldn't bring myself to open the door. I was afraid of how he might react to me barging into his private space.

If I didn't want him, would that change anything? Would he just do the same as my professor had and fuck me for being *that kind of girl* in the first place?

But hypotheticals hardly mattered. The fact was that I *did* want him. I wanted him so much it made my teeth hurt. I'd never wanted another human being the way I'd wanted Shannon. And now that I had my history back, I could say that with some authority.

I thought back to our last time together earlier in the night. I tried to determine if his body inside of mine had created any lasting trauma... in light of my new memories. But I couldn't find any. Still, I couldn't bring myself to go in there. Shannon hadn't invited me to start sleeping in his bed like his girlfriend or anything. Whatever thing he felt for me, it was something new to him, and visiting him with my problems would likely only push him further away. After all, feelings were only really desirable if they were good, and

Shannon was still so new at any feelings at all. Maybe he would determine human entanglements were far too much trouble—that I was too much trouble—and just shut the whole thing down.

Finally, the white cat became annoyed with my pacing back and forth in indecision to the point that she was ready to do something about it. She stood up and let out that long, insane Emergency Broadcast Meow—the one that could probably wake the dead with its length, volume, and insistence.

Shannon stomped over to the door and ripped it open. "What!?"

I jumped, and the cat fled.

His tone softened. "Oh. What is it, Elodie?"

I shook my head and turned to go back to my room. "Nothing. It's... it's nothing." What the hell was I going to say to him? I didn't know even now the full extent of what he wanted from me. But I was pretty sure what he wanted wasn't to have to become my therapist. He wouldn't know what to do... how to erase this, fix this, make it all go away. Assuming he wanted to.

As far as I was concerned, losing my memory was perhaps the best thing that had ever happened to me, and even the ugliness of the theme park months with Trevor didn't erase the soundness of that basic principle.

Shannon caught my hand and pulled me back. "What is it?"

Could there really be concern in his eyes? Concern for my welfare? Or did I just want it to be there? Was it a fake emotion he'd practiced with the dedication of a theatre major, or was there the kernel of something genuine behind it? Weren't even actors so good at faking an emotion because they understood how it felt to begin with?

"Nothing," I said. "Just... I'm going back to sleep."

But Shannon wasn't having it. He pulled me into the bedroom with him and nudged the door shut behind us, which set off shrill outrage from the white cat, who by this point had come back only to realize I was being allowed into the one room in the house she was consistently barred from.

"Shut the hell up!" Shannon barked at the closed door.

The cat made one last angry snippy yowl, then shut up.

Without another word, he guided me to the bed and pulled back the blankets. He wrapped his body around mine like a guy who understood how comfort worked.

And in that moment, I believed him.

He didn't push or pry or ask for anything, either physically or emotionally, from me. He just held me and let me sleep. In his arms, I didn't worry about Professor Stevens coming back, not even in dreams. Because if he did, I knew Shannon would fucking kill him without a second thought.

8

I woke the next morning to a tray of coffee and toast in bed. This might seem like the most mundane and bland thing. For a normal man in a normal household, this would be just something moderately nice and considerate that nearly anyone would do for someone they cared about if they were sick or had a bad night. But Shannon wasn't exactly normal by anybody's metric. It was huge that he'd broken his *no food outside the kitchen* rule for me. At least I thought it was. If I hadn't been sure before that he truly did feel something toward me, I was sure now.

I was beginning to see sociopathy as not a black or white—either you are or you aren't—kind of deal, but rather a spectrum. On one end were your serial killers who didn't have a single thing in their life that wasn't entirely for show—every displayed emotion carefully calculated for the maximum socially appropriate impact. Then on the other extreme were the people so empathetic that they were too sensitive to ever watch even a single bit of news on TV without bursting into tears and being depressed for the rest of the day.

Most of us lived somewhere in the middle of all this. We

didn't cry when random people got swept away in a tsunami on the other end of the world, but we'd be upset if our neighbor's kid skinned his knee in our backyard. In a way, human nature seemed to have designed us for sociopathic indifference toward distant strangers from other tribes and caring empathy toward our own small group. Toward that end, Shannon was just extremely fine-tuned for survival.

Being with him made me wish I'd majored in psychology rather than botany. Knowing with more authority than hunches and mere guesses how the human mind worked might come in handy here. But if it was like the other sciences, nobody really agreed on any but the most basic principles. There were theories and notions and people in this camp and others in that one. Nothing prepared one for the live study of a thing or person right there in front of you.

I was beginning to firmly believe that Shannon did in fact feel real emotions, and not just selfish ones that only pertained to himself and his own outcome. He might not have a big circle of people he would protect and defend, but he had one. I still didn't fully understand—and I don't think he did either—how I came to be in it, but nevertheless, there I was.

And despite his warnings to scare me before going to his parents' house, I was convinced he felt more than casual disinterest toward them as well, even if the feelings were vague and not strong enough to fully quantify. Like he'd said, their parenting had made a difference in the type of monster he'd grown into. He had to feel *something* with regards to that. Didn't he? Also, I was pretty sure if his house were on fire, he'd grab the white cat on his way out the door.

Shannon sat in a sleek gray chair across the room, quietly observing me while I had my coffee and toast.

"Thank you," I said.

He just nodded.

The tray was a simple white porcelain. Plain. Zen. Minimalist like everything else he owned. The plates were square and white as if ready for gourmet edible art to be splashed across them to the delight of some food critic somewhere. The coffee cup was plain and white as well, steam still rising up off the hot black brew.

Along with the toast, he'd brought raspberry jam. He'd already slathered the butter on, so that it would soften and melt against the heat of the bread. I spread the jam on top and poured some cream he'd brought in a tiny white creamer into my coffee. He knew by now that I didn't take sugar, so he hadn't brought any.

Shannon watched me like this for a while, but he didn't speak until I had finished both my toast and my coffee. When the last crumb of toast and the last drop of coffee were gone, he finally spoke.

"What was it about this new nightmare that was bad enough for you to come to my room? You never came to my room before." His words didn't seem accusatory or annoyed, merely curious.

I looked up, startled. "You knew I had nightmares before last night?"

He nodded. "I've heard you scream in the night."

I hadn't realized I'd called out in my sleep.

"And you didn't say or do anything?" I asked.

He shrugged. "You didn't call for me. You didn't come to me. I assumed that you wanted to deal with it on your own and that you required space."

This was exactly why I wasn't a useless ball of human rolled up in the fetal position on the floor all the time. Shannon had the most amazing sense of space I'd ever encountered in another human being. It occurred to me that some measure of his coldness wasn't garden variety coldness because he was *dead inside* or whatever, but was instead an expression of trying to project what he would want onto someone else. It just seemed to him like the natural thing to do.

I had the sense that, in general, Shannon didn't give a damn what other people wanted in any circumstance really, but if he *did* give a damn, it seemed more likely he'd think about what he would want instead of trying to guess at how other people's minds and emotions operated.

It was only the fact that what he wanted was so very different from what the general population wanted that someone could interpret it as a total lack of empathy—or at least this was what I kept telling myself.

"What was different about this nightmare?" Shannon asked again.

I hesitated, unsure if I should tell him. But in the end, I faltered beneath his hard, expectant stare. "The other nightmares were about the park. This one was something that happened in my life before the park."

His position against the supple leather shifted ever so slightly, his calm exterior disturbed by the tiniest ripple... of something. "You remember? Your life?"

I nodded. "A lot of it is still fuzzy, but I imagine that's probably true of a lot of normal people, too. Nobody remembers everything that ever happened to them. But I remember who I am, and all the major highlights of my life, and all the important things leading up to the accident."

The thought suddenly struck me that before my memories came back, I had been a pure human expression of minimalism. Just like his house. Simple. Clean. But now I was complicated and messy, and I wasn't sure how Shannon would take that.

"And this dream..." he persisted... "What happened in it?"

The way he asked the question was as if the option not to answer him didn't exist. He expected to know. He demanded to know. And yet I knew that if I told him, I would be at least partly responsible for what happened next, because I couldn't pretend there wouldn't be something that happened next. Shannon loved to kill people, and he had a whisper of feeling toward me. It didn't take a genius to figure out where that magical combination would lead. Telling him would be like giving him a big present with a giant red bow on it. I might as well gift wrap Professor Stevens and hand Shannon a knife or a gun or whatever it was he liked to kill people with.

Against my better judgment and my better angels, I told him the dream. Telling it seemed to unlock more details of the memories I'd been trying not to see when I woke, memories that had fled in Shannon's arms the night before but came roaring forth now that I allowed them.

I squeezed my eyes shut as tears slipped down my cheeks. I couldn't stop hearing the belt coming down on me. I couldn't stop feeling the violation that I would have given anything to forget about, and for a brief shining moment in my history, I actually had. Why had it come back after so long? I knew things I'd done with Shannon must have triggered it, but why did it have to be triggered at all?

I'd been hopeful that everything would just stay dead and buried. Some part of my subconscious must have been well aware of how much I wanted to forget and keep the past locked away in boxes I could never open again. Why hadn't my mind listened? Things had been just fine as they were. It had seemed so unlikely after so long that I'd have to worry about any memories surfacing. But then, I'd never been in the situation to have it triggered by just the right activity before.

"He touched what's mine," Shannon said quietly.

I wasn't sure how to feel about that response. It made him seem even more inhuman than he ordinarily seemed—and yet, a deep dark part of me liked that irritated sense of possession in his voice.

It didn't seem to matter to him that I hadn't been *his* back when these events had originally unfolded. As far as Shannon was concerned, I'd been set aside for him from the moment of my creation. And someone else had the gall to touch me. I felt it would probably be unwise to go through the laundry list of men I'd consensually fucked, lest they end up on Shannon's shit list as well.

I looked up to find his blue eyes burning with an icy-hot intensity I'd never seen there before, and quite honestly hoped to never see again.

"I have to go away for a few days. I have business to take care of."

At first I thought he meant my professor, but then I remembered he had a job this week. I'd forgotten it in everything that had recently happened between us.

"Will you be okay alone a few days? Or do you want to come with me?" he asked.

Part of me wanted to go with him, but I had the sense that he wasn't going to *not fuck me* on this trip if I joined him. I'm not sure it would even occur to Shannon that such a thing might create more damage in me. I wanted to believe he cared—at least where I was concerned—but I wasn't sure how his mind processed such things.

I remembered the night in the castle, how intense he'd been after killing Trevor. And that had been self-defense. I imagined the whole event was even more of a rush when he stalked and hunted his prey first, when there was a bigger intentionality behind it. I wasn't sure I could deal with being his victory fuck right now.

"C-can I stay here?"

Shannon nodded. "I think that would be best."

Without another word, he got up and dragged a suitcase out of the walk-in closet and started opening drawers and pulling out clothing. He neatly folded several nondescript and mostly black outfits and put them in the suitcase, then he pulled out a few large hard black cases that contained several guns and a few knives.

I sat dumbfounded in bed, wondering if he'd forgotten I was there altogether while he checked each blade—for what, I couldn't imagine... sharpness? Acceptable murder ability? Then he went through some kind of function or safety check for each of the guns. I'm really not sure. I watched as he dropped magazines, pulled parts of the gun back and looked inside, flipped small plastic switches on and off, racked slides, and finally pressed each trigger. Satisfied with whatever he was checking for, he replaced his weapons in their cases. He added several boxes of ammunition to the suitcase with his clothes and sealed everything up. I was pretty sure he wouldn't be flying commercial with this load of weaponry—if he was going far enough away to fly at all. Maybe he'd take the car.

He lined his bags up by the door and peeled his clothing off. I flinched at his nudity. And it made me angry at myself. I was starting to not even give a shit what he did for a living or how much he liked it. I'd wanted Shannon. I *liked* Shannon. Way more than I should. And I still wanted him, but in light of my memories... I just wasn't sure if my present with Shannon and my past traumas could play well together—or at all. I was hoping to have a few days' break from him to sort myself out somehow.

He came over to my side of the bed, moved the breakfast tray out of the way, and offered me his hand. "Come shower with me. Then I have to leave."

If he noted my hesitation, he didn't say anything. He just patiently waited for my inevitable capitulation. Finally, I took his hand and let him lead me to the bathroom. I leaned against the counter while he got the water to the right temperature and got towels ready for us.

When he was finished, he gave me a once over. "Are you planning to shower with your pajamas on?"

It didn't seem to occur to him that my memories might now affect what happened between us. I mean, Shannon is not a stupid man. Surely, if he sat down and thought it through, he could at least intellectually grasp the situation. Or maybe he was already well aware and just didn't care because he'd determined that I was *his* and that was that.

When I didn't reply or start to remove sleepwear, he came over and did it himself. Again, I flinched, and again he ignored it. There was a part of me that was somehow offended that his entire reaction to my traumatic retelling of what had happened with my professor had elicited nothing more than mild pouting on his part.

Even though I knew it was wrong, I'd briefly fantasized that he would go kill that bastard. And a part of me *liked* that fantasy. I very much doubted Shannon would let me leave to go finish my degree, but Stevens should fucking pay either way. And I knew there was no way he'd end up paying through the criminal justice system. I wanted him to have to pay through Shannon's justice system because I imagined it was far more satisfying and that it was a system that wouldn't victimize me yet again in the quest for a *fair trial*. Fuck a fair trial. I knew what that monster had done, and that was all that mattered to me. Why should I have to prove it to a bunch of random strangers who weren't there? Why couldn't this be my business? Mine and Shannon's.

It was unnerving to fully realize I felt this way because I'd told myself that I didn't want Shannon to do anything. And yet... with his reaction so minimal, I found I really *did* want him to do something. I was tempted to flat out ask him to do it. Hell, I had money; I could pay his fees. I mean, he had access to my money, so he could just steal it, I guess. But I could be a paying customer, no problem. It didn't have to be some personal favor or lover's vendetta.

"Elodie," Shannon said, snapping me out of my thoughts.

"Hmmm?"

"Get in the shower. I don't have time for this."

By this point, I was past flinching and cringing. I mean, realistically, I shouldn't be. But I was so caught up in this revenge fantasy that I couldn't be bothered with the supposed trauma of Shannon touching me.

I can say one thing with certainty. If Shannon were a normal man handling me like something breakable, trying to soothe all my damage and trauma, trying not to *trigger* me, I would never have been able to let a man touch me again. I would have built it up too far in my head. I wanted to believe Shannon knew this, but I'm not sure he did. I'm not sure he cared. And I'm not sure I cared because the fact that he wasn't coddling me and treating me like a fragile piece of china was likely the only thing that made his touch okay.

He took my hands and pressed my palms flat against the shower tile.

"Do not move your hands. Do you understand?" he growled against my ear.

"Y-yes, Sir."

I lowered my head to let the hot water hit my neck and roll down my back as Shannon ran his soapy hands over me. I tensed, waiting for something dramatic. A panic attack. A sobbing fit. Begging and pleading.

But instead of crying or begging, what came out of my mouth was a low, throaty moan. My body reacted to him just as it had before without even the slightest hint that there was any reason for it to behave differently. My body and mind stubbornly clung to and affirmed Shannon's possession of me.

He grabbed my hair and pulled my head back and to the side out of the way of the spray. "You are mine. My filthy little whore. Say it."

Those words shouldn't have had positive results, but when Shannon said it, he wasn't judging me. There was no hatred or disgust in his voice. It reflected nothing more than a sexual kink that helped him get nearer to feeling something more human.

My body happily skipped along to his beat, the warmth and tingling already starting between my legs. My nerve endings didn't give a shit what Professor Stevens had done and refused to let my conscious brain fuck up whatever this thing with Shannon was. Good. Because before that incident at school, I'd secretly and maybe not-so-secretly longed for a relationship like this one. Private kinky parties at the frat house and a little bit of play at a few clubs here and there just hadn't been enough. I'd wanted something more stable and lasting.

"I'm your filthy little whore, Sir."

"No one else will *ever* touch you again, do you understand?"

"Y-yes, Sir."

Shannon released my hair and detached the shower head. It was the massaging kind that could easily be maneuvered to ease sore muscles in hard to reach places, but every woman in the world knew what that kind of shower head was really for.

Shannon knew, too. He held the pulsing spray between my legs, a few inches away so that the pressure of the water beat down against the swollen, aroused flesh between my thighs. After the first orgasm, he took the shower head away for a moment to let me semi-recover, then he started in on me again. He repeated this several times until I barely knew my own name and wasn't sure I could hold myself up any longer.

But that wasn't a problem. After reattaching the shower head, Shannon held me strongly against him while he fucked me, finally seeking his own release. When he pulled out of me, he shut the water off and I slid to the floor of the shower, no longer trusting my legs, or even my voice.

Shannon got, toweled off, and went back into the bedroom to change. I stayed where I was like this for several minutes—

leaning my head against the tile, willing my legs to support me when I stood.

He'd left a second towel for me next to the sink, and I secured it around myself. It was an extra large fluffy towel probably meant for someone much larger than me. I loved the quiet luxury of Shannon's towels, the way they wrapped me up like a cloud on a warm sunny day.

When I finally emerged from the bathroom, the towel wrapped firmly around me, both Shannon and his bags were gone. I went out into the hallway to find the white cat bitching at me because she always blamed me for everything as if every aspect of her little furry existence had gone horribly wrong the second I crossed the threshold into Shannon's life.

There was no sign of him downstairs, either. I made my way back to the main part of the first floor. He wasn't in the kitchen. I glanced at the front door to find the security system armed, the red light blinking. I ran to the door and peered out the window to find the tail lights of Shannon's shiny black Cadillac disappearing around the corner.

I heard the faint sound of a cell phone ringing on the second floor. I took the stairs two at a time to get to Shannon's room. The phone rang from a pair of pants draped over the dresser. I dug through the pockets and found the red phone—the one he used with his family—shrieking incessantly at me.

"Shannon?" I said, hoping it was him. He hadn't even said goodbye. Why hadn't he said goodbye? *Because you don't matter. Nobody matters to him. Look at his non-response to what happened to you?*

"It's Millie, dear. Is Shannon around?"

I pulled back and just gaped at the phone for a moment. Was she serious? Why would I say *Shannon* into the phone if he was with me?

"I'm sorry, he just stepped out," I said, biting back all the sarcasm that wanted to come spilling from my mouth. None of this was Millie's fault.

"Oh, Elodie, I wanted to tell you... those green beans I sent home with you, you want to add a little bit of sugar and a little bit of olive oil to them and then cover them and let them boil almost down to no liquid. Leave a little bit in there, but not much. It'll make the flavors kick more, like Shannon likes them."

"Okay, thanks."

"Do you know when he'll be back?" she asked.

"I'm not sure. Do you want me to have him call you?"

"Yes, thank you, dear."

I disconnected the call and sat on the edge of the bed wondering if I should do what I really wanted to do next. I knew the number for Shannon's most recent burner phone. I'd been nosy and snooping, and he'd left it out. I don't even know why I searched the phone's information and wrote down the number. I probably would have never done it before I was reasonably confident he wouldn't kill me. It was telling that instead of using the burner to call for *help*, I used it to find out what number I could reach him at. Of course, Shannon had been in the house at the time, and I'd only had a few moments to scribble down the number—not long enough to communicate with the police even if I'd wanted to.

Despite my better judgment, I dialed the number.

"Hello?"

"It's me," I said.

"Are you calling from my other phone?"

"Yes."

"How do you have this number? More importantly, *why* are you calling this number? Do you realize I now have to get rid of that phone, too, and get a whole new *permanent* number for my mother? She'll ask endless questions about why I have a new number. I'm going to have to ditch this phone and get another one. When we hang up, take the battery out of that one."

"Your mother wants you to call her," I blurted.

"Of course she does. Was that all you wanted?"

"A-are you mad at me?" I felt like an insecure schoolgirl asking that, but what else was I supposed to think? He'd gone so cold and distant. I tried to shake that thought out of my head. He'd been cold and distant from day one. This was all just my own weirdness about us sleeping together and then him leaving like this without saying goodbye. It was hard to know how to behave when a sexual relationship was new, even under the best circumstances. And I had no idea how the script worked with Shannon. Maybe he was already regretting moving things to this level. Maybe he thought I was going to be nothing but drama. He was probably already rethinking whatever spark of feeling he'd thought I'd inspired in him.

Maybe now that he knew what had happened with my Professor, he saw me as *tainted* somehow and didn't want me anymore. That last thought felt too true, and I quickly pushed it away. I hadn't sensed any of the ugly weight in Shannon's words compared to Professor Stevens', but maybe I was only hearing and seeing what I wanted and needed to hear and see to survive.

"Why would I be mad?" He sounded genuinely confused. "Did you do something for me to be mad about? Besides calling from that phone?"

"No. Why did you leave so fast? You locked me in. What if I need something?"

He'd always locked me in, but it was never for very long. Not like this.

"I told you. I have a job. I'm running late. I'll talk to you when I get home in a few days. Remove the battery and do not use that phone again."

"Why am I removing the battery?"

"So no one can triangulate the signal."

"But why would they do that? Who would do that? Is somebody after you?"

"No. Not that I know of. These are just basic precautions. This is a normal part of my world you need to get used to."

"But..."

Shannon sighed. "Elodie, just do what I say."

"But what if I need something?"

"For God's sake, the house is stocked with everything you need to survive without me for a few days. You spent months in an abandoned theme park with one other psycho and no access to the civilized world, and you survived that just fine."

Rationally, I knew he was right. I was actually sitting there panicking, worrying some unforeseen emergency would happen and how would I get medical care? I'd lived for months in a world where hospitals weren't even an option, and yet this was my first worry locked up in Shannon's clean, well-stocked house? I had a quick flash, wondering what Trevor would have done with me if I'd had a medical emergency. Probably let me die, but then I remembered he was a doctor and likely could have handled most things.

"I'm sorry," I said.

"What are you apologizing for?"

"I don't know. You're mad!"

"I'm not mad. Goodbye."

"Bye." But I'd already heard the connection go dead before I said it.

As soon as I hung up, I did what he'd asked. No matter how paranoid I thought his caution was. Though maybe it wasn't over the top. He *did* kill people for a living. One didn't exactly want to leave a trail of bread crumbs behind them while doing that. I wasn't sure there was any level of paranoia that was too much under those conditions.

I stared at the phone sitting on the bed with its guts spilled out. At least his mother couldn't call back again. I didn't want to have to start coming up with excuses for why Shannon wasn't there to take her call. I didn't know what he'd told her as his cover story for what he did now, and if she thought he traveled for business. Maybe she thought he worked in an office somewhere now.

As I stared at the phone, I finally realized what I had. A link to the outside world and plenty of time to utilize it. I could call for help. I could get away from Shannon if I really wanted to. The trouble was, I didn't want to.

And while I still didn't want to deal with the police and a million questions, the idea of such a thing didn't seem as traumatic with my memories back in their proper storage lockers in my brain. I just... didn't want to go. Shannon's house was a clean, safe cocoon from which I wasn't ready to emerge—even if Shannon's emotional range left something to be desired.

I crossed to the balcony and, without thinking, opened the door and stepped outside. Winter in southern Georgia was pretty mild, unless this year was a fluke. I didn't know. It was my first Georgia winter. I actually stood for a good five minutes breathing in the crisp morning air before it suddenly occurred to me that Shannon hadn't armed the balcony door. The main door, the back door, and every single window was always armed, but almost never the balcony door. Shannon liked to go out there a lot and didn't want to bother inputting the code to get in and out each time.

I wondered if he'd forgotten about it in his rush out the door. Surely he normally armed it when he'd left me in the house all those times. But today, for whatever reason, it was unarmed. The wheels in my head started turning. Was this a test? It had to be a test. *Or he doesn't want you. He's dismissing you from his life, you little idiot. If you don't leave while you have the chance, he might just kill you and dump your body off with his buddy at the crematorium when he gets back.*

I know people can make mistakes, but Shannon... Shannon was the most precise person I'd ever met. He had a system for everything. He had a protocol for everything. He covered every single track he left no matter how minor or discreet. Shannon didn't *do* mistakes like this. If he did, he'd be sitting in a prison cell right now.

All I could conclude from this was that he'd purposefully left me a phone and an exit. The insecure schoolgirl part of me thought he was tired of me, done with me, and instead of tying up the loose end, he'd decided to give me a chance and let me go while he wasn't looking. But then... the way he'd looked at me, even this morning. It was impossible to think something that intense could fade so quickly to casual disinterest.

Or at least this was what I told myself. Maybe fucking me after knowing ugly parts of my history was somehow less satisfying to him. He'd left so quickly afterward. What did that even mean? What else could it mean but that he'd wanted to get away from me?

But despite my negative inner monologue, I knew he wouldn't release somebody who could destroy his neat, minimalist life. And I didn't think Shannon could even pretend to be the noble type who would let me go because it was the *right thing to do*. Shannon didn't give a shit about the *right thing* beyond the basic desire to keep his life as uncomplicated as possible. If someone or something got in his way, I was sure he would take care of it, and there were few if any laws or appeals to reason and morals that would sway him. He may not have killed an innocent *yet*, but that didn't mean he wouldn't or couldn't. If I pushed beyond my fears and insecurity, I just didn't believe he intended to let me go.

So that only left one option. It was a test. He wanted to see what I would do with the temptation of freedom. Would I try to escape? Fuck no, I wouldn't. Even if I hadn't grown stupidly attached to this man, no way in hell would I run. I had no doubts that Shannon could track me anywhere. He'd built that dossier on me, after all. And it hadn't seemed too difficult for him to map out my whole existence. The news stories were months ago. I had no idea how he'd managed to piece it all together so quickly and easily, but clearly he had.

Before my memories had started coming back, I could have said that he'd simply invented much of the dossier, but that was no longer true. And either way, he couldn't invent my fluency in French. I'd planned to move to Paris before the accident had landed me in the hospital under Trevor's care. I'd decided there was no future for me left here, and not enough people I cared about to warrant my staying. I'd known Trevor was dangerous. And I'd had the money to get far enough away from him that he would no longer be a threat. I *did* have friends in France.

I'd wanted a new start. I just made the mistake of telling Trevor that. It had slipped out because I couldn't resist the urge to let him know just how little control he had over me or my life. He'd manufactured this story in his head about how our life would go, how we'd get married and live happily ever after—us against the world. It hadn't initially occurred to him that I actually could escape him, that I had the means and ability to be free. I didn't need him.

He'd flown into a rage and actually got into a car chase with me like right out of some cheesy movie. How smug he must have been when I woke in the hospital for that brief moment without a single memory in my head, with no way to know I'd wanted to leave him and the country. Now I could again. Technically.

But all those plans were from my life before. While the idea of Paris still sounded nice in theory, I didn't want to leave Shannon. And if I ran away, I'd no doubt make some amateur move, and he'd see it in plenty of time. And even if he didn't, he would find me. He probably already suspected I'd go to Paris based on what he'd learned about me. And unlike Trevor, Shannon had the means and ability to follow me and drag me back. Realizing all this should have disturbed me. But for whatever fucked-up reason, it didn't. The only thing that bothered me was the continued nagging fear that he might not want me anymore.

There was a fine sheen of frost on the ground. It glittered like starlight under the weak rays of the sun. I leaned over the balcony railing. There was a trellis I could climb down. A fucking trellis. Like he'd set it all up for me. I went back inside before I froze to death. Winters in Georgia might be mild, but I was only wearing a towel, and my hair was still wet. I didn't want to tempt fate.

I went back down the hall to my room and quickly got dressed in some jeans, sneakers, and a light sweater. Back in Shannon's room, I noticed the nightstand drawer beside his bed was open. I pulled it out the rest of the way and gasped. Holy shit, there was a lot of cash. Small bills, mostly twenties. There must be a few thousand dollars in there. It's not that I considered this an inordinately large sum of money. My bio-dad had given me a staggering amount after all. This was small potatoes by comparison. But my interaction with money had always been through the medium of plastic cards and distant vague numbers on bank computer screens, which my brain refused to fully process as money—even though it could buy me things. So this was a large amount of *cash*.

This was definitely a trap. It was all too convenient. Him abruptly leaving me, creating an emotional reason for me to leave... money in the dresser. Cell phone left behind—though that had been hidden in his pants and could have been an accident, but it also could have been intentional. Shannon never left his clothes lying around. Then there was the unarmed balcony door and the trellis with an easy way to the ground level and freedom outside.

There was still a part of me that feared he wanted me gone from his home. Like he was tired of me, and maybe he did feel some spark of something that made him not want to kill me, but nothing else beyond that to make him want me to continue invading his personal space like this. But if he didn't want me gone, it was definitely a test. Either way it was orchestrated, everything laid out so simply and enticingly.

I grabbed a few hundred out of the dresser and put half in one pocket and half in the other. It wasn't like I was stealing it. He had full easy access to my accounts if he hadn't already drained them. I could pay him back. Though I doubted he cared if I did.

I searched for a spare set of keys and was happily surprised to find one in the drawer with the money. I stepped outside and locked the balcony door behind me, then climbed down the trellis to the ground. Child's play.

I wasn't going to run, but I sure as shit was getting out of the house for a while. If he wanted me gone, he could have a conversation with me and tell me himself. Or he could put a bullet in my head. Whatever. But fuck this. Even if I wanted to go, I wouldn't leave this way. He had to be smart enough to know that by now. Maybe in the first day or two in his care I would have, but over weeks my feelings had changed.

I'd known in a vague way that Shannon lived in a nice neighborhood, but now I was walking through it, experiencing it live. I wasn't even sure what month it was, which, now that I had my memories back, seemed extra disorienting. I was sure it was after Christmas, though.

I'd had opportunities to learn the date, but each time I'd only realized after the fact. Like when I'd been shopping online for clothes that first night... all I'd had to do was glance into the bottom right corner of the screen, but I'd been too flustered by everything. And the time I'd checked Shannon's phone for his number. There wasn't much time, and it just didn't occur to me until Shannon's phone was back in his pocket that I could have easily read the date on the phone. And even this morning with the red phone. I could have checked that, but I'd already taken the battery out when it occurred to me yet again. And by now I was too paranoid to put it back in. I was determined to remember to find out the date while I was out.

I hadn't realized how close Shannon lived to town. He lived in a small town near Savannah, called Stoney Oak. From what little I'd seen in the car with him, there might be fifteen thousand people here, if I was being generous in my estimation. His parents lived inside Savannah proper, but it was still an easy drive to get from one place to the other. I wondered how he felt about his parents living so close. They could just drop in on him at any time, but so far since I'd been here, they'd maintained a polite and respectful distance.

It was maybe a mile walk into the main part of town—twenty minutes or so. Or it was that far into what had been the original downtown area at least. I wasn't sure how much urban sprawl had overtaken the edges.

There was a small old-fashioned grocery store on the corner of a strip of buildings that looked like they'd been built maybe around the mid-eighteen hundreds. Next to that were several boutique stores that ranged in offerings from tourist-y gift shops to clothing stores.

I wondered what would ever possess Shannon to live in such a small town. Small towns were nosy. Everybody wanted to know everybody's business. And if you weren't involved enough in town stuff, people always wanted to know why. I would think Shannon would prefer to get lost inside a big city.

"Hello," a woman said from behind the register inside one of the boutique stores. Her name tag read, *June*. "Can I help you find something?"

"I'm just looking, thanks."

June had short pixie-cut graying hair that fringed delicately around her face, and reading glasses perched on her nose. The glasses were on a chain so she could wear them around her neck when she didn't need them. She was dressed smartly in a black leather skirt that ended mid-calf, covering the tops of chic black boots. A somewhat fitted black top completed the look, accentuating the gentle curves on her slender frame. She had this freaky sort of old-lady/young hipster combo going on that made it impossible to tell if she was twenty or two hundred.

Sure, I'd met Shannon's parents, but it was so weird being *anywhere* without Shannon or Trevor and being around strangers. This was my first *unsupervised* visit anywhere since the car wreck. And it made me want to climb out of my skin.

I know I'd decided I wanted to be with Shannon, and it seemed nothing could drag me from that determination, but it was unsettling being in this little boutique shop outside of Shannon's direct grasp and *not* asking for help. Like, if I were a sane or rational person, shouldn't I realistically ask this woman to call 911 for me? Shouldn't I make some token effort? But even with how our relationship had shifted, I had a hard time realistically seeing my life with Shannon as imprisonment—despite the extremely limited times I'd been allowed to venture outdoors.

So instead of doing something rational, I wandered toward the back of the store to the lingerie section. I didn't even know if Shannon still wanted me, and yet the first thing I did as a supposedly free woman, was shop for lingerie for him. Well, for me... but you know... for him.

The sales lady by this point had migrated back to the lingerie area as well. If I were a teenager in a baggy overcoat, I'd assume she was shadowing me for fear of shoplifting. But I was pretty sure it was more general nosiness. This suspicion was confirmed a moment later.

"Are you new to the area, or just visiting?" June asked.

I was tempted to insist I was just visiting, but instead I said, "New."

"Oh? Do you know anyone here?"

"Shannon Mercer." I had a momentary fear that he might murder me for bringing his name up, but hey, he chose a small town to live in. And frankly, if he was going to end up killing me, I wanted him to have to work up an explanation about my disappearance and sweat a little over it.

"Ooooooh," she said. I swear, I thought she was going to start singing the *kissing in a tree* song like a grade school child. She got a sort of blushy dreamy look on her face. "He is *so* beautiful."

In spite of everything, I found the grin inching up the side of my face, followed by a nervous giggle. "Yeah. He *is* pretty hot."

"You did good, honey."

I was pretty sure she wouldn't maintain that position if she had more facts about Shannon. This made me wildly curious about what *she* thought Shannon did for a living.

"And he's such a *good* man," she continued. "But I don't have to tell you. I guess you'll be going on the trips with him?"

"Ummm, yeah, the trips. Sure." I had no idea what this lady was talking about, but I was fascinated to know more about the saintly portrait Shannon had painted of himself.

"I think it's just so lovely that he donates so much of his time to helping all those poor people in those destitute countries."

Oh, dear lord. It took all my powers of self-control not to bust out laughing at the deranged idea of Shannon doing extended charity work like some black-clad special ops Mother Theresa.

The sales lady sized me up and then handed me a sexy little black lace number. The lace was elegant and made me think of something a Victorian-era courtesan might wear. "He'll like this," June insisted.

I checked the size. It was my size, all right. She had a good eye. "I'll take it."

"You don't want to try it on to make sure?"

"No, I'm sure." I kind of needed to get away from her. This lady had a crush on Shannon and thought he did charity work. If only she knew. I would never do it, of course, but there was this sadistic part of me that wanted to tell her the truth about him. Just to watch the color drain out of her face.

I frowned, realizing the dark road my thoughts had turned down.

"Something wrong?" she asked.

"Oh, no. I was just thinking about something else."

"Now, I've got all sorts of fun and interesting toys and edible body paints and..."

"No, the lingerie is fine."

"Is it for Valentine's Day? That's right around the corner, you know. We have some cards at the register if you want to pick one out."

"That's okay, I've already got a card." I couldn't imagine ever giving Shannon a card for any reason. I was tempted to ask "how right around the corner" Valentine's Day was. But at least now I had a better idea of what month we were in.

June took the lingerie to the register and rang it up. She quirked a brow briefly at my shopping with cash, but it was probably just more nosiness. With a card she could learn my name. Without one, I was still a mystery. I was surprised she hadn't just gone ahead and asked. Maybe I should have offered a name. I wasn't sure about the small town meet-and-greet protocol.

She carefully wrapped the lingerie in tissue paper and put it in an elegant black paper bag with shiny silver accents. Then she added some additional gray tissue paper in the top, tied the handles together with some curling ribbon, and handed it to me like it was the holy grail.

"Have fun," she said, winking at me.

I looked at my receipt. The date was February third. Okay then, another piece of the *what the hell is happening in the real world* puzzle solved.

I stopped in a few other shops on the block and got some apple cinnamon bubble bath which I felt tempted to just go ahead and eat instead of bathe in—it smelled that real. Then I grabbed a few fashion magazines and some stationery and a roll of stamps and some fat white candles.

Finally, I stopped at the corner grocery and got a few snacks I missed now that I remembered I liked them... like kettle corn drizzled in dark chocolate and a bottle of Merlot.

Since I didn't have a car, I stopped buying things at this point. I still had to carry it all back.

It was tricky figuring how to get everything back up into the house since I couldn't use the front door. The security system was like an extra lock. If you didn't know the code, it didn't matter whether you had a key or not. It wouldn't just sound an alarm, the door or window wouldn't even open. The balcony door was therefore the only door I could still get into.

I ended up having to throw the bags one at a time onto the balcony from the ground. Except the Merlot, which I carried up. I was glad there were some trees around the house and that Shannon's nearest neighbor was more than a block down the road. I didn't need anyone asking why I was tossing stuff up onto a balcony, or climbing the trellis to get inside the house. I looked like a really inefficient cat burglar. And even from my perspective—knowing the back story—the whole thing seemed absurd.

Once inside, I still felt antsy. The freedom of finally being able to come and go in a civilized world was not lost on me. I grabbed some more money from the drawer and after a quick lunch, I went out the balcony and climbed down the trellis.

This time I went into a florist shop a block over from where

I'd been earlier. As soon as I stepped inside, I knew this was what I'd craved. Plants. Living green things. Shannon didn't have a single plant in his house. Given my history with the study of them as well as being surrounded by greenery constantly in the abandoned park, it was almost distressing not having any of my own. They changed the energy of a space, making it more alive than it might otherwise be. It was the kind of thing you didn't notice unless you were used to it and then suddenly it was gone.

In the company of so many options, I went a little crazy, buying up almost everything in the front part of the store. I was, however, careful to only buy plants that were non-toxic to cats. There may be no love lost between me and the white cat, but if I killed her, Shannon would be livid.

"No flowers?" the old florist asked, disappointed. "I haven't gotten to make a fresh arrangement since Tuesday." His name tag read, "Stanley."

"I'm sorry, not today." I made a mental note to come back for flowers at another time, assuming Shannon was just testing me and not trying to get rid of me. "Can I get these delivered?"

The old man pulled out a large sales pad. "Address, please?"

I gave him the address, and immediately a large smile broke out over his face. "You're Shannon's girl. June told us about the mysterious new girlfriend. Finally domesticating him, are you?"

I just smiled.

"I can have these out on the van to you in about an hour. Will that be okay?"

"That would be great. Thanks. I'll probably still be out and about, so could you just leave them on the front porch, and I'll bring them inside when I get home?"

"Certainly, Ma'am."

I paid him in cash, to a raised eyebrow similar to June's. He didn't ask personal questions of me, but I was almost sure he realized he didn't even know my name as I made my escape from the building.

I went straight back to Shannon's after that. When I got inside, I poured a glass of wine and ran a bubble bath in the master bathroom and lit a few candles and soaked and read. I stared at the stationery and stamps still in one of the bags on the bathroom floor. When I'd bought it, I'd planned to send Professor Stevens an anonymous threatening letter. I wasn't sure if he'd even know who it was from.

I really just wanted him to fear it might be from me, that I was coming for him. But I was afraid that the postmark would just lead back to Shannon.

I heard the old white van with the plants pull up. I waited until they were unloaded and I was sure Stanley was gone before I went outside. Getting the plants inside was even trickier than the rest of my purchases had been. Thankfully, I hadn't bought any really big plants. I could just imagine Shannon's irritation if I broke my neck falling off the trellis with these.

When they were finally inside, I went about the house, finding a window for each of the bright light plants. I'd bought a few low light plants for the coffee table and some end tables that had nothing on them. I wasn't sure I wanted to imagine Shannon's reaction to all this when he got home. I imagined he'd lived in this cold, minimal, antiseptic house with the white cat as his only other living companion for so long, that bringing this much life into the house might not go over well. They might clash with his energy. Plants were quiet at least. Surely they could find some common ground with Shannon there.

I needed to be surrounded by green things if I wanted to not lose my mind. And with the trees bare of leaves and everything so bleak and gray all the time, this was a necessary evil. I couldn't stay by myself in a house where the only other living being hated me. I needed something friendly.

9

Without Shannon in the house, the nightmares came back even darker and more detailed than before. This time, I couldn't will myself awake in time. I had to relive the whole fucked-up thing. Somehow the worst of it wasn't the too-hard whipping that exceeded anything I'd previously experienced. The worst part of the memory/dream was his voice and the awful words he said, blaming me over and over again for what he was doing as he made sure I knew what a filthy, disgusting little whore I was. Without that, I might have been able to pretend it was someone else, anyone else.

I jolted awake and scrambled to sit up. It was too quiet in the house without Shannon, and I knew the white cat wouldn't comfort me. She hated me. That feeling was mutual.

I'd moved all my bags from my shopping excursion into the bedroom except the snacks, which were in the kitchen. I turned on every light in the house as I made my way there now.

I opened the dark chocolate drizzled kettle corn and took a bottle of water from the fridge and sat at the kitchen table with it. Shannon might kill me if he ever found out I'd been drinking red wine in the tub. I wasn't even sure candles were allowed because wax could drip. I was pretty sure the coffee and toast in bed kindness had been a one-time thing. After my snack, I finished up the bottle of wine from earlier.

On a lark, and pleasantly buzzed, I checked Shannon's office door. I couldn't believe it when the knob turned easily in my hand. He never left this room unlocked. Even when he was home. It wasn't as if there were any remaining doubts that he was trying to get me to leave, but why the fuck would he leave his office accessible?

Of course, inside the office itself, pretty much every drawer and filing cabinet, as well as the closet were locked. The only thing that wasn't locked down was his laptop on top of the desk. I booted it up. There was a split screen, one was a login for Shannon, and I was sure I'd never crack *that* password. But next to it was another login for "guest". That must be me. But what was the password?

If he'd really set up a login for me it would have to be a really simple password I could easily guess like my name or admin or... I typed in *password*. The screen changed, and I was in my own desktop and internet connection.

It was yet another link to the outside world. Another window of escape I was just going to go ahead and ignore, self-preservation be damned. Maybe it was the effects of the Merlot, but I knew exactly what I wanted to do online and it wasn't ask for help.

I typed in my old university's web address. The screen loaded surprisingly quickly. I scanned around the site in the faculty section. Exactly what I thought. Professor Stevens was still there. Fucking tenure. Probably still assaulting students and getting away with it right under everybody's nose. I could send him an email. But I didn't know enough about computer security. It might be traced somehow back to Shannon. I was sure he had to have some really beefy internet security, otherwise there was no way he'd give me access to an internet connection at all, but still.

Besides, email didn't have the satisfying physicality of a real paper letter.

I went back upstairs and got the stationery and the magazines I'd bought earlier and brought them down, trying to will my hands not to shake. But the adrenaline was surging full throttle now, and I couldn't get the tremors to stop. I took several deep breaths and then went to the sink and splashed some cool water on my face. After several minutes, I felt myself begin to relax as my body realized I was in Shannon's house. Safe.

When I felt calm enough, I put on some gloves from under the kitchen sink and found a glue stick and some scissors in a drawer in the kitchen. I began cutting out letters from the magazines and gluing them onto the stationery.

It took about an hour, but when I was finished, it said: "You must have been relieved when you thought I was gone for good. Watch your back. This isn't over, fucker."

I folded the crude note, put it in the envelope, sealed it, addressed it, stamped it. I didn't put a return address on it, but I was back to the trouble of the post mark. If I were in Savannah, it might not be as big of a deal, but I knew I couldn't mail it from Stoney Oak, though I *really* wanted to.

I was tempted to get dressed again, sneak out, and walk back to town. I was sure there would be a mail drop off box somewhere outside one of the stores, maybe outside the courthouse a couple blocks over from where I'd been shopping earlier. But Shannon would kill me. Besides, what was I going to do besides mail a stupid, pointless letter? I was afraid to even ask Shannon to kill him for me, not just because it was crossing a line on a whole other level I didn't know if I could cope with morally, but because I was afraid he would say *no*.

So maybe my problem with it wasn't morals at all. Especially now with my memory back, knowing how Trevor had died safe in the knowledge that I was *mourning* him. I just didn't think I could let someone else get away with hurting me like that. And yet, so far, Professor Stevens had. He'd gone on with his life in his cushy little tenured teaching position, smug in the knowledge he'd gotten away with it.

I wasn't sure if what I wanted was justice or garden-variety vengeance, and I didn't really care. Whatever it was, I wanted it so much I could taste it. It tasted vaguely like apple cinnamon bubble bath.

I ended up ripping up the carefully constructed anonymous threat and throwing it in the trash. I was careful that no part of the address or name was visible or could be reconstructed. Shannon was rubbing off on me. I cleaned up the mess in the kitchen and went back to bed.

~

EVERY NIGHT WITHOUT SHANNON, the dreams came, each time more awful than the night before. I was sure that if he were here—if I were in his bed—the nightmares wouldn't have the nerve to disturb my sleep.

On Sunday morning, Shannon returned.

"Elodie?"

I could tell by the sound of his voice that he wasn't sure if I was there. Though surely he couldn't think I would fill his house with plants and then run away.

I practically flew down the stairs to meet him even though I was afraid to see that deadness in his eyes that I was sure he reserved for most everyone else.

When he saw me, the hint of a smile appeared on his face, and I let out a breath. He *did* still want me here. So it must have been a test.

He seemed so much calmer and more relaxed than he'd

been before. I'd always thought of Shannon as calm and methodical, but now, by its absence I realized there had been a buzz of restless energy below the surface. He might not give it away overtly, and he might not react strongly to things, but wheels were turning behind the scenes all the time. Now it seemed some tightly coiled thing inside him had been released and a reset button had been pressed.

"How was the job?" I asked.

He seemed caught off guard, surprised that I'd ask or care about *the job*, particularly since I knew what kinds of jobs he did.

"Satisfying. Everything went smoothly. The target knew he was being hunted. It's always better when they know. It's a bigger challenge. More fun." He looked nearly giddy. Like a kid on Christmas morning discovering Santa got him everything he wanted, even though he'd asked for crazy things he shouldn't expect to receive.

I must have made a bit of a freaked-out face at this display of *too much information*, because he noticed and changed the subject. "Jesus. It looks like a fucking greenhouse in here."

"I need them."

He took a moment to look around, assessing the changes to his space. "What about the cat? Some of these might be poisonous."

"They aren't. Botanist, remember? I know my plants. I considered that when I bought them."

"Okay. But you are the one who has to water and take care of them." His eyes narrowed. "So you obviously left the house. I see you came back."

"I want to be here with you." It sounded so childish when I said it out loud. So nakedly hopeful. For a moment, I worried he'd laugh at me, but it was a wasted worry.

"Good. If you'd run, I would have come after you. I just wanted to know if I could trust you to leave and return on your own. It's simpler if I don't have to keep you on lock down. Did you say anything stupid to anybody in town?"

I was sure my face went a little white at that because I could feel the blood draining out of it.

In contrast, Shannon's expression darkened. "What did you do?" The muscle in his jaw clenched.

"N-nothing."

"What did you say?"

"J-just that I was staying with you. Somebody from town asked me."

He stared at me for a good, long several minutes as if trying to determine if he believed me. "And that's all you said? Nothing incriminating?"

"N-no."

"No, what?"

"N-no, Sir."

In his absence, I'd been cavalier about his anger. I'd forgotten how completely terrifying he could be if he was displeased about something. And I wondered again at my sanity in staying or even wanting to. One would think, with my memories back, that I'd want to stay the hell away from men, especially men like Shannon. But I didn't think Shannon was anything like Professor Stevens or Trevor. In his way, he was more terrifying than the two of them put together, but he was scary in the way live volcanoes and tsunamis were scary. It didn't feel personal. He was a force of nature to be respected, but despite everything I knew about him, I just didn't believe he was *evil.*

I know that's stupid. But I couldn't help how I felt. There wasn't a deep core of malevolence in him. He just didn't have as strong of emotions or empathy as everybody else. Certainly it could be turned toward evil, but the military had used it as a tool, presumably for good. And when Shannon said the people he killed were bad people, I believed him.

"How much of my money did you spend?"

"M-most of what was in the drawer. You can take it out of my account. I wasn't trying to steal from you."

"That doesn't matter. Besides all the plants, what did you buy?"

"Umm... snacks, wine, candles, magazines, stationery..."

"Candles? You burned candles in my house?" His voice rose the most subtle degree higher.

"Y-yes, Sir."

"Candles drip."

"I-I know. I didn't make a mess." I didn't mention the fact that I'd spilled a bunch of dirt all over the house, getting the plants in and set up. I didn't want him to have a heart attack. And I'd cleaned it all up.

His eyes narrowed. "We'll deal with the candles later. What was the stationery for?"

"It's stupid."

"Tell me."

So I told him the whole inane thing about the letter to my professor, just wanting to scare him, and ripping it up and throwing it away because I didn't want to risk Shannon's location. He smiled at that, obviously pleased. At least I'd done something right. I didn't tell him the nightmares were getting worse. I told myself it was because I didn't want him to go *do something* about it. But really, I was afraid if I told him, he would barely react again and not care and refuse to do anything at all except tell me to stop whining about it.

"Is that all you bought?" he asked, oblivious to my internal struggle.

I felt heat flood into my face. "I bought some lingerie," I mumbled.

An eyebrow raised. "Oh, really? Put it on. Now. Then come back downstairs. And bring the candles with you."

My heart was nearly throbbing out of my body. I felt like I

was vibrating from the inside out as I changed out of regular clothes, and into the lingerie. I added a swipe of cherry red gloss to my lips. I put the candles in the paper shopping bag the lingerie had been in and descended the stairs back to Shannon.

But he wasn't in the living room.

"Shannon?"

"I'm in my office. Come on back."

He glanced up when I walked in. "Are those the candles?" he asked, indicating the bag I carried.

"Yes, Sir."

"Good. Put them there on the side table."

There was a large glass table next to a window with a white leather chair beside it. On the table stood various decanters of alcohol that appeared to contain different types of whiskeys—bourbon, scotch, all the usual suspects. Next to that were glasses of varying shapes to allow the flavors to do whatever magic thing they seemed to do in just the right glass. Next to all this was an empty space where I put the bag.

"You can sit," he said, indicating the white chair I stood beside. I sank into the leather. On the ground at my feet was a thick black shag rug.

Meanwhile Shannon clacked away at the keys on his laptop. Every now and then he'd make a *hmmm* sound, but other than that, he just stared intently at the screen. I had no idea what he was looking at, and although I was deeply curious, I wasn't foolish enough to ask.

I also tried not to be too put off by the fact that he hadn't had any strong reaction or even any *discernible* reaction at all to the lingerie. Did he not like it? I hated the way this made me feel. For weeks before our relationship had changed, I'd felt comfortable and safe with him. But the moment things had shifted... he made me so nervous now. Those nerves were no longer about what he might do to me but about what he might *not* do. I couldn't stand the idea that he'd lost interest in me, not because I thought he might get rid of me in some gruesome way but because I couldn't stand the idea of losing him.

Shannon's eyes narrowed, and he looked up at me, accusation in his gaze. "You drank red wine in my bathroom." When he spoke, the words came out in that scary dead calm of his.

"I-I'm sorry. I was taking a bubble bath."

"Yes. I can see that."

"What?"

"Oh, you thought I'd just leave you alone in my house without monitoring the situation? There are hidden security cameras all over this house. I'm watching the footage. Additionally, I'm confirming all the places you've said you've been. I can't know what exactly you said or did while there, but I know everywhere you went and when you went there."

"How?"

"I put a tracking device in your shoes."

"But... when?" He'd left so fast that day.

"The night before I left. I set up the money and everything else the night before as well."

So... if I'd run, he would have just brought his little computer with him and tracked me down that way. I had no doubts that Shannon could find me anywhere. I just hadn't thought he would do it in such a literal tracking device way.

"I can't believe you put a tracking device in my shoes."

"Be glad I didn't insert a chip under your skin. I'm still considering it."

This was the kind of thing that always brought home to me what an idiot I was where Shannon was concerned. I thought he had no malevolent intentions and that I could trust him, and yet he was calmly considering implanting me with a tracking device. Wasn't that evil? If Trevor had done it? Yes. If Professor Stevens had done it, no question. But my mind went out of its way to give Shannon a pass for everything. As long as he was feeding me, caring for me, not hurting me, and giving me orgasms, my brain refused to register him as a threat—at least for more than a couple of minutes at a time anymore.

And he wasn't hurting me. Outside of sex games, he'd never raised a hand to me. He'd never lost his temper in any measurable way that would give the average person pause. And I really, really liked being here with him, despite all the fluttery nervous fucked-up feelings he made me feel. And half of that I would have felt with any man I was so attracted to.

Shannon closed the lid of the laptop and slid it into the middle desk drawer. Then he opened another drawer and pulled out some scary looking chains and cuffs and a collar.

"Come here."

I swallowed around the hard lump in my throat but went to him. When I reached him, he finally took a moment to appreciate the lingerie. He drank me in slowly, his eyes roving over every inch of me as if trying to mentally capture the image forever in his mind. His hands followed his gaze, skimming over me.

"I like this. We have to buy you more beautiful things that you can barely wear in my presence. And once we have these things, I expect you to only put normal clothes on to leave the house. Is that clear?"

My breath got stuck in my throat for a moment. "Y-yes, Sir."

"Good."

His hands traveled under the sheer black lace. He ripped the panties off. "No panties," he said. "I don't care if it comes with it. No panties. I don't want anything ever in my way."

When his hand moved between my legs without any obstruction, I started to grind against it, unable to help myself. He pulled away.

"No, not yet. Down on your knees."

There was a second black shag rug underneath this desk. I knelt on the thick carpet and waited for further instruction. None came. Instead, he took the black leather collar off the desk and secured it around my throat. The chain that was attached made a sharp clanking sound against the desk as it was dragged along.

Shannon undid his pants and freed his cock. He didn't have to say anything else. I took him into my mouth and sucked like my life depended on it. I dragged it out as long as I could, teasing and pulling away whenever he seemed close to the edge. I licked and stroked and caressed him until I'd worked him into a state I'd not yet seen him in. His fingers tangled in my hair as he groaned and came with a shudder. But I didn't let up until he was finished and pushed me away.

His breathing came very heavy for several minutes. I felt flushed and pleased with myself as I stared up at him from the floor.

"Your punishment is going to be worse, now," he said.

"What? Why?"

"Because you thought that talented little mouth could lighten your sentence. Well, you *are* quite talented, but that sort of manipulation doesn't work on me."

"I wasn't trying..." We both knew I was lying.

"Of course you were."

Shannon put the cuffs on my wrists and ankles, then he stood and pulled me up with him by the chain.

"Bend over the desk and spread your legs wide."

When I did, he moved the chain out of the way, and he took my arms and spread them out to either corner of the desk. He attached the cuffs to discreet metal rings that were attached to the corners. I hadn't noticed them before, though I was sure they must have been there the other night when I'd used the computer.

Off my confused expression, he said, "I put them in the day after the party."

I was stupidly happy that he hadn't done this with another woman in here.

He similarly attached my ankles by the cuffs to the rings at the bottom corners of the desk. Then he moved behind me and shoved the lingerie up over my hips. I thought he was going to fuck me like this, but instead, he went to the side table and withdrew the candles one by one from the bag. There were six in all. He brought them back to the desk and put three on either side of me in the large empty space of the desk that my body wasn't occupying. He lit them.

"Elodie, you know how much I dislike messes. You knew I wouldn't approve of candles burning all over my house. Or you drinking red wine—or any wine—in my bathroom."

I was about to protest, but yeah, I knew. And I'd done it anyway. But sometimes a girl needed a glass of wine in the bubble bath and candles.

"I just needed comforting things. And you weren't here."

An odd expression moved over his face, and for a moment, I thought I'd somehow moved him to compassion, but in the next second, it was gone, replaced with the kind of devilish glee I imagined he got on his face moments before he completed a job.

"Be that as it may... candles drip."

"Not the fat ones." If they were taper candles, I'd see his point, but he was being over-the-top about this issue.

I shrieked when his hand came down hard across my ass without warning.

"Don't talk back," he said.

"Yes, Sir."

I let out a hiss and gripped the side of the desk as hot wax landed on my flesh right where his hand had been a moment before. I glanced over to find Shannon holding one of the candles with an almost maniacal look on his face.

"Like I said, candles drip."

I wasn't nearly stupid enough to ask why he wasn't worried about the mess he would no doubt make by intentionally causing the candles to drip. I just kept my mouth shut about that one.

"All of these candles drip," he said, as if this were some novel discovery the world should know about.

He shoved the lingerie farther up my back, giving him a nice expanse of flesh to work with. I felt another sharp sting as what seemed to me like molten lava dripped down my back. I squeezed my eyes shut, whimpered, and tried to breath through it.

"Please, Sir, it hurts."

"I know it hurts. Punishments are meant to hurt. That's why we call them punishments." He poured the remaining wax out of that candle onto my skin to the sound of my shrieking protest. Then he blew that candle out and set it on the desk. "Only five more to go. You can take it."

He pushed a finger inside me. "Maybe I should punish you more if this excites you so much."

I shook my head furiously. "No, please... no. I can't help how my body reacts, please, please Shannon."

He smacked my ass. "Sir," he corrected. "Don't try to get personal with me. I know what you're doing. If you'd been a good girl in the first place, this wouldn't be happening."

Shannon moved on to the second candle and a new fresh piece of skin. I gripped the edge of the table as he poured all the wax over me at once.

"Shit!" I shouted.

"Tell me you're sorry, Elodie."

"I'm sorry, Sir. P-please. Please, I won't do it again."

He moved close to my ear and whispered, "You may as well have a little fun occasionally, I'll probably do this to you anyway."

"N-not this much, okay?"

"Be good and we'll see."

After the third candle and a lot of panicked tears and pleading, Shannon did something miraculous. He showed mercy and blew out the other candles.

"T-thank you, Sir." In some strange way I was sure this meant something. Why should he show me any mercy when he liked this so much and when it wasn't going to actually harm me? Did my distress bother him now? Was that possible?

In moments like this, he was more human to me. It seemed as though we had some sort of real connection. It wasn't hard to imagine he was a regular guy, and I was his regular girlfriend. No trauma or skeletons in our respective closets

My hands went limp, no longer clutching at the desk. Despite how much it had hurt, I was humiliated to realize how wet I was now. Shannon chuckled as his hand moved between my legs.

"Despite your protests and begging, part of you likes that," he growled.

I didn't bother denying it. For better or worse it tripped my wires, and delivering it tripped Shannon's. With the fingers of one hand, he stroked my clit, and with the fingers of the other, he penetrated me. Both of those large, strong hands touching me like that had me gripping the desk and begging again, this time for more.

"Please," I panted as I moved with him.

"I want you to come for me. Come harder than you've ever come. I want to feel it. If you don't, I'm going to have to relight those candles."

The panic of that possibility sent me spiraling into the strongest, hardest orgasm I'd ever had, not only with Shannon, but ever.

"Good girl," he whispered in my ear. "You know I hate messes." He held his hand next to my face and I obediently licked my juices up.

While my breathing went back to normal, he uncuffed me from the desk and peeled the hardened wax off my skin. He ran his fingertips over the places where it had dripped. "You've got a few burn marks, but they aren't serious. Go get cleaned up and I'll take you out for dinner. There's a nice little Italian place on the other end of town. Do you like Italian?"

What the fuck? Not that I was complaining about being taken to a nice dinner, but what the actual fuck was going on? I wasn't stupid enough to verbalize this, however.

"Yes, Sir."

"Good, then we'll go as soon as you get ready." He put everything that looked like an impromptu dungeon, back in the lower desk drawer and gave me my lingerie, then took out his laptop. "I need to make a private call, so if you'll close the door behind you."

I nodded absently, still not sure I'd heard him right about going out for dinner. Though why shouldn't we go out? I'd already proven, given total free reign and him probably out of the state somewhere for days, that I would return right back to my crate like a good dog.

"Do you want me to take the candles?"

He glanced up sharply, that look of disapproval on his face. That would be a no.

"O-okay." I bumbled awkwardly out of his office and shut the door. Now with my memories back, I knew I'd been somewhat sexually adventurous. At least before Professor Stevens. And I'd been largely comfortable with my own nudity even outside of a sexual context.

A lot of people separated nudity into categories. There was shower nudity, always okay. There was sex nudity... largely essential and normal and nobody felt uncomfortable because everybody naked was engaged in a shared naked activity. And then there was random walking around the house nudity, which most people were only okay with inside a long term relationship involving plenty of random nudity.

I had been okay with random nudity, even in a full frat

house after all the sex and games were over. I was just that way. But with Shannon it was different. I felt so overwhelmingly awkward when he looked at me that way outside a specific sexual context. If we were engaged in some naughty activity, fine, but otherwise... let's just say I was more than relieved to close his office door and be outside his line of sight.

The white cat gave me a dirty look and stalked me up the stairs. I'd meant to ask Shannon how nice the place was and what I should wear, but I'd been caught off guard by his continued irritation over the candles, the way he watched me move, as well as knowing that this *private call* most likely involved his latest hit.

There was no way I'd go back in there and interrupt such a call to ask about wardrobe, so instead, I selected a simple navy summer dress with a cardigan to go over it. It *was* still winter... if you could call it that. The temperature had peaked at fifty-five, and wouldn't drop below forty until well after midnight.

I took a quick shower and got ready, pausing only briefly in front of the bathroom mirror to inspect the burn marks left by the wax. I'd played with candles and wax before. Most of the time, it wasn't nearly so scary because we usually used soy wax since it melted at a much lower temperature than paraffin. So it stung a little, but didn't usually leave marks behind.

In truth, I kind of liked these marks. And if I took care of it, they wouldn't linger very long. I applied burn cream from Shannon's first aid kit and finished getting ready.

When I descended the stairs, he was waiting for me on the living room sofa, stroking the white cat, who had rolled onto her back so he could rub her belly. She hissed at me.

"Ready?" he asked.

"Yeah."

The cat jumped off the sofa and flounced off to another part of the house in full-on diva mode.

Shannon input the code, and I followed him outside to his

nondescript black hitman car and got into the passenger side. I managed to wait until we were out of the neighborhood before I asked the question that had plagued me for days now.

"Why did you leave so fast that morning? Was it because of what I told you? About my professor?"

Shannon didn't reply, but he gripped the steering wheel harder, and the muscles in his jaw and running down his neck tightened noticeably.

"Let's just have a nice dinner, and we'll talk about it when we get home."

I was sure I couldn't have a *nice dinner* until after we'd talked about it, but I didn't want to ruin things.

"Are you going to let me leave the house more?" I asked.

"Of course. You're not a prisoner." But the way he said it wasn't very convincing.

Sure, I wasn't a prisoner. He'd just made clear on more than one occasion he was never letting me go and stated in pretty absolute terms that he felt I belonged to him. Why would I think I was a prisoner?

"Are you still mad at me about the candles and wine?"

"No. I wasn't mad to begin with. But you knew I wouldn't like it."

I was quiet for another ten minutes until he pulled up beside the restaurant and turned off the ignition. The restaurant was in what had once been a somewhat old-fashioned cottage in the historic district.

"Oh my God, Shannon. Please, please for the love of God, talk to me about it now! I can't have a nice dinner if I don't know what the fuck is going on. You just ran out right after fucking me, and you didn't even say goodbye. You were just gone. *Whoosh.* Then you were mad when I called. And then I thought you just didn't want me at all because the balcony was unlocked and there was money and it was just all too easy. Does what happened to me change how you feel?"

At this point, I was sure I just honestly didn't care if he dragged me out and strangled me in the parking lot. There was no way I could sit in a restaurant and politely eat pasta in romantic lighting without knowing what the fuck was going on.

Shannon, for his part, looked perplexed. He turned in his seat to face me. "Why would it change how I feel? How I feel about what? About you?"

I nodded. And all of a sudden I felt like a complete moron. Whatever he felt had to be infinitely smaller than what normal humans felt in romantic relationships, and here I was cornering him... asking him to define everything. To explain himself. I was being the *where is our relationship going* girl to the last guy on the planet who wanted to hear it.

"Why would it change how I feel about you?" he asked quietly. He seemed to really be struggling trying to figure out the complex algebra I'd laid out.

"You don't think I'm dirty or tainted somehow? Like... like damaged goods?"

"No."

As much as I was grateful for the silence with him, for the lack of intrusion and overwhelming emotion and smothering, I needed more than one word. Damn.

Shannon's expression darkened. "I left because I was losing control of my emotions. I never lose control of my emotions. It disturbed me that I didn't feel I had control of myself, and it's always been the one thing I've felt sure of, that I was in control. Knowing what he did... I thought sex in the shower that morning would take the edge off, and it didn't. Then I thought the job would. The job helped some, but not nearly enough. I'm going to kill that motherfucker."

It was like a chorus of angels singing. *I'm going to kill that motherfucker.*

I couldn't help the smile creeping up my face. No matter how hard I tried, I couldn't mask the utter joy at the idea that not only was Professor Stevens going to pay for what he'd done, but Shannon was going to do it. It almost made up for the tragedy of crying for Trevor. Almost. I would have given almost anything to go back in time knowing the truth, and to coldly watch Trevor die without mourning him.

"I want to go with you," I said.

Shannon hesitated. "I really work better alone."

"I have a right to be there. This is my vengeance. Not yours."

For a moment it felt as though the two of us were two pieces that came together to form one whole, that nothing made sense without both of us together as one unit.

"Let's eat dinner. Let me think," Shannon said.

I didn't push further because I knew that ultimately he would decide if I got to go or not. Even if I ran away from him and tried to do it all on my own, I wouldn't know where to begin, and I would very likely get caught. And I wasn't going to do time for my bastard professor.

It was hard to appreciate the restaurant. I wish I could have. It was warm and cozy with what seemed like endless candles. There were some low lights recessed into the ceiling, but the sheer proliferation of candles made it seem as if the space was lit entirely by candlelight. The food was amazing, authentic. I felt as though I were actually in Italy.

But no matter how nice the atmosphere or how good the food, my mind kept going back to Professor Stevens and the giddy sense in my stomach that finally, finally, something in my life was going to go right. Finally, someone who had hurt me would pay. Finally, there was a man fully in my corner and on my side who was focused on the same dark goal as me.

Neither of us spoke much during dinner. Shannon seemed in his own world, planning this impromptu pro bono job. I didn't even have to pay him for it. He was clearly set on doing this no matter what. Even through just the course of one dinner, I could see how his energy shifted to this one idea. I wasn't sure if all of his thoughts were about planning the logistics or if he was also considering my involvement—perhaps running parallel scenarios in his head of how it would go down with just him versus adding me to the mix.

I was surprised when he ordered us dessert. I'd expected, with his current intensity level, that we would eat quickly and leave.

I was sure the other patrons in the small restaurant were looking at us strangely. I wondered if they thought we were in a fight or something. It was extremely odd to be in such an intimate setting sharing a romantic dinner in utter silence. Then I started to worry. Wouldn't the people of Stoney Oak gossip? This was such a small town after all. Shouldn't we at least make the pretense of small talk?

But before I could make any real effort in that direction, we'd finished dessert and the check was unobtrusively placed on the table.

"I'll take that when you're ready, Mr. Mercer."

"I'm ready now," Shannon said, pulling out his wallet and sliding a credit card inside the payment folder.

When the waiter slipped away to process the payment, I noticed a familiar person amble over. It was June from the boutique near Shannon's house.

"Shannon! I thought that was you! I can't believe you missed the last town meeting. We were discussing whether or not we should cut down that huge diseased eyesore of a tree in front of the courthouse. The historical shade tree committee was there, and put up quite a fight, but we won in the end. After all, it might be a three hundred year old tree, but it was well past the point of survival, and we all knew it. It would have been nice to have you there. I know you would have been on our side."

"Absolutely, Mrs. Privet. I hate that tree. It should have been cut down years ago," Shannon said, his voice soothing and warm. It rang a little hollow to me, but June didn't seem to notice.

I was certain that Shannon didn't give a shit about whether or not the tree in front of the courthouse was removed. I was surprised he actually attended Stoney Oak town meetings. It didn't seem like the kind of thing Shannon would do. But then I remembered how he'd said he wanted to fit in when he was a kid, and I thought maybe there was a part of him that still did. Though, I was sure it wasn't *just* that.

All at once his choice to live in a small town began to click together for me. These were the *he was such a nice man, I can't believe he would do that* people who always seemed to pop up out of the ether to defend serial killers and other violent criminals. The people of Stoney Oak were an unwitting line of defense for Shannon. Should suspicion ever fall his way, they would instantly leap to his defense as character witnesses and alibis—unwitting accomplices to his illicit jobs.

"I noticed you two weren't talking much. Everything all right, I hope?" she prodded.

Shannon smiled, a practiced friendly smile. I couldn't believe he could actually pull this off. Ladies and gentlemen of the academy, give this man an Oscar.

"Everything is wonderful," Shannon said without missing a beat. "I'm afraid I'm a bit pre-occupied planning our next trip."

June appeared immediately interested. "Oh? What exotic locale is it this time?"

"Thailand. We're going to a small village that is in need of clean water and helping with the effort there."

"That's just lovely," June said, clasping her hands to her chest. I thought she might swoon at any moment if someone didn't show up to catch her. "When do you leave?"

"A few days," he said.

I wondered where *Mr.* Privet was. Shannon had given her

the married form of address. I wondered if her husband knew how she pined for Shannon.

She turned to me, suddenly, "This one's a keeper. You hold onto him. I don't believe I caught your name?"

Smooth. No, I hadn't told her my name during my earlier visit to the boutique. I imagined she'd already asked half the town trying to gain that information to no avail.

"Elodie," I said, forcing an artificial smile that didn't seem to come as naturally to me as it did to Shannon.

Before June could intrude further, the waiter rematerialized with Shannon's card and receipt. He signed and added a tip, then stood.

"Well, Mrs. Privet, I'll see you at the next town meeting, after we return from Thailand."

"I hope you're bringing Miss..."

Damn, she did not let up.

"Evans," Shannon supplied. Not my real last name.

"Elodie Evans, yes we do hope to see her at the meeting."

Shannon navigated the social etiquette of disentangling ourselves from the curious Mrs. Privet, and we made our way out to the car.

"I don't think you should have given her your real first name. It's too uncommon," he said.

"I was put on the spot. What was I supposed to do? Besides, if I'm going to live here, it makes little sense to give a fake name I won't remember to answer to. It's not like *nobody* has my name. Besides, if somebody did remember it, they probably remembered it wrong. They probably think my name is Melody. People called me Melody all the time."

Shannon was quiet as he started the car and we pulled out onto the road. Finally, he said, "I'm just careful. You know that."

"I like that about you." I'm not sure why that popped out of my mouth. It just felt like the thing to say. I *did* like that about him. It made me feel safe because he always thought of everything. I felt as though nothing could ever thwart or harm me while Shannon was around thinking so many steps ahead, always on high alert.

There was a little moment between us that I can't quite describe—as if he were trying to determine if he should acknowledge that I'd said I liked something about him.

Apparently deciding against it, he instead said, "I hope you know, she's going to Google you the moment she gets home. Let's hope if there's an Elodie Evans, she proves interesting. But not too much."

10

A few days later, Shannon had worked out all the logistics of killing Professor Stevens and had agreed to let me join him. He left a large amount of food and water out for the white cat and left all the toilet seats in the house up in case she knocked her water over. For someone with no soul to speak of, he had grown skilled at caring for small animals.

We pulled out of his driveway all packed, at eight that morning. He made it a point to drive through the middle of town to wave at Mrs. Privet. She waved back from behind her shop window, a dreamy smile on her face.

It occurred to me that June Privet was now part of Shannon's alibi should something go wrong. I wondered how else he'd secured his Thailand alibi. I was sure he must know someone overseas who would claim he was there, helping bring clean water to some poor village. What a saint. He probably had a whole back story. Without a lot of tedious emotional baggage and drama to deal with, Shannon had lots of mental space to concoct all sorts of alibis and backup plans for every possible contingency.

Though I reminded myself it was just a contingency. Shannon planned things too well to have need of any of them. We couldn't fly with the weapons, airport security being what it was. He told me that when he did big jobs overseas, he was sent by private plane. There was nobody bankrolling this job but Shannon, so we wouldn't be flying private, though a part of me thought we probably could if he really wanted to.

I was sure he had a stockpile of money hoarded away somewhere. He lived nice, but modestly and didn't appear to own anything too extravagant. But I knew being a contract killer wasn't like being an accountant. There was some big money sitting around somewhere. It was possible that Shannon only did enough work to keep him in a modest comfortable lifestyle, but I had begun to be able to see the itch creep over him. It seemed increasingly likely to me that he took nearly any job that came his way just so he could feel like a normal person for short stretches of time and convince the rest of the world of the same.

It took nearly a week—with stops at night to sleep—for us to reach our destination on the other end of the country. I hoped my plants would be okay. Most of them could go a while between waterings without freaking out, but I was still concerned. I couldn't help it. I'd say it was an occupational hazard if I'd ever gotten the chance to use my schooling in an actual occupation.

Every night during our journey, Shannon stopped at a rundown motel in some out of the way place, just before the front desk closed for the night. He always went in. I stayed outside. He always paid cash, and I was sure he was using a fake ID. Just like that first night, he always got a room around the back, away from any possible passing traffic, and backed the car into the parking space so the license wasn't visible to anyone else who drove around for a secluded room in the back.

The primary difference in these nightly stops was that he

didn't seem paranoid if I took a longish shower. He no longer assumed I was fashioning weapons out of bathroom pipes, and he didn't tie me up for the night. Well, he did one night, but that was sex games, and it wasn't as if he made me sleep like that.

On Professor Stevens' Day of Reckoning, we arrived at our destination a little after midnight. The Professor lived a few blocks from the university campus in a heavily wooded neighborhood. It was a full moon, but the moon was obscured by thick cloud cover, making the street even darker than it would normally be. There were no street lights on Professor Stevens' street, which was just fine for our purposes.

Shannon backed the car into an unlocked empty garage at a house two doors down with a *for sale* sign in the front. He'd done meticulous research. Even if the garage had been shut and locked, we could have still parked close enough to the abandoned house—given that there was a high row of hedges beside the house that allowed cover. But happily, the garage was open.

I thought it was dangerous doing this so close to the campus, but Shannon reasoned that if Stevens was able to commit sexual assault here and get away with it, that it was as good a place as any to kill him. And Stevens did have that horrible basement he'd taken me to. Of course Shannon was right, but I still looked over our shoulders from the front porch, paranoid someone would come up the path. But it was late on a weekday. Surely everyone was asleep already.

Shannon rang the bell, dragging Professor Stevens out of what must have been a sound sleep from the bleary-eyed grumpiness that answered the door. Shannon had instructed me to wait behind the bush until he was inside. So when the door opened, a strange man dressed in black was all the professor saw on the darkened porch.

"This better be good," he snarled at Shannon.

"Trust me, it is." Shannon lunged forward and knocked the professor out with a chloroform soaked rag, then with speedy smooth practice, he handed it out to me all while he kept the Professor from hitting the ground. I disposed of the bag in Stevens' trash at the end of the drive. Both Shannon and I wore gloves, appearing as shadows everywhere except for our faces.

We'd talked about this in the car on the way over. It wasn't all chloroform, but I wasn't sure about the other ingredient. He'd assured me the concentration and mixture he'd made would keep someone unconscious for about fifteen minutes—just enough time to move things to the next phase.

I went inside the house, trying not to flashback to the last time I was brought in here. It looked much the same—exactly like one would imagine a stuffy botany professor's house might look. Lots of old books. Lots of plants—many exotic and rare. There were several plant lights for the exotics that needed a high amount of light but weren't close enough to a window to get it. These were turned off for the night.

I felt as though the plants watched me. As if they'd been awakened from their sleep by our intrusion. The average person might think this completely crazy, but when you study plants, you realize they are even more alive than you imagine. They simply exist on a different time scale than us. On time lapse photography, they seem to live with purpose. A few might even be said to have goals. During my time at the University, I'd anthropomorphized plants to a degree I couldn't back away from, even though as a scientist I was meant to look at things coldly and clinically. I wasn't sure how I could have ever done science that required animal experiments since I now saw plants as nearly sentient.

This sensation wasn't minimized knowing what I was about to do. The creepy feeling that Professor Stevens' plants watched me accusingly only escalated as I made my way through the main level of the house. I briefly panicked about what would happen to the plants when Stevens was gone. Would they all die? Would a relative or some students at the university take them under their wing and care for them? Could I orphan all these plants? Now I *was* being crazy. Because surely I still prioritized people over greenery.

But I knew even if I got cold feet, Shannon was determined. After all, he hadn't decided to kill Professor Stevens as a favor to me but because he was angry and wouldn't be satisfied until the man was dead. Maybe I should have stayed home. During the trip I'd shoved any doubts or dread into the back corners of my mind as if shoving it back there often enough would somehow make the issue vanish altogether.

It's one thing to think about killing someone. It's another to actually do it. Most of us have the good sense to know that the reality won't be anything like the fantasy. I had that good sense, but I'd acquired it far too late in the game for it to do me any good.

I quietly crept down to the basement where Shannon had made use of Professor Stevens' bondage equipment to tie him up.

My heart thundered in my chest as though race horses galloped through my veins.

Shannon took out a small 22 caliber handgun. He attached a silencer to the barrel and inserted a magazine, slamming it a little harder than was necessary.

"It's quiet anyway, but with the houses so close together here, it's best to be careful," he said, almost as if he were talking to himself. "They call this an assassin's special. The mob used to use these for hits because they're so quiet and discreet. You can come right up behind someone, and shoot the back of the head. The bullet's so small it just ricochets around in there. They never see it coming, and there's no exit wound. Neat. Clean. If I'm not using a sniper rifle, I prefer this. Keeps it simple. And I like the challenge of having to get so close into their space to pull it off."

"Shannon?"

"Yeah?"

"Could we not... with the commentary?" I was sure I was going a little green. We shouldn't have eaten so close to this event. But of course Shannon wouldn't be bothered by things like that.

"Too much for you?" he asked.

"Yes."

"You wanted to come."

Because it was my revenge. Not his.

"So... you don't want him dead now? Is that it? You want him to just waltz along through life thinking he's gotten away with it? You want him to victimize other women?"

"What do you care what he does to other women?" I asked.

Shannon rolled his eyes. "Just because I don't feel all the range of emotions you feel doesn't mean I don't know intellectually if something is right or wrong. You might not think I have a working moral compass, but I was trained to take out the bad guy. And this guy is as bad as they come. I can smell it on him. It wasn't just you he's done this to. And he'll keep doing it. He can't help it. Someone like me needs to remove him from civilized society."

I sank into a red velvet chair in the corner and didn't say anything else while Shannon pulled a bundle from his bag and unrolled it with a flourish on a small table he'd dragged near the professor. From my position, I could see several gleaming knives and other fun little toys I didn't want to think about.

"Shannon?" Was this normal for him? In my head I'd managed to convince myself his job was some sort of necessary evil and that all his kills were quick and clean like hunting a deer for dinner. Did he need them to suffer first?

He looked up. "I'm taking my time with this one. This one is personal. You can go wait upstairs if you need to."

I wished again that we hadn't had dinner so recently because now it was starting to get real. It wasn't some abstract notion. There was a living person sitting a few feet away who was going to be carved up like Christmas ham, and I was going to watch it happen.

"I'll shoot him when I get bored. Or you can do the honors when it's time if you like."

I shook my head vehemently. When he'd been gone on his last job... when I fantasized about taking Professor Stevens' out, in the fantasy, I'd actively participated. Shannon and I had been like Bonnie and Clyde—two disaffected sociopaths who didn't give a shit about playing by the rules. Now I didn't want anything to do with it. I wasn't sure I could even stomach being down here.

"What if he screams and wakes up a neighbor? You can't afford that," I said, hoping Shannon would change his mind and just make this quick.

"I'll use one of his ball gags. Besides, look at the walls. This place has been soundproofed, and it's underground. How else do you think he got away with what he did to you?"

I shuddered at that, and for the smallest moment, my reservations melted away. But then Professor Stevens regained consciousness. His eyes widened when he saw me sitting across the room.

"W-what's happening? Elodie? I-I thought you were dead."

"Why would you think that?" I asked. I at least had the courage to have a conversation, even if I couldn't bring myself to rip and tear skin.

"You were missing. I saw you on the news. That hospital.... that doctor..."

I could see from the look in his eyes that he'd been thrilled when he thought I was dead.

"How many others besides me did you do this to?" I asked, my voice getting a little stronger. I wasn't sure if I was just trying to get some sort of closure or if I was stalling Shannon.

A smug, satisfied expression, spread over Stevens' face. "My relationships with other students are none of your business. Jealous, you little slut?"

I leaped out of the chair and across the room so fast that, for a moment, I didn't realize I'd even moved. But all at once, I stood in front of him inches from his smarmy little face. Did this asshole not realize what was about to happen? But no, his eyes had found mine immediately. He hadn't yet noticed Shannon, who'd somehow seemed to dissolve into the shadows behind him. He hadn't noticed the table with the instruments of pain. He hadn't noticed the gun. He was too fucking stupid to know this was his last night on earth.

I hauled back and slapped him so hard my hand stung. "You fucking piece of shit," I spat.

He just smiled. "Oh, so you want to try role reversal? I like a good round with a dominatrix as much as the next fellow. It must be why you have me tied to the chair." His eyes widened suddenly as if only now realizing he was tied up in his own basement. "T-there was a man... before..."

Now it was coming back. The effects of the drugs were wearing off enough that his rational faculties were returning. He looked around and noticed the table with gleaming knives and the gun. He craned his head around, and Shannon seemed to materialize from the shadows.

It was as if Shannon's energy had been so deep in predator mode, so silent, that you couldn't see him unless he wanted you to. Now that subtle energy had shifted, and he suddenly seemed larger and louder even before he spoke.

"Hello," Shannon said, mildly. "I hope all your affairs are in order."

For the first time since I'd known him, Professor Stevens

looked afraid. The air of smug condescension and power abuse that clung to him like too strong perfume finally shed its scaly skin.

"Do you want to get some of your anger out first?" Shannon asked me.

I shook my head. Now that Stevens had stopped being so aggressively nasty, now that he looked scared and about to start begging for his life, I once again didn't have the stomach for it. I wished I did. I wanted to have the strength and courage to make him pay directly by my own hand, but now that the moment was upon me, I shrank away.

"Very well. Do you want to watch, or do you want to go upstairs and wait for me?"

I stood for a moment in indecision, and then there was a sound upstairs. The front door opened and shut. It was after midnight. Who the fuck had a key?

"Professor Stevens?" a young woman called from the first floor. "I finished grading those papers you wanted. You said you didn't care how late it was. Hello?"

Fuck. It was his TA.

"Professor? Are you downstairs?" I realized then that the basement door was open and the light was filtering up. It was just a matter of seconds before she came down here and saw all this.

I could sit by and let Shannon hurt Stevens. I wasn't sure I could sit by and watch him kill an innocent. But Shannon didn't do loose ends.

"Yes, I'm down here!" Professor Stevens shouted from the ground. "Go get help! Call the police!"

Somehow during all this and perhaps even while I'd been waffling on whether or not I was staying to watch, Stevens had managed to work the knots behind his back loose. He lunged for Shannon and the two of them started to struggle on the ground, knocking the gun off the table. Shannon kicked it to a far corner so the professor couldn't get to it.

Then that stupid fucking bouncing blonde innocent TA bounded down the stairs to investigate like the dumbass in every horror movie.

"Professor Stevens?"

It only took her a moment to take in all the necessary details of the scene and to process what was going on.

"Call the police, you stupid girl!" Stevens shouted.

I couldn't help but wonder how the hell him talking to her like that was going to motivate her to help him. She hesitated for just a moment before she ran up the stairs. Shannon still struggled with the professor.

Stevens was an old guy, and Shannon was young and strong, but it was amazing the kind of fight he could manage with so much adrenaline surging through him.

I stood frozen for only a microsecond. And in that tiny window of time it seemed like everything stopped as my mind ran through all possible options. Shannon couldn't go deal with her; he was busy with the professor. She was going to call the police. I was sure she was. I'd seen the determination on her face.

Without wasting another precious second, I grabbed a large knife off the table and ran up the stairs after her. She hadn't stopped upstairs to use the phone. Instead, she'd run outside. Of course. Only a few blocks from the university. The main campus security station was on this end of the campus. She'd be safe there.

I chased her down the road, toward the light and hope of the school. Realizing I was gaining on her, she got off the road and darted into the overgrown backyard of the abandoned house. I took a leap for her, tackling her to the ground. I clamped a hand over her mouth to keep her from screaming and waking a neighbor. I was paranoid someone might already be up and looking out their window.

Her eyes were wide, pleading with me, as the hand holding the knife seemed to act of its own accord.

~

I SAT IN PROFESSOR STEVENS' basement, the cold sweeping over me, the tremor moving through my limbs like a serpent. I was going into shock. Didn't we do this already? Shannon had gone back to laser focus. He chopped up the drained bodies as if he were cutting meat in a butcher shop. This time he wrapped them in plastic he'd brought and took them out to the car for later incineration.

I felt as though I kept zoning in and out of time. Time as I perceived it was like a bunch of tubes I kept hopping in and out of. Sometimes it moved faster sucking me through and causing life to blur around me. Sometimes it moved so slow that I zeroed in on the tiniest details—like the incongruity of the delicate hand-painted teapot that had been upstairs on Professor Stevens' fireplace mantel. What would a man like Professor Stevens want with such a thing?

I'm missing a few pieces as well. There are gaps. I just sat there, staring at the blood on my hands, shaking, moving in and out of the surreality. I worried somebody else would show up unexpectedly. How high would the body count have to get for us to get away tonight?

I'd just wanted Stevens gone. Not her. But I had to. I couldn't let Shannon go to prison. Would I have gone to prison as well just for being here? I didn't know. Probably. I had clearly been helping. I couldn't pretend to be the victim.

Killing him, making him pay, had seemed like the perfect fantasy, the best ending. The deserved ending. And yet, I was right back where I'd started, staring at all the blood, trying to remember how to breathe in and out, how to make my heart beat, how to feel something besides completely numb and terrified of the killer I found myself alone with.

I couldn't even decide if I was glad Stevens was dead. The event was too clouded by the unexpected intruder, by the sickening slice of the knife. I should have felt relief he was gone. Instead, there was this complication. This complication that Shannon seemed perfectly calm and serene about. I was sure I would never feel calm and serene again.

I had no idea what had happened with Stevens during my absence. I wasn't even sure how I'd gotten the TA back to the basement by myself. I couldn't remember anything from the moment I'd started stabbing. All I knew was that there were two bodies, and I'd been responsible for the innocent one.

Now I was on to worrying if we'd get away with it. It would be the cruelest irony for that bastard to get away with what he'd done to me only for me to be punished for his murder. My mind kept spinning around and around all these things, and in the end, I decided Stevens' early departure from this world hadn't been as satisfying as I'd hoped—like longing for a favorite food, only to find it not as sweet or rich or delicious as you remembered. But disappointment after dessert was a wholly different thing from disappointment that killing someone hadn't turned out as great as you'd imagined—that the fantasy couldn't live up to the reality, that unless you were someone like Shannon, it would infect your soul and begin to rip it apart from the inside like a closet full of tiny moths quietly eviscerating clothing.

Finally, it was done. Shannon felt my skin and shined the flashlight in my eyes. He hurried me along to get me moving to get me engaged with the physicality of the world, as if I might float away otherwise.

We got cleaned up and changed clothes. He made sure nothing was left behind, no evidence, no hair, no fibers, nothing incriminating. Though I wasn't in any database anywhere, and I was sure Shannon was fully off the DNA grid as well.

I got into his car, and we drove. As lights blurred past my window, I fantasized that Trevor's world in the theme park had been the real one, that that simple, yet terrifying, life had been true. A part of me wanted that world back—the post-apocalyptic wasteland that at least left me virtuous and untainted by my memories or the future actions I'd take.

Shannon patted my knee. "Don't worry. Things don't always go as expected on jobs, but we won't be caught. There's no reason to worry." He looked electric, alive, pulsing with energy as if he'd just gotten off a roller coaster. His cheeks were flushed, and his lips kept inching up in a smile.

"I could go for some pizza, how about you?" he asked. "I always get pizza after."

I just stared at him in horror. This was what I'd tied myself to. This was who I had somehow started to love, who I wanted, who I felt safe with. This monster who was happy and excited and ready for some celebratory pizza. And yet, at every turn and bend, I'd chosen him. I no longer had the will to choose differently.

I couldn't stop silent tears from sliding down my cheeks. Shannon finally realized I was crying when we stopped at a red light.

"What's wrong?"

He really didn't know? He really couldn't comprehend?

"I just *killed* someone." Never mind that he had. I'd never expected him to cry over it. But I at least expected him to understand on some basic level why I might, particularly since my victim was an innocent. The sick idea slid into me that she could have been the professor's victim, too. And I'd killed her. To protect Shannon? To protect myself?

There wasn't a flicker of anything human in him. Nothing

registered with him. He didn't get it. How could I ever be safe with him if he didn't get it?

I managed to collect myself by the time we got to a small pizza parlor a couple of towns over. We sat in a booth in a back corner where patrons were smoking, even though I was sure it was against the law. They didn't care, and nobody else seemed to, either.

"You're glad he's gone, right?" Shannon asked after our pizza and drinks arrived. "I couldn't let him..." he trailed off, remembering we were in semi-public, and maybe not as completely anonymous as we'd like to be.

"Yeah," I said. "I just... I wasn't prepared for how I would feel or for... what happened." I had to speak in code, too, now. Even in my darkest fantasies, where I was more active in Stevens' murder, I couldn't have anticipated an unexpected visitor. An innocent bystander. The way *I* had made metal rip through flesh, and blood and life spill out in such sweeping finality.

I closed my eyes against the images that came unbidden, filling in some of the gaps, leaving no doubt that it had been me doing that awful thing. In a twisted way, I almost wished Shannon had gone after her and left me to deal with Stevens. Maybe I could have reached the gun and ended him quickly. Maybe then I wouldn't feel like a shadow about to be destroyed by the light.

"Shannon?"

"Yeah?" he said between bites of a fully loaded pizza.

"Don't you feel..." I trailed off, wishing we were having this non-conversation in the car, but also knowing that possible witnesses in nearby booths were the only thing forcing me to keep it together.

He looked at me blankly. "What should I feel?"

And there was my answer. I knew I would be haunted by this for the rest of my life, and tomorrow Shannon would get up, have a hearty breakfast, breathe in the crisp air, and just go on, not a single ruffle against his soul. I envied him that.

"Hey, do you want to go to Paris? It'll be spring soon. I've heard Paris is nice in the spring. You could see some of your friends," he said.

I had never before seen him this happy and animated. This peaceful—like all the pieces inside him suddenly fit together right.

"What about my plants?" Once again, my mind wandered to the fate of all of the professor's plants. And now I was worried about leaving my own for an extended time.

"We'll be gone a couple of weeks maybe."

"Yeah, Paris sounds great." But my voice was flat. I didn't even bother asking how we'd accomplish that. He'd figure out fake IDs and passports or whatever we needed. I was sure he *knew a guy*, and all would be taken care of as if by the wave of a wand.

"Good. We'll make a quick stop at the house when we get back and check on the cat and your plants. We'll get in late—well after all the nosy neighbors are asleep. We can let them believe we're still in Thailand."

I wondered if he'd planned this all along, to get me somewhere off far away for a week or two to distract me from what I'd participated in.

When we stopped for the night, it wasn't a run-down motel. It was some place much nicer. It was the kind of hotel you take someone you love, though by this point I was sure, if Shannon didn't understand regret, he could never understand love.

More than ever, I saw him as a wild animal trying to live inside an artificial habitat. He was a predator who didn't belong here in our world. It wouldn't matter if he was ever caught and put in jail. He was already caged just by the constraint of trying to blend with society, to look normal.

I stood in the middle of the hotel bedroom while steam

from Shannon's shower poured out of the bathroom. I stared at the gleaming gun on the bed. He'd removed the silencer.

I felt at that moment, that it was me or him. It had to be. I wasn't sure which outcome was worse.

I didn't think, even after everything, that I could pull the trigger to end myself. And if I killed him, here, now, in this nice hotel, I'd go straight to prison unless I could convince them it was self-defense. A credible story started to unfold in my mind. I would tell them I was that missing girl. I would make them remember. He had kidnapped me. I took the one opportunity I had to free myself. I had to do it, don't you see? I had to. It was me or him.

I picked the gun up and pointed it at the bathroom door in time for Shannon to emerge from the mist.

"What are you doing, Elodie? I thought we trusted one another." His voice was calm and steady, and I knew he wasn't even a little worried I'd shoot him, which only made me want to pull the trigger more. I inched my finger closer to the small lever that would end him.

"Do you even know how to use that gun?" he asked. "The safety's on. You might want to take care of that."

I was afraid to look too closely at the gun, afraid Shannon would rush and tackle me. And then what? I flicked the safety off with my eyes still on him, the barrel of the gun still pointed at the center of his chest... the chest water was dripping off of down into the folds of the towel secured around his waist, while he stood serene. Confident.

"Is it hot?" he asked.

"What?"

"Hot. Is a round chambered or do you need to rack the slide? You don't know, do you?"

I didn't. And I wasn't sure how to find out. I could just pull the trigger and if nothing happened, then I'd know.

"What's your plan after you shoot me? You want to go to prison? Haven't you been in enough of those lately?"

"I already figured that out. I'll tell them who I am. I'll tell them you were holding me prisoner. They'll find all your weapons. They'll believe me."

Shannon nodded. "Very good. And the questions? The media? I thought you didn't want that."

"I've got my memories. I can handle it now."

"Can you?"

My arm was starting to feel weak from holding the gun up, so I steadied my grip with my other hand.

"I don't think you can pull the trigger. You don't have it in you. You already proved that once tonight while I cleaned up your mess."

"I was protecting you."

"Great job," he said. The sarcasm dripped off him as he stared bluntly at the gun. He sighed. "Well, do it if that's what you want."

Did he have no self-preservation instinct? I knew he did. He wouldn't have been so careful, so meticulous if he didn't care about his fate. But I knew why he wasn't troubled. We both knew. I couldn't shoot him.

I turned the gun on myself, and for the first time since this drama had started, Shannon looked scared.

"Elodie, point the gun back at me," he said urgently.

"So you know I won't shoot you, but you're not so sure about whether or not I'll shoot myself."

And then it happened. Shannon cried. They were silent stealth tears creeping down his cheeks, but I knew he felt them drip down and fall off his face.

"I can't lose you, Elodie. You're the only thing human I have to hold onto. If I don't have you, then I don't know what anything feels like. I need you with me. I need you to translate all the things I can't feel."

"What good could that possibly do? You couldn't even process my guilt over killing an innocent person."

"I'm not stupid, goddammit! I know how you felt. I just can't feel the same thing directly."

An unjust mercy. I should be the one who could happily skip along without a ripple.

"Maybe you will if I pull the trigger. Maybe this is the final lesson in how to be a real person. How to feel actual pain and empathy."

The expression on his face was like a wounded animal, looking at his attacker in disbelief. "You knew what I was. I never lied or pretended with you. I let you see it all."

And then, against all I thought I was capable of, I pulled the trigger. Instinctively I flinched, but nothing happened. The chamber had been empty. Shannon lunged for me, and the gun slipped out of my hands as his full weight settled on top of me on the bed.

"Is this how it's going to be now? Am I going to have to keep you on suicide watch?" he asked, his breathing coming out wild and heavy.

"I can't live with what I've done. I can't stop seeing the things you've done."

"I won't involve you ever again. I shouldn't have brought you along this time. I thought I was doing something good for you so you could get your revenge."

In fairness to him, I'd thought it was something good for me, too. I'd thought I needed to not just be told or hear that Stevens was gone, but to see it happen with my own eyes, to watch him struggle, to absorb his fear out of the air as if it might energize and sustain me. To watch the light go out of his eyes and see for myself that he couldn't hurt anybody else again and that he'd gotten what he deserved. But the actual cold reality of death and murder wasn't the glamourized fantasy of the movies with no emotional consequences. It was harsh, brutal, awkwardly violent, and poisonous to all who participated.

Except that Shannon didn't seem affected. How could he be? I was sure he didn't have a soul to damage. He was impervious to all this inconvenient humanity.

"But you're not going to stop doing it," I said.

"Of course not. I told you... everybody I kill deserves to die."

"But not that woman," I said.

"I didn't kill her."

"But you would have. She would have been collateral damage."

"I was too focused on the results and not focused enough on the planning. It was because I cared more this time. But yes, I would have done what was necessary. Whatever you believe, I'm sorry you had to make that choice tonight. But I'm glad you made it. Aren't you glad you made it? Would you rather I go to prison?"

"I don't know anymore. I don't think I can live with who you are. Or with who I am now."

"You're the same. One moment doesn't change that."

"It changes everything."

Shannon eased off me, and pulled me into his arms. I thought at first he might squeeze me to death, he was holding me so tight.

"I wish I could take this for you," he said, quietly. "I could handle it. I would take the guilt and pain so you wouldn't have to feel it."

"I wouldn't have to feel anything if you'd let me..."

"No. We'll go to Paris. Everything will be better there. You'll see. A trip is what you need. You can see your friends. You can show me the sights."

"You've never been to Paris?" I asked.

Shannon shook his head.

"But you speak fluent French."

"No. I've been learning it ever since I found out you spoke it. I have CD's in the car. I know just enough to get by."

His mouth found mine, and despite what I wanted to be true, I still wanted him. Sex with Shannon that night wasn't the victory fuck after a fresh kill that I'd feared it would be. And it wasn't ropes and whips and power games. It felt like making love. And I wanted to believe it, that this was real, that it was something he was capable of feeling with me. Even seeing him cry wasn't enough to fully convince me that I was some magical exception to the cold deadness inside him.

Afterward, he held me for a long time until I had almost drifted off, surrendering to dreams to make me forget for just a little while how badly everything had gotten fucked up.

But then, moments before I reached that happy release, he got up, unzipped a bag, and pulled out a coil of rope and tied me to the bed. My heart rate picked up. "Shannon?"

His answering expression was grim. "I don't trust you with loaded guns lying around. This is for your own safety."

When he'd secured me, he got back into bed beside me and pulled the covers over us. "Go to sleep. Things won't seem so bad in the morning."

Whoever had first coined that phrase was an idiot.

A WEEK LATER, we were in a hotel suite in Paris. Shannon seemed weirdly happy traveling with me, as if he could tick off the box marked *romantic vacation* on his normalcy checklist. I sat up in bed and drank coffee and ate pastries off the room service tray. Shannon stood beside the window looking out at the breathtaking view of the Eiffel tower.

"Do you want to go to the Louvre today before we meet your friends for dinner later?" he asked.

"Yeah."

Shannon had taken a softer turn with me since the night we killed Stevens and his TA. As if almost losing me had snapped something into focus for him. At least where I was concerned. Or maybe it was that he thought I was too fragile to handle anything that would remind me of who and what he was. Or what I'd become in his care.

"Shannon?"

"Yeah?" He still stared out the window.

"Why did you stop? The kink stuff?"

"I don't know."

"Can we go back to it?"

He turned sharply from the window, his gaze now intently focused on me. "You want that? After..."

"I need it. I mean... if you want..." More than ever, I needed that release from everything that those games brought. I couldn't say it out loud, but I needed to be punished, no matter how hollow the effort.

That dark intensity came back to his eyes. "Yes. When we get back home."

I let out a long breath. "Good. Thank you."

"Sir," he corrected.

Despite everything I was dealing with and all the things I thought I'd never get over, the feeling of safety and security wrapped around me again like the warm, inviting smell of the coffee on the tray in front of me.

"Sir," I said.

I went back to my breakfast. I'd momentarily forgotten the previous night's dream, but now it rushed into my mind with the force of a typhoon wind, practically leaping into vivid color right in front of me. I was back in the theme park with Trevor. The dream replayed that last day before Shannon had shown up. Yet somehow, the dream version of me had seen the future already. Half of me lived the reality as it was, knowing nothing of myself or the truth, and another half of me seemed to be off to the side watching, already knowing everything that was to come.

Shannon's dark clad figure filled the doorway. Gunfire sounded. Trevor crumpled to the ground, blood spilling out of him. I ran to him on autopilot, trying to stop the blood, trying to keep him there, trying to hold the lie of our life together, all while trying to remember I'd already done this, and Trevor wasn't the good guy.

But neither was Shannon. I watched it all play out again. And then, the choice... do I go back out into the world not knowing who I am, or do I go with this man?

Shannon held his hand out, and all the knowledge of everything that was to come flooded into me, and the two parts of myself merged. And once again, I knew everything. I looked at him for a long moment, frozen in this space, this fork in the road. Finally, I took his hand, and we walked out of the castle into a future that only felt real with him.

EPILOGUE

SHANNON

I'm whistling as I step out of the shower, buzzing from a fresh kill, but I stop cold when I reach the main part of the suite. Elodie lies in wait, pointing the gun at me. But she won't shoot. She can't. I see it in her eyes. She can't kill yet another person—especially when that person is me.

We both know it.

I ask how she'll get away with it, what she'll do. How will she handle the police? She has plausible responses, I think. I'm kind of proud of her. The only problem is... she can't do it. But then she turns the gun on herself, and the bottom drops out of the world.

What is this feeling in my chest? Is this... terror? Can you die from it? Oh, fuck this is awful. I've never felt anything like this. I feel cold and hot at the same time. Clammy. There's a loud high-pitched ringing in my ears, and I panic, thinking the gun has already gone off, and the ringing is from gunfire exploding into such a small indoor space. But no, it's just my body discovering adrenaline—the bad kind—for the first time in my life.

I've never had anything I was scared of losing before. I've

never had real skin in the game. It was all just things. I could get them back, replace them. I could find a way to win the next round. I could be stronger, better, faster, more brutal the next time.

But this? Elodie? I can't replace her. Fuck, I can't remember if the gun is hot. I always clear the chamber and do a function check after a job. Always. But this wasn't a normal job. She never should have been there. I should have locked her up in the house with no convenient balcony escape and taken care of it myself. She could have been mad at me as long as she needed to, but she'd be safe, and not a killer like me.

If I had made that one simple choice—the right choice—we wouldn't be here.

"Elodie, point the gun back at me!"

She pulls the trigger. I'm standing close enough that the blood spray hits me in the face, her blood mixing with my tears. Tears. I didn't even know I could cry before this moment. Maybe I'm more human than I thought. What a fucked-up way to learn that.

As soon as her body hits the ground, I bolt upright in bed, a noise like a wounded animal tearing out of my lungs. My heart pounds so fast and hard in my chest. I take several long slow breaths, willing it to calm and return to its normal cadence.

Just a dream, Shannon. Everything is okay. She's okay.

It's the same nightmare I've been having for the last six months, ever since we got back from Paris. I don't bother her with them, and she doesn't know because she sleeps in her room down the hall.

Sometimes it's Elodie who has bad dreams and comes to me in the night. I never turn her away. We usually try to fuck it away, and then I hold her until she calms and falls back asleep in my arms.

We both keep dreaming about that night—her about what *did* happen, and me about what could have happened. I don't give one shiny fuck about that stupid TA, but Elodie is a real person, and real people care about things like that. I just wish I'd been the one to do it.

I open my door to find the cat glaring up at me. I probably woke her. She has her own comfortable cat bed that she refuses to sleep in. Instead she keeps vigil outside my door and has every night for the past eight years since I brought her home with me.

I don't let her in my room. I'm allergic to cats.

It's not a bad allergy, but I've seen how they sleep right up next to their humans' faces, and… I'd rather not. As long as I keep her out of the bedroom and clean like a maniac, I don't even have symptoms. She follows me down the hallway, complaining the entire way as I descend the stairs down to the main level and then down into the dungeon.

I don't think I'll be able to get back to sleep tonight. The only solution is to clean—to try to erase the image of Elodie dying from my mind. Of course that's not how it went down. I have to keep reminding myself of this. Thankfully I did keep to my routine that night. I *had* cleared the chamber and run the function check.

But what if I hadn't? What if I'd forgotten to do it? In that moment in the hotel room when I'd frantically demanded she point the gun back at me, I couldn't remember if I had or not. The only thing different in the dream was whether or not the gun was hot. That one tiny fuck up and I could have lost her forever.

I sit on the dark hardwood, unpack my cleaning supplies, and start polishing. I run my bare fingertips over a few of the twenty-eight dents Elodie left in my floor with her high-heeled boots. I've played dark and dirty games with many women in the past. Subs love their marks.

Rope burns. Whip lashes. Cane welts. Bite marks. Candle wax burns.

Before I met Elodie, the women I played with loved the evidence of what we'd done together, to see how I'd claimed them, how I'd owned them—this dark secret they'd carry until the marks faded away. And even though I'm not a sub, I clearly have my own version of that as I look at these marks Elodie made on my floor—the marks I ordered her to make—then punished her for.

I smile at this. She only got to look at and touch the marks I left on her for a week. But I've had these marks in my beautiful hardwood for much longer. I'll keep them forever, just like I'm keeping her. Touching them, feeling the sharp indentations, soothes me.

I still can't believe she killed someone to protect me. An innocent. I really never have killed an innocent. I've been so careful; I've never had to.

I *would, w*ithout blinking or remorse. I just haven't *had* to.

The stupid fucking professor. He had way more fight than I expected for an old guy. He thrashed about and fought and wriggled like a slimy fish trying to escape my hook.

I'd wanted to take my time with him, and yet as I slid my hunting knife into his side, it gave me that same satisfying release, that warm glow and buzzy feeling. It was what I always thought happiness must feel like for normal people.

At least the professor knew Elodie was alive and that she'd come to claim her revenge before he died. Maybe it was better that he felt so close to escape—so close to rescue before the knife slid in and twisted. If I'd played with him, he could have kept hoping until the moment he lost consciousness. And that wouldn't have been nearly as satisfying for me.

I pushed his carcass off me, letting him thud heavily on the basement floor, and let out a long, contented breath. And then I remembered Elodie ran after that fucking TA.

I had the presence of mind to grab a rag and the bottle of my own special sleeping potion before I left the basement. I needed to find that TA and knock her out for later disposal. Elodie would be too upset if I killed the girl right in front of her. I didn't like to remind her of what I was.

But it was too late. When I got outside, Elodie was covered in blood, screaming.

Fuck. Fuck. Fuck.

I ran to her, soaked the rag in the drugs and covered her mouth and nose with it.

"Shhhh. It's going to be all right. I'm here." I rocked her as she lost consciousness, like the crazed psychopath I am.

I didn't know how her screams hadn't woken anyone, but we'd gotten lucky. Every single light in every single house was still off. I glanced up and around at the street-facing windows, but not a single curtain was disturbed.

I carried them one at a time—first Elodie, and then the dead TA—back into the professor's house. One of the side effects of the drug is memory loss. I hoped she wouldn't remember killing the girl.

But she did—not all the gory details, but enough to know. Later, after her suicide threat, when she was calm in my arms, her breath evening out in sleep, I dosed her again, hoping to take just a few more memories, to make it just a little more fuzzy, just enough so she could carry it. So it wouldn't destroy her.

I couldn't let her destroy herself for me. I think it helped some, even though she still has the nightmares. Hers aren't as often as mine. That's how I know the drug helped. I just wish it had taken more. Even as I think it, I know how fucked up that is, given her state of memory loss when I first found her in that theme park.

The cat winds in and out of my arms as I polish the floor, her yowls getting louder and louder. She wants me to feed her, I think. I stroke behind her ears, and she purrs. Or maybe she just wanted attention. She meows a question at me, but I don't speak cat, so I just go back to cleaning.

An hour later, the floor is about as shiny as it's getting, and I'm tired enough I might be able to drift back off. I climb the stairs, the cat trailing behind me, asking a million feline questions I don't have the language to answer.

I go into Elodie's room, shutting the door behind me to another irritated yowl, and I watch my girl as she sleeps.

"Shannon?" Elodie says after several minutes.

"Yeah?"

"Stop being creepy."

I chuckle. At least it's not a nightmare tonight for her. I cross the room and get into the bed, pulling her against me, making her my little spoon.

She sighs and turns on the lamp. The diamond on her finger nearly blinds me as it catches the light. My parents were thrilled about the engagement. Neither of them seemed to think it was too fast. My dad just said, "When you know, you know."

And he's right, I knew Elodie was mine from the moment I saw her.

My mom just wants us to give her a pack of Mini-Mercers. I'm not sure if that's such a good idea. What if the kid is like me?

Fathers daydream about taking their sons fishing, teaching them to play ball. If I had a son like me, maybe I could teach him dismemberment and disposal. Could be fun. But Elodie probably wouldn't like it.

"Did you hear me, Shannon?"

"Hmmm?"

"I want to sleep in your room," she says.

"Tonight?" Maybe she *did* have the nightmare.

"No, not tonight. Every night. Am I still going to be in a

separate room when we're married? That's weird, Shannon. I don't like it."

"I don't want to keep you up with my insomnia."

"Maybe you wouldn't have it if we were together. I don't have nightmares when we sleep together, and you don't either."

I absently stroke up and down her exposed arm. "You know about my nightmares?"

I can almost feel her eyes roll when she answers me. "The wall between our rooms isn't soundproof."

She doesn't ask what my nightmares are about. I'm sure she knows. She knows she's the only thing I really care about.

"It'll piss off the cat," I say.

"Fuck the cat."

I kiss the back of her neck. "You know I want my girls to get along."

She snorts.

My fingers trace her fingers and we lay quietly together until finally she speaks again.

"Shannon?"

"Yeah?"

"I don't really remember most of that night. I don't remember killing her. I don't even think I made a choice to do it. It just happened, but I don't completely remember it happening. Is that normal? To not remember like that if you do something really bad?"

I think it might be normal. But I've never lied to her before—not outright. If I start now, it will change something between us in a way I don't want.

I sigh. "I drugged you."

A long spiraling breath escapes her. "I thought you might have."

"And again later that night after..." I trail off. Maybe this is too much honesty.

She tenses beneath me, and I lean in close to her ear. "And I would do it again. I would do anything to erase that night from your mind, anything to take that pain and guilt away from you. You never should have had to do that."

"You intentionally took memories from me." Her tone is accusatory, but I don't think she has the energy to be truly angry about it. I think part of her is glad I did it. Part of her feels safe inside my ruthlessness.

"It's not like I got to hand pick and remove them," I say. "I didn't even know if it would work. And it didn't work nearly as well as I would have liked. I just want you to be happy, to have the fairy tale."

She deserves so much better than I can give her, but I'm far too selfish to ever let her go.

"Well you did literally rescue me from a castle I was being held prisoner in, so, that's sort of the fairy tale."

"It's not enough." I bury my face in her hair and inhale her strawberries and cream shampoo.

There's something darkly poetic in our relationship being bookended by murders, though I'm sure of the two of us, I'm the only one who would see it this way.

That night I found her... sure, Trevor would have shot me, so I had to do it. But I took one look at Elodie, and my heart started to beat in a different rhythm. I wanted her. I needed her. Before that moment I had no idea that I was missing her. I would have destroyed anything and anyone that kept me from her.

There's another angry yowl out in the hallway and then a thumping sound as the cat settles against Elodie's door, taking up her new guard position.

"Okay," I finally say. "We'll try sleeping together in my room." I extract myself from her warmth and tug on her hand.

"No, not tonight, the blankets are already snuggly. Stay here."

I strip off my clothes and get into the bed, pulling her back into my arms. I slip my hand under the blankets, finding and stroking her most recent cane welts—the punishments I give her to make her feel right again.

She sighs contentedly and goes back to sleep.

I can't sleep, so I just lie there, holding her, listening to her breathing. I've been in denial about this for a very long time, even though I've known since the night I thought I could lose her.

I love her.

ACKNOWLEDGMENTS

Thank you to the following people for their help with Tabula Rasa:

Amy Martin for her help with French translation.

Robin Johnson @ gobookcoverdesign.com for the fabulous cover art!

Thank you to Cathy for copyedits!

Thank you to Michelle and Karen for their great beta read suggestions on the original version! Special thanks to Michelle for all the body disposal help. Who knew getting rid of bodies was so much work! ;)

And thank you to M for digital formatting of the original version! Love you!

Printed in Great Britain
by Amazon

41331898R00142